Merry Chris ♥ YO-EHC-558
from Leroy 1993

ACROSS THE WHEATGRASS

1889 · 100 · 1989
NORTH DAKOTA
CENTENNIAL
1985 North Dakota Centennial Commission

An Approved North Dakota Centennial Commemorative

ACROSS THE WHEATGRASS

—A Collection Of Hearthside Stories About Uncommon People, Wildlife, Days Afield, And Things, Times And Places Of Some Centennial Years —

By
H. Ted Upgren Jr.

Illustrated
By
Burdette Calkins

Cover Art and Layout-design
By
Mike Bruner

Windfeather
Press

P.O. Box 7397 • Bismarck, ND 58502

ACROSS THE WHEATGRASS

Copyright © 1988
by H. Ted Upgren Jr.

International Standard Book Numbers:

0-9620122-1-1 Softcover

0-9620122-0-3 Hardcover

Library of Congress Catalog Number:

88-050045

Published by

Windfeather Press
P.O. Box 7397
Bismarck, N.D. 58502

Printed in U.S.A.

2nd Printing

ACKNOWLEDGEMENTS

The publisher thanks Random House, Inc. and Alfred A. Knopf, Inc. for permission to quote from *The Time of the Buffalo*, copyright 1972, by Tom McHugh, *This Reckless Breed of Men*, copyright 1952 by Robert Glass Cleland and *The Great Buffalo Hunt*, copyright 1960 by Wayne Gard. Thanks are extended to Charles T. Bradford Co. for use of excerpts from *Lives of Game Animals*, copyright 1953 by Ernest Thompson Seton, to Tumbleweed Press for use of quotations from *Recollections*, copyright 1975 by John W. Robinson, to the N.D. Historical Society for use of quotes taken from *North Dakota History, Museum Review* and their *Official Newsletter* as cited in the references of various stories. Other sources listed in references or elsewhere occur in the public domain or are used conservatively under journalism's fair-use doctrine.

TO

Kaye

CONTENTS

DAYS AFIELD

THINGS, TIMES AND PLACES

FOREWORD

North Dakota is a state poorly understood by those who haven't lived here. It is a land that lends itself to stereotype easily grasped and readily dismissed. Far too many folks see North Dakota as the nation's ice box — a cold, flat, and desolate place that warms enough in summer to allow its small population time to do "whatever it is they do up there."

This perception of North Dakota as a land unvarying in form and pattern is one that we who live here have learned to take in stride. The North Dakota stereotype has enough simple fact to sustain false impression and discourage all but the most curious from seeking the truth about our state and its people.

An understanding of North Dakota can be imagined by evaluating facts available in history books and statistical compilations, but it is a canvas without life. To add life and meaning to the picture of our state you need people, and people are basic to what H. Ted Upgren Jr. offers us in *Across The Wheatgrass.*

Across The Wheatgrass is a book about natural resources and the outdoors. It offers opportunity to learn about wildlife management through activities of managers, both public and private. There are hunting and fishing stories, as well as interviews with old-timers about their early day activities . . . what drew them to the prairie and why they stayed.

This publication contains 38 selected stories presented in four sections for convenience. Each selection, complete unto itself, speaks to some facet of prairie life. The voices are those of North Dakota men and women blended by the author into an entertaining and enlightening volume, particularly timely coming as it does during North Dakota's Centennial.

The year 1989 will be a year of celebration and reflection as thousands of visitors seek to rediscover North Dakota and the qualities many of us take for granted — open spaces and an infinite variety of outdoor opportunities — qualities once common to many places but now becoming increasingly rare.

There is a powerful connection between prairie dwellers and the outdoors. To begin to understand the power and importance of that relationship to North Dakotans, one need look no further than *Across The Wheatgrass*.

Harold Umber, editor
North Dakota OUTDOORS
April 12, 1988

PREFACE

The effort I have made here with *Across The Wheatgrass* is the offspring of anxiety. In the closing months before North Dakota's 100th Birthday I began to ask myself if I was to see the Centennial come and go without having made some contribution to its celebration. I am not an artist so I can leave no legacy in oils; I am no sculptor so I can leave no legacy in bronze; I am no cinematographer so I can leave no legacy in film. If I were a rich man, I would buy the state a huge prairie, a Centennial Grasslands, but . . .

Finally late in 1987 it dawned on me that I might be able to leave something like *Across The Wheatgrass* as some sort of literary account reflective of the way at least I interpreted a thin slice of some Centennial years.

Though *Across The Wheatgrass* talks about prairie people, prairie wildlife, and their relativity, the marrow of these accounts has to do mostly with the rapport between people and the prairie. This collection of stories recognizes people who have chosen to live in this rigorous land of four seasons because they have found something captivating in the breadth of the land, something enduring in the sunsets; and even in the monotonous whine of the immortal wind, the prairie offers a musical rhythm to those who listen. And something of these qualities is found in the people that make them resilient — like the wheatgrass.

The people you will read about on these pages are uncommon, either by achievement, background or perhaps in time and circumstance. I would like these people then, to represent all those who have escaped one Centennial scribe or another — but deserve similar acknowledgement — to be the example by which we know something extra of the ways of people past.

I would like to thank my patient and loving wife, Kaye, without whose lightening fingers this manuscript would yet be undone, and for her faith that the contents of this book deserved to be presented as a Centennial publication. I am appreciative of Harold Umber's words in the Foreword which will direct people to turn the page to find an "enlightening volume." Thoughts like that from a fellow writer whom I highly regard are indeed comforting: to me and, I am sure, to my banker as well. The beautiful artwork of Burdette Calkins lengthens considerably the imaginative reach of the text. I am indebted to "Burt" for his willingness to work hard on these pen and inks and keep the schedule. Mike Bruner's cover art and his layout and design has made this author a happy person and I thank him for his sincere interest in getting things right.

Stories in *Across The Wheatgrass* have been previously published in *North Dakota OUTDOORS* and a number of other magazines, the names of which are indicated at the end of each story. They have been edited somewhat, but principally stand as they were initially written. In several instances, particularly in PEOPLE, I have added *Postscripts* to provide current information about some story subjects.

This effort in self-publishing has been an interesting experience. It has provided a lot of fun, but caused just enough trouble to transcend the hobby category and qualify as a project — as an Approved North Dakota Centennial Commemorative project — and, I hope, as a suitable contribution to the amusement and education of a wide variety of North Dakotans, and to our 100th Birthday as well.

H. Ted Upgren Jr.
May 5, 1988

ACROSS THE WHEATGRASS

PEOPLE

FIELD NOTES FROM ONE OLD HUNTER

The sunrise was a half hour old when the first flock of Canada geese rose from a willow-flecked sandbar and labored for altitude to pass above the rugged east bank of the Missouri and return to the wheat field they had feasted in the night before, only a couple of miles from the river and just north of the Robinson Stock Farm. A brisk northwest wind helped move the heavy-bodied birds through cloudy October skies that spit the season's first snow flurries.

In a pit that he had dug the night before, young John Wade Robinson sat holding a borrowed 12-gauge hammer gun. On horseback he'd spotted this place the evening before. Twenty yards away his father, John J. Robinson, crouched in another pit. Several yards in front of them 40 sheet metal, silhouette Canada goose decoys stood planted in the near-virgin prairie.

Young John shivered. He wondered, was it the raw, humid cold or just apprehension that chilled him? He'd hunted with his father on many previous occasions, but this was the first time he'd been granted the responsibility of handling a firearm and the opportunity to bag the magnificant goose. It was a paradox. How could you love to kill such a bird? The question bothered him. It was a question that would surface repeatedly to haunt him for the rest of his life. It was a question he would never fully rationalize. John shivered some more.

The man and boy could hear the honking goose sounds now, carried on ahead of the flock by the driving northwester. Shortly, black specks appeared. Then they grew in size and took form until eight majestic honkers made their graceful debut. They slipped south a bit to better investigate the black metal profiles that had expropriated their prime stubble ground. They dropped lower and began a glide. The only movement was the slight dipping of wing tips. But they moved too far south and passed the spread. Finally they made the turn which put them squarely against the strong headwind requiring deeper more powerful wingbeats. Two hundred yards, 100 yards . . .

Despite German socks and overshoes, young John's feet were cold and his fingertips were numb. But in the excitement of the moment he forgot his discomfort. He reviewed quickly all the important things his father had lectured him on about guns and safety and goose hunting. His father glanced at him with an urgent expression that communicated those instructions. Fifty yards in front of them . . . young John thought they should be shooting. They looked huge, even too close. Another instant and he heard the roar of his father's Daly. John raised on his knees shouldering the long 12-gauge. An enveloping explosion followed. Black powder smoke filled the air as the no. 1's connected with one of the giant birds and brought it down amongst the metal decoys. A seventeen pounder, easily! John was ecstatic. Aglow with excitement and a new indescribable feeling he ran across the stubble to retrieve the first Canada goose of his hunting career.

John was 12 years old on that day. The year was 1891, and the place a quiet stubble field near the Robinson home only a mile from the present town of Riverdale. Thus began a lifelong love affair with the outdoors, particularly waterfowling, that put him close to his natural heritage and forever bound him to an appreciation of North Dakota's wildlife resources. Today young John is 97 years old, three years short of centurial status.

Recently I sat with Dr. John Wade Robinson (a title legitimately earned through his education and experience in the veterinary

3

field) and his son John Paul, a retired Garrison pharmacist, for the express purpose of recording our conversation about early North Dakota and particularly about his experiences as a pioneer hunter and waterfowl enthusiast. We sat in the old, but well-kept frame house he had built in 1909 for his new bride. He had moved to Garrison in 1905 from the Riverdale-Coal Harbor area he'd been raised around. For the last several years he has been living in the house alone, still able to care for himself, although son John Paul, next door, looks in on him often.

Time appeared to have been very good to Doc John. Nearly a century old, he seemed mentally keen. A hearing impairment required me to speak to him in a somewhat exaggerated volume. The major affliction of his age was his eyesight, and that had failed him only recently.

Doc John came by his avid interest in the outdoors honestly. Responsible was his father, John Sr., a professional market hunter and butcher who operated out of the St. Louis region before coming to Dakota territory in 1884. John Sr. was a noted scattergunner and a crack trapshooter. If you were good enough to shoot jacksnipe off horseback, you had to be good at shooting live pigeons released from the trap, and, with your two feet on the ground. On at least one occasion he demonstrated his trap shooting prowess by winning the Abbey Cup at a tourney in St. Louis on June 10, 1866. Doc John also recalls his mother talking about her husband doing battle with Captain Bogardus[1] who was one of the period's best trapshots. "He was referred to as the Great Captain Bogardus," Doc John said, "and he outshot my father, he won the top trophy."

"My father was a great hunter, he was a good shot, but that was with the shotgun, he wasn't much of a rifleman." Of his experience in goose hunting with his father Dr. Robinson said, "It was a common thing for him to kill two birds with his first shot and one with his second."

"Do you recall any accidents or any close calls you had with firearms," I asked.

"No," replied Doc John, "my father gave me a thorough train-

[1]Captain A.H. Bogardus was classed with well known exhibition shooters of the post-Civil War period to 1900 which included William Cody, Doc Carver, and Annie Oakley. Of these and others, Bogardus was best known of the early exhibition gunners. An Illinois native, he had acquired his smoothbore skills in the duck blinds along the Mississippi. Using a 12-gauge breechloading shotgun Bogardus' best record was the breaking of 990 glass balls out of 1,000 thrown. (From: Askins, Charles J. 1950. All-Time Rifle Champ, American Rifleman, June, 1950, p29).

ing before he let me handle a gun at all . . . on how to go through a fence and always to have the hammers down and never go into the wagon or sleigh without unloading the gun . . . always point the muzzle towards the ground . . . one man per pit while goose hunting . . . he taught me all that stuff . . . and that's probably why we had no accidents."

So, young John had an expert teacher in his father. Importantly too, John Sr. hunted for the love of it, so he was able to communicate ethics as well as the mechanics of hunting to son John Wade.

The Robinsons were some of the first North Dakotans to practice shotshell reloading for sporting purposes. They loaded 10, 12 and 16-gauge brass shells. "We had a regular loading outfit," Doc John related, "loading block, gauges, powder measure for different drams of black powder." But the brass shells couldn't be crimped and this presented a special transportation problem. They had to be carried topside up or the weight of the charge would push the wad out and escape to the bottom of their shell pouches.

I asked Doc John if they ever made any mistakes, any overcharges. They never had any problem, but ". . . my father warned me and told me to turn that loading block upside down and tap it every time before you put a shell in . . . you might have a shot down in the bottom that will fire the cap." Doc got by alright, but a neighbor friend didn't. "He went to put the mallet on the wad and the cap fired and blew a piece of the shell brass into his eye, and he lost that eye."

A strange assortment of firearms were used by the Robinsons. For waterfowling the 10-gauge brought up from St. Louis was first popular. Then John Sr. acquired a Daly three-barrel that had two 12-gauge barrels on top and a .40-70 cal. rifle barrel beneath. Doc John's first gun of his own was a 16-gauge double-barrel hammer gun. An old .45-60 Winchester was used by his father for deer and Doc John recalls his love for a borrowed little Marlin .38-55 with Lyman sights he used for deer hunting. "I also remember going down to the woods along the Missouri with a .22 in the wintertime to hunt grouse . . . found them in the bullberry bushes."

Hunting trips were constantly being planned and executed from early fall, when the first young waterfowl left the brood waters of the abundant prairie potholes, then through winter in pursuit of resident game. Evenings inside the large cottonwood log house were taken up with shell loading and making hunting plans. Then, young John would retire to the attic and crawl into his bulky featherbed. There beneath the bare rafters he tossed and turned with anticipation until sleep finally claimed him.

And, they did it about the same as any crazy, modern-day wildfowler. "I 'spose you and your father were up early in the morning?" I asked.

"Oh boy, yes, getting up in the dark."

"How about your mother, was she very happy about that?"

"She didn't mind . . . didn't ever complain . . . never scolded us much about hunting . . . never scolded us about going on Sunday or anything." She appreciated the game too, that is, as long as the men skinned or picked it.

John Sr. was hooked, just like he was back in St. Louis, even though his horse farm was now his main occupation, not market hunting and butchering. Nonetheless, he couldn't shake his love for the field – he never got all the black powder residue wiped from his hands. His enthusiasm spread to his children, his two sons John Wade, older son George, and his four girls, and on almost all his outings one or some or all were his constant companions. But, there were some limitations.

"Do you remember playing hookey from school in order to go hunting?" Doc smiled a bit and shook his head as if he thought I might be surprised at his answer.

"No, my father would not allow that. We'd go on weekends and sometimes after school."

"How about deer hunting when you were gone several days, what did the school marm think of that?"

He hesitated a minute and finally admitted, "Oh, I guess I'd have an excuse, I don't know how I'd fix that up."

Scores of hunting trips were made, but a few stand out in Doc John's memory as being a bit special. Most deer hunting was done on the bottomlands of the Missouri, where John Sr. felt at home, like on the Mississippi flood plain around St. Louis. But one day in late November, 1893 a friend, John Reuter, who lived up north of Turtle Lake talked a cautious John Sr. into making a prairie hunt for deer. "My dad was reluctant," Doc indicated, "he didn't think many deer would be on the prairie. But more than that he didn't think much about running the risk of getting caught out there in a storm so far away from everything . . . wasn't nobody in the country then, nobody to help."

But they did go. Doc John was 14 at the time. They made the 15-mile trip to Reuters, then put a triple box on the wagon and loaded it down with supplies; a canvas tent (without floor), a steel camp stove, wood poles for firewood, bedding and hay for the horses, and bedding and food for themselves. Only light snow covered the prairie but the marshes were covered with eight inches of ice. They were gone four days up in the beautiful rolling prairie country around the present town of Ruso. They shot five whitetails and had a splendid time except for one incident that could have cost John Sr. his life. Ironically, his initial judgement regarding the feasibility of the trip considered the very circumstances in which he found himself.

John Sr. had shot two deer, one which required tracking for about four miles. He forgot the time and the November daylight drained beyond the distant horizon just as he finished dressing the last animal. Darkness had overcome him and he was several miles from camp. Nowhere could he see a guiding light. The prairie expanse was not unlike the vacant sea. He remembered his earlier fear of being caught out on the prairie with no guideposts. He wandered ahead for two hours or more and in what he thought was the right direction. He was tired from the day's activities, but if he stopped he would only cool off. He had to keep moving. Finally, he saw a faint yellow glow. He geared up to a brisk pace. Within minutes he was back at camp, cold, scared, but safe.

Doc John recalls this experience vividly. "We became alarmed because darkness overtook him and we knew he only had on walking clothes, hunting clothes . . . we were fearful that he may not be able to survive a night on the prairie without better clothes, shelter, and without firewood." The camp lantern made the difference. Tied to the longest firewood pole they had, "We took it to a nearby knoll and raised it high above our heads. Father saw that lantern and it guided him into camp."

On another deer hunt, that Doc John was not on, his father and a neighbor, Enoch Otis Vaughn, crossed the Missouri to hunt where the grass was greener and in an area where they had previously constructed a crude log shelter. The trip was destined to end in frustration. On recounting the incident Doc explained, "Otis was rockin' the boat, so dad told him he'd have to lie flat down or they'd tip over . . . that's the only way they made it across."

But that scary trip across the treacherous Big Muddy wasn't the end of it. A cold snap put ice in the river channel, the jagged rotten kind, and perimeter ice appeared unsafe too. They couldn't get back. They had to spend two weeks in the log hut. Finally the food was gone so Otis was elected to walk to Stanton, several miles north, to get food to tide them over until the river froze hard enough to cross safely. Doc John can't recall whether or not Otis' 8-gauge or his father's 10-gauge, both loaded with buckshot, took a single deer. "But I laugh everytime I think of that little bit of a man, Otis, huggin the floor boards in that tiny two-foot-wide duck boat . . . don't see how they made it." The Robinson's real bag was waterfowl hunting. Duck and goose hunting. Doc's boy, John Paul testified, "Grandpa and father were more bird men, and me too. Today if I go out and I run into a duck flight I'll quit deer hunting in a minute and hunt ducks." John Paul is in his middle 60s and his interest in waterfowling hasn't been dampened yet. And his father, Doc John, carried the fever late into life. He was over 92 years old when he participated in his last duck hunt. "He wasn't walking too much then, but he was pass shooting," John Paul said. Douglas Lake had some of the best shooting in the area.

"Oh yes," Doc sighed, "I shot a lot of ducks on that lake." Goose hunting was probably their favorite. Canada geese were abundant and competition was nil. There were few avid waterfowl hunters in those days. Hardly anybody had decoys or used pits, and without know-how you didn't kill many geese. Seldom were they without targets. There were no limits and few regulations. On one outing in particular Doc John remembers he and his father bagged over 35 geese. "I'm sure he killed probably all but one or so himself, I spent my time chasing wounded ones."

On a fall day in 1904, just a year after Doc John had graduated from the Chicago Veterinary College, he and brother George had an exceptional goose hunt on a Missouri River sandbar. After spotting the flock the night before the boys rose early the next morning and traveled to the spot between the mouths of Wolf and Snake Creeks. They took tubs along and dug them down into the sandbar next to the willow brush. The decoys were arranged. It was a perfect setup. The action started late but by 11:00 a.m. they had shot over two dozen big Canada geese. As they prepared to leave, an unexpected visitor approached from down river in a gasoline boat (one of the size used to ferry wheat down the river) and pulled alongside the sandbar. "The guy yelled, 'give me a goose will ya', and I threw two geese over onto the deck of the boat," Doc John said. "It was our father's friend Captain Grant Marsh,[2] and we knew him as some kind of hero from when he ferried casualities of the 7th Cavalry back to Bismarck from the Little Bighorn Battle of 1876." Grant assured

[2]*Captain Grant Marsh was the pilot of the steamer Far West that carried wounded 7th Cavalry troops the 710 miles from the mouth of the Little Big Horn to Fort Lincoln at Bismarck also bringing the word of Custer's fatal encounter with the Sioux. The ferrying time of 54 hours remains a feat unparalleled in steamboat history. (From: Piper, Marion J. 1964. Dakota Portraits, 231pp.)*

the brothers that he'd properly care for the geese.

Doc John recalled a comical incident that involved his father that he and his brother witnessed on a favorite duck slough near Falkirk. John Sr. was having good shooting. In fact, it was an impossible situation. The senior Robinson, his doublebarrel 10-gauge pounding the skyways with chill shot at such a wicked pace, finally found the barrels too hot to touch and it became . . . necessary to open the gun at the breech, take out the shells and dip the barrels in slough water to cool them.

And of course, they had their share of prime upland game hunting. Dr. Robinson lived at a time when prairie chickens and sharp-tailed grouse were abundant. The foreign pheasant and Hun had yet to appear, but there wouldn't have been room for them anyway with all the grouse in the country. "I'd drive the buggy for my father," Doc said, "and that old bird dog would go out and set and my father'd get out and shoot."

"You had a regular bird dog then?" I asked.

"Setter, Gordon setter, black with brown around the eyes . . . it'd be nothing for us to go out for a half hour or so and come in with 20-30 grouse."

I'd listened for more than an hour now to hunting stories and outdoor experiences that Dr. Robinson could recollect from nearly a century back. They hunted an awful lot. They took large amounts of game. And now I began to wonder to what use they put the harvest. I finally laid out a question that I really hadn't wanted to ask — I was afraid the answer might stain the creditable testimony I'd heard so far. "Dr. Robinson," I said in a somewhat apologetic tone, "did you hunt for fun or food?"

"For fun," he blurted out, "we hunted for the sport of the hunt and not so much for the eats." I wasn't sure that was what I wanted to hear either. I just assumed that pioneer people might hunt mostly out of necessity.

"Did I hear you right?" He adjusted his glasses, probably out of habit, for they couldn't have been doing him much good — he'd been looking past me during most of our conversation.

"Oh yes, yes, father was a great hunter, loved to hunt, and I loved it too." Still I wasn't satisfied. He fiddled with the buttons on his gray sleeveless cardigan sweater. Earlier I had asked about any tough times the family might have experienced. Many settlers had lived from hand to mouth. I wondered how the Robinsons had managed.

"Father was a pretty good provider, he seemed to have money all the time, but we had lots of people that couldn't afford sugar," Doc John said. But I was still confused about their need to hunt.

"What about all the meat then," I cross-examined, "what did you do with it?" By his expression I felt that he had finally got the drift of my questioning. He looked me squarely in the face, his eyes missed me, but his voice was well aimed.

"We cleaned and used it all, none was ever wasted!" He made his point. My question was answered and I felt better at once.

Doc John continued and I began to find out why possibly they did have a bit more money on hand than some of their surrounding, mostly non-hunting neighbors. I asked about their use of venison. "Yes, we used a lot of venison, more than beef."

John Paul interjected, "beef they could sell for income, and venison I 'spose was their meat staple." And, John Sr. being a butcher and knowledgeable in the care of meat didn't hurt a bit.

It turned out that from midfall until late spring, the period of the year when refrigeration was weather-provided, game was a mainstay in the Robinson's diet. But in summer they were back to cured pork, what other people, less handy than these Robinson hunters, lived on year around. "In summer you couldn't keep meat over three days . . . on account of weather and flies." But in early fall when temperatures dropped and insects collected on southern exposures, you could find the first of the season's ducks and geese. ". . . hanging by their throats on nails on the north side and along the eaves of the granary." On hunts where they experienced exceptional luck and there was a surplus of game, beyond the family's needs, they shared their harvests. "Our neighbors loved goose, but few of them hunted," Doc said, "but often father sent extra geese on the stage down the line to people he knew enjoyed roast goose."

Early in the fall deer were taken as they could be consumed. Later, bigger hunts with bigger harvests worked out alright because the carcasses would cool and finally freeze in the tool shed. The tool shed was their "fridg." When they needed meat John Sr. would butcher a quarter. "Mother would fix roasts, soups, fried chops, or whatever cut father would bring in for her." Upland game was similarily used. Yellow legs and "regular" grouse and some rabbits too, provided additional table variety.

"Do you recall any special recipes your mother prepared that you especially enjoyed? What was the best game dinner she could produce?" A kind of drooling smile developed on Doc's face folding the lines of his cheeks together like the leather bellows of an accordion.

"Oh, roast goose, yes goose with bread dressing, seasoned bread dressing! And visitors thought so too . . . they thought it was a luxury to have a good piece of mother's roast goose."

10

Some of the critters they hunted had other uses. Ducks and geese came not only with that delicious, dark, juicy meat, they also wore a feathery wardrobe that Mrs. Robinson turned into warm featherbeds and feather ticks. "Everybody in the family had 'em . . . one to sleep on and one to cover up with."

John Reuter from over at Turtle Lake taught Doc John how to tan deer hides. "What did you use the tanned hides for?" I questioned.

"Made gloves and mittens out of them."

"You mean your mother did that," I corrected.

"No," Doc John emphasized, "I did, my brother and I both sewed them. Sometimes we'd sell them for $2.00 a pair . . . made baseball covers with deer skin too — buckskin we called it."

John Sr. had a whole suit of buckskins that he got from the Indians at Fort Berthold. ". . . he liked to hunt in it because it didn't make much noise going through the timber . . . warm and windproof too."

Another hour had gone by and I was beginning to appreciate more and more what hunting meant to the Robinsons. It seemed to me that they had the right kind of relationship with their wildlife. They were lucky because they were hunters not just shooters — sport hunters not just meat hunters. They were fortunate to be able to supplement a cured pork diet with a veritable wildlife smorgasbord. They used the prairie and bottomlands to their advantage, but they didn't appear to take unreasonable advantage of what lived there. They needed the meat for food, but this need provided their recreation, fed their conscience and enriched their lives by association with the natural world. They could have made reckless assault on their wildlife, unnecessary shooting, wanton waste, Instead they chose a different way. It's called sportsmanship. The Robinsons were surely some of the first North Dakotans to practice it.

Maybe that's why he was asked to be a deputy warden back in the 1930s. "They needed a man with some prestige, some principles," son Paul explained, "so they asked dad and he broke more than one poacher with just plain diplomacy."

Three and a half hours earlier, at a local gas station, I had asked directions to the Robinson home. "Ya gonna talk to ol' Doc, huh?" the attendant pried, "Well," he lectured with a head shaking routine, "he's a wonderful man, but he'll take care of the talkin' — you're gonna have your hands full just listenin'!" That I did and I enjoyed every minute of it.

For a mid-November day it was unseasonably beautiful and sunny. Sounds of kids at recess across the street at the grade school drifted through the screened door while Doc reviewed a final experience. As I'd watched the old man relive all those experiences, I realized that his childhood, the times when he ran and yelled and played on a country school ground, predated North Dakota's statehood. I was sitting here before a grand old gentleman whose memory spanned an era of time greater than the history of our state. It was a sobering thought.

The conversation slowed and changed to the present. It was like a trip had ended. We had talked for over three hours without a break. It was time to end our visit. A nod from son Paul conveyed agreement, even though I had the feeling that Dr. Robinson would have been more than happy to carry on. He wanted to share his memories, for that's what his waterfowling was now, memories. He knew his hunting days were over; he knew, in fact, that most all of his days were over. But he had alluded to his age at no time. He'd made no exhibition of his survival. This slight man, no taller than a lanky fifth grader, no heavier than a wiry welterweight, had triumphed over time. He had enjoyed extra-productive years, more years than most of us figure on existing, let alone living.

I packed up, thanked the doctor for his time and for sharing his recollections with me. I wished him well, said goodbye and slipped out the screened door onto the wooden-floored porch.

I overheard Paul talking with his father. "I'll stop by later dad," he assured his father, "gonna get out and do a little walking before sunset, last day of deer season coming up ya know."

Longingly Doc John asked, "Where ya goin'?"

"Over near George Bovkoon, south of him there."

"Oh . . ."

North Dakota OUTDOORS, February, 1977

Postscript

Dr. John Robinson lived to be 100 years old. He died February 26, 1980 at Garrison, North Dakota. The pioneer veterinarian and druggist was past Grand Master of Masons, a charter member of the North Dakota Livestock Sanitary Board, Garrison Civic Club and Garrison Sportsmens Club. Son John Paul is also retired after a career in pharmacy in the same business started by his father in 1905. Dr. John worked at the drug store and as a veterinarian until he was past 90.

Spring, 1988 H.T.U.

WOOD CARVING
SPOONER STYLE

Vern Spooner always has liked wood. As a youth he enjoyed whittling small figures with his pocket knife. He graduated to wood after perfecting his technique on hundreds of Ivory soap bars. Later, he moved to bigger wood projects as a carpenter with his father. Together they created dozens of homes for residents of Casselton, the prosperous Red River Valley community 20 minutes west of Fargo where Vern has spent all of his 52 years.

Major heart trouble in 1969, however, forced his early retirement from the carpentry trade. Suddenly, Vern Spooner, barely over 40 years old, found a lot of time on his hands. Fortunately, he knew exactly what to do with it. Vocational rehabilitation occurred almost overnight. He exchanged 20-foot construction lumber for small pieces of Minnesota basswood, a framing hammer for a small hobby knife, then he plunged impetuously into wood carving, the artcraft of his youth, and started putting out the miniature wood figurines he'd always dreamed of producing.

My first contact with Spooner carvings came relatively recently, in August, 1976. Norman Paulson, museum curator at the Liberty Memorial Building in Bismarck, pointed out Spooner's collection of art objects. Behind a 12-foot-long glass display case where the museum features "North Dakota's Artist of the Month" was a sampling of wood-carved animals and birds—in miniature. I was elated to learn we had such a North Dakota artist.

And so had been the Smithsonian Institute, Washington, D.C. In December, 1975, they sent a representative to Casselton to visit with Spooner and critique his carving. In May, 1976, a letter to Spooner from this eminent institution invited him to Washington, all expenses paid, to participate in an international Family Folklore Festival. In July, 1976, he did just that. There he met with artists and craftsmen from around the world. Only a few wood carvers had been invited: a man from Kansas, a decoy carver from the east coast, a Californian, and Spooner.

While demonstrating his carving technique in Washington, several passersby were impressed by his display and ordered different figures. One especially well-groomed and articulate gentleman requested the beagle dog figure. Vern indicated he didn't want to sell his display figures but would be happy to carve him another within the next several weeks and ship it to him U.P.S.

No problem. But it turned out there would have been a problem—the man was the East German Consulate. So, Spooner's wood carving fame was about to cross international boundaries.

It's hard to keep a good man down. It wasn't long before Vern Spooner's artwork was noticed by Les Kouba, Minneapolis-based and nationally recognized wildlife artist/painter. Coincidentally, both men shared interest in the artistic renderings of the same life form—wildlife. Somehow they got together and Kouba has helped Vern break into some of the bigger national art shows. One, Ducks Unlimited's Midwest Art Show, held in Kansas City in mid-March, 1977, accepted Spooner's woodcraft into competition. The Kansas City event featured about 90 artists, 14 were wood carvers.

Yes, the exposure has created big orders. Vern finds himself working 12 and 14 hours a day, but he says he loves every minute of it. He says he has only one major conflict and that's pro football. His carving suffers quite a bit on football weekends.

Is woodcarving an infrequently practiced art form in this part of the country? Apparently not! Vern is a member of the Flicker-tail Wood Carvers of Bismarck and the Minnesota Wood Carvers of Minneapolis. He is also president of the Red River Valley Wood Carvers' Association and last November this group held its First Annual Wood Carvers Show in Moorhead. Spooner is also a member of the National Wood Carvers. It looks as if there is plenty of local and regional interest in wood carving.

Vern Spooner was at one time an avid waterfowl hunter, and his dad was too. It used to be, according to Vern, that little carpentering got done on fall days. Instead, they pursued ducks and geese in North Dakota's wonderful outdoors. Vern can't do that anymore. But maybe one of his ways of staying close to the great outdoors and the creatures he found there is to recapture his recollections in wood. Today, he's an indoor outdoorsman, appreciating his wildlife heritage in a different way.

North Dakota OUTDOORS, April, 1977

Postscript

Vern Spooner, 64, has not been dealt the best hand in life, yet he's played it admirably. First heart trouble forced a change in his ways. Then in 1979 complications of hip surgery left him confined to a wheelchair. "But, so what," Vern says, "I have a son and daughter living in town and they both cut out forms on the band saw and I just keep on carving. It is the best form of therapy that I know of."

Vern's incredible wildlife miniatures remain award winners and are highly desired by clubs and organizations for fund raising. Some he donates to his favorite group, the Cass County Wildlife Club. Last year a carving of a pointer and flushing pheasants brought the club $1,000. Vern is invited annually to Nebraska where he instructs in techniques of miniature carving. Bismarck and Fargo see him at their annual shows as well.

Vern Spooner is widely acclaimed for his wood carvings. They are things of art and beauty. But more than that he is respected for the Spooner trademarks of perseverance, discipline and positive attitude that he has developed. Despite his lingering handicaps, these attributes have kept Vern Spooner a productive North Dakotan.

Spring, 1988 H.T.U.

WALLACE SPRINGER
– DAKOTA GUNMAKER EXTRAORDINAIRE

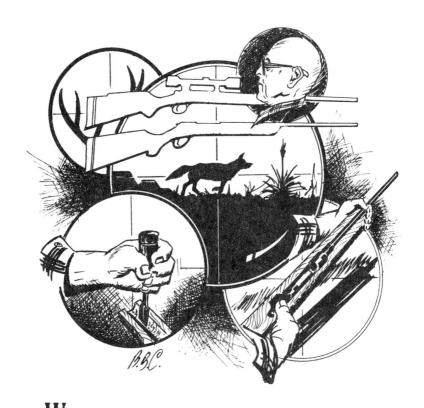

Wally Springer is doing today what he wanted to do full-time 35 years ago but didn't dare. He's a gunsmith. He's a gunstocker. He's a 67-year-old master craftsman with over 45 years in the gunmaking business — a firearms expert of rare ability, whose craft, historically practiced in one-man shops with distinct individuality, is passing from the American scene.

In the 1930s and 1940s shooting recreation was a relatively expensive sport involving a mere fraction of the people it does today. Making a living gunsmithing then would have been a struggle. It was too much of a gamble. Springer had more than himself to think of. To support his wife Bernie and their growing family (eventually four boys and four girls), he hired on with the U.S. Post Office in Hettinger. After 12 years office work and 28 years on a rural mail route, he retired in 1975 and turned his lifelong interest in firearms into a booming gun business.

A couple years back I heard of Springer's gunstocking skills from a friend who said, "He can turn a blank piece of walnut into a gunstock, sanded and finished in a single afternoon." Last fall I heard it again. Jack Samuelson, big game biologist, told the story of how he finally got his cal. 22-250 from Springer several years ago.

"I'd had the order in all summer," Sam said, "so I finally called Wally in August and he assured me he'd have it done any day."

At that time Springer was still working full-time with the Post Office so he had little time to be really productive in the gun-making business. Sam called again in late August.

"No," said Wally, "I've just been swamped — but when do you have to have it?"

Sam told him that he had drawn an antelope permit and would like the rifle by September 1. Sam called on September 1.

"Guess what," Wally said apologetically, "I'm really sorry but I just haven't been able to get to it."

Sam reluctantly indicated that he understood.

"When do you absolutely need it?"

"Next week Wally, the doggone antelope season opens then!"

Sam was sure that he had impressed him with the urgency, so he didn't call again until two days before opening of antelope.

"I couldn't believe it — he still didn't have it done, in fact he hadn't even started! What's more he told me to stop by the next afternoon on my way to Bowman and the rifle would be ready!"

The next day Sam borrowed a rifle, packed his bags and headed for Bowman. For the heck of it he went via Hettinger and stopped by Wally's place in late afternoon.

"I couldn't believe it, I was stunned. Wally handed me the finished product!"

The fast-drying lacquer finish was still slightly tacky.

"Probably better stop by a clay butte and tune her up Sam, didn't have quite enough time to get that done."

It's true, what Wally Springer can do with a hunk of walnut in four hours is simply amazing. In fact, what he can do with a rugged, knotty piece of birds-eye maple in 12 hours is even more astounding. I found that out for myself.

I made arrangements to spend a day with Springer to observe and photograph this gunstocker at work. I arrived in Hettinger shortly after lunch on a beautiful, warm afternoon, located his home and adjacent shop and met this Wally Springer.

A short, stout, thick-chested man with heavy wrists and muscled knuckles, Wally cordially welcomed me. His unpretentious manner was relaxing and I felt at home almost immediately. An old fur hat covered his bald head and a plaid flannel shirt and light vest, a pair of colored jeans and western boots made him look more like a badlands rancher than a gunsmith. But wait! No metal-oxide smudged apron or old wire-rimmed spectacles? No drawn and haggard look? No cranky disposition? Somehow this was my stereotyped image of a gunsmith, but Wally didn't fit it at all. He was, however, a west-river rancher by background, coming out of the Slim Butte country south of Hettinger and east of Buffalo, South Dakota. He'd been in this country all of his life.

"Lots of people head south when they reach my age. I like fresh air – like a tough ol' winter – that big city stuff's not for me?"

"I've gotta' birds-eye maple blank here ready to go. It'll take a bit longer than regular 'fast' walnut, but I promised a friend up northwest of here I'd get it done."

First, I wanted to see his lash-up. I followed Wally as he happily led me on a tour of the five-year-old, well-equipped shop. My eyes bugged at all the gadgets and guns. I must have looked like a kid in a candy factory. Two of the nicest olfactory pleasures in the world are the smells of bakeries and gunshops. Wally's place had that hallucinating aroma of burnt powder and gun solvents.

I could tell this place wasn't your ordinary basement gun repair shop. It was filled with speciality tools collected over the last four decades and included tiny tap-and-die sets and a large precision metal lathe, and all the tools in between. A heavy turret rifle press hung over the edge of a massive wood bench. Above it, protruding from either side of a storage rack were more than 60 dies for reloading various rifle and pistol cartridges. The whole set-up, including building, Wally figures, is worth at least $100,000. With this equipment and his experience, he does virtually everything but barrelmaking (boring and rifling). His complete service includes stocking, barrelworking, action work, part fabrication, blueing, and his own barrel-bedding technique he calls "accurizing." He knows of no one in the state who offers as complete a gun service.

And guns, why they're lined up on four or five gun racks, most waiting repair, some for sale and some ready for customers who come from miles around to avail themselves of Wally's expert gun service. He figures he's made guns or stocks for people in every state in the Union, and "made'em for some Europeans too."

While I was there a Bismarck man, employee of a notable gun dealership and repair business in that city, walked in carrying an armload of firearms for Wally to repair – work that required

18

the services of a real gunsmith not just a gun repair man.

"You can pick 'em up next week on your way through, I should have most of them done by then."

One needed a barrel straightening job, another had a bad headspace problem.

"Say, by the way," Wally said, "I might be interested in buying this one if the price is right."

It was an old military carbine with a mauser-type action, and it was only the action he really wanted. According to Wally the mauser action is the strongest and most durable around. Most of his custom-made rifles include mauser-type actions.

Later, a young man came in to pick up a rifle that had some kind of cartridge ejection problem. He also wanted some powdered graphite for the action. Wally spent ten minutes looking for a small container in which to put some.

"What do I owe you?"

"Ah, get'cha next time — didn't take much."

I could see that the young fellow was quite surprised — so was I! Wally was a businessman too, and one from the old school.

One part of his shop housed his personal collection of firearms. I soon found out that Wally is no armchair hunter, he's an avid participant and still going strong. He loves North Dakota falls when he can take his English setter, "Gyp," out after sharpies and pheasants. What kind of shotgun does he use? He owns not one, but two Winchester 21 doubles, one 20-gauge and one twelve. Shotgun fanciers recognize the "21" as the gentlemen's scattergun. New, they sell for nearly $5,000. His greatest love is big game hunting and he has spent several falls in the Canadian and Alaskan wilds after moose, elk, bear, and goat.

A tragic accident several years ago almost ended Wally's hunting and shooting career. A cartridge accidentally fired, before it was completely chambered, tearing the brass apart and sending one piece deep into his eye. He lost that eye — his right eye, his shooting eye! Somehow he developed an excellent shooting ability using his left eye. He made a custom rifle featuring a one-inch off-set (to the left) scope and a one-inch off-set (to the right) stock to compensate for sighting problems. With the shotgun he lines up on his thumb which he sticks out and away from the left side of the forearm. Now, some 20 years since the accident, he says he shoots as good as ever.

We finally finished the tour. Wally was probably worn out from my constant interrogation. I was worn out from seeing so much, so fast, and from trying to ask questions and record answers about one thing while looking at some other intriguing appointment.

"Better start on that piece of birds-eye or I'll never get it finished."

"What time do you predict you'll finish it?" I asked.

"Should be done by midnight."

He wasn't working late just to please me. Wally frequently puts in days that start at 9 a.m. and don't end until 11 or 12 p.m. "Like it," he says, "and it keeps me out of mischief, too."

It was 1:30 p.m. when the barreled-action of the cal. 300 H & H was centered on the smooth-planed surface of the maple blank for the initial measurements. I loaded my 35mm camera, mounted the strobe and got ready to record the unusual metamorphosis the maple blank was about to experience.

Springer's stockmaking tools are basic. In fact, they're essentially no different than those used by biblical wood craftsmen — a couple of chisels, a one-and-a-half pound oak mallet, and an assortment of rasps and files. A table saw is used once to make a clean cut of the stock butt and a drill press is used to drill two holes, the rest of the work is all hand-accomplished.

Wally worked steady, conversing freely, and I kept him talking answering my nagging questions. We talked about the gunsmith business and its future, especially for young men.

"It's a good business," Wally assured me, "but where is a young fellow going to get started — there are so few craftsmen left for them to work with and learn from. Take me, I can't possibly have anyone in here and be training and paying him. Hell, I'd be violating half the federal government's safety and labor regulations, and I surely can't afford to revamp this place just to do that. If we had the old apprentice system, like the Germans started, we could still put out craftsmen. Some of the gunsmithing schools are alright for what they do, trouble is, it takes years to acquire the skills of a craftsman. Where are they going to go after they leave school? Unless they can somehow keep close to an experienced gunsmith, they'd never make out."

All the time the maple blank was being worked. The roughed out bed for the barreled-action was nearly complete. By now Wally had shed the fur cap and vest. Tiny sweat beads rose on his bald head. He was working, getting to know that piece of wood. By 3:30 p.m. the barrel was bedded properly and the floor plate was just about in place.

"Pretty soon we can start moving the wood. That's fun, just like sculpting."

Two neighorhood kids came in. Tiny fellows, they looked up at Wally, then longingly eyed the pop machine (those kids were probably the only reason Wally had that machine in the shop).

"What are ya having?" Wally asked, digging into his jeans for a couple of quarters.

"Haven't seen you guys all winter, takes a nice day like today to bring you boys out of hiding, huh?"

The kids took off, each with a large bottle of pop.

"Those little rascals make my day."

In another hour Wally started "moving wood" with a chisel and plane. It came off slowly, the maple eyes popping and splintering when the tools moved too fast.

"I can see already this miserable hunk of wood has its own ideas about being worked. You know, I've had this piece of wood for two or three years and I've been putting off working on it a long time. One guy wanted to buy it — way it looks I think I should have sold. She's a mean one!"

We covered a lot of subjects, from gun dogs to chickenpox, Wally chiseling away, the mallet jarring the steel chisel, the chisel stealing short thin slices from the obstinate maple. But it was starting to show. I wondered though, how he could complete it by midnight.

". . . Ya, I knew old Bill Weaver when he lived in El Paso in the 1920s . . . he got started in his garage back then."

We talked about his three-point bedding system using fiberglass because it was more inert than wood — how he firmly bedded the barreled-action in the glass and later during fine tuning, or as Wally called it, "accurizing," how the glass is removed until the barreled-action rest on only three critical points.

"All barrels are different though, you never get two the same."

This happens even though Wally buys Douglas barrels — considered one of the best barrels around.

"Occasionally, well, in fact darn seldom, a barrel comes along, about one in 200, that we call a "gilt-edged" barrel, which turns out to be super-accurate. But they're rare and when you do find one you don't realize it until you're on the bench with it and then it's too late because you've made it for someone."

Wally related a story about one "gilt-edged" barrel he stocked for one of his rancher friends. "He told me he wanted a rifle that would tip over coyotes from his yard down to the fence corner, about 250 yards. Well, I built him a beautiful cal. 25-06 on a mauser action. I'll never forget the day I finished it and took it to the range to test fire."

Holding up his thick thumb and indicating the thumb nail, he said, "that son-of-a-gun shot a group no wider than that. That, was one accurate weapon. But he ordered it, bought it — it was his, darn it! I didn't say anything about it being a gilt-edged when he picked it up. But it wasn't two weeks he came back ranting and raving about the terrific rifle I'd made him."

"Those coyotes don't sit out by that fence corner no more," he bragged.

Wally leveled with the guy and offered to buy it, but it wasn't for sale.

It was getting late. Supper had come and gone. The stock was taking shape but that burly maple would change only with Wally's ruthless, incessant tooling. He kept chiseling, planing, filing. I was on my fourth 20-exposure roll of film.

At around 9 p.m. a mixture of Hettinger-area gun buffs strolled in and out, each taking his turn to peer over Wally's shoulder and offer some comment about that nasty piece of maple. It was obvious that this gun shop was a collecting place for those who wanted to argue shooting and firearms. A particular subject was argued back and forth until no further headway could be made. About then, Wally would settle the argument with some obscure fact. Through it all Wally persisted. His head was wet with sweat. His thick forearms and hands seemed thicker yet, swollen from the constant isometric exertion.

I tried to qualify the demand that damnable piece of birds-eye was making on Wally. I tallied some data, averaged it and came up with some staggering figures. The 1.5 pound mallet was being swung an average of about 70 times per minute. He'd been working on this particular aspect for about three hours — therefore moving an equivalent of 18,900 pounds in that time and mostly with shoulder, arm, and wrist action. No wonder his arms looked like fence posts!

Midnight arrived. The job was not complete. That birds-eye maple was the problem.

"A normal piece of walnut I would've completed, sanded and finished by supper time. But it won't be long now — noon tomorrow, should have her done by noon tomorrow."

I grabbed the last motel room in town. I was exhausted and I couldn't imagine how Wally felt. I konked out and eight hours later awoke to a three-inch snowfall. Up at the shop Wally was ready to go, having just finished his routine, morning constitutional with dog Gyp.

The gunstock was ready for glass bedding of the barreled-action. It was a messy job and one that required quick work because of the fast-setting glass. After bedding, the curing was to take about an hour or so. Unfortunately, my time was up. I wasn't going to be able to see the finished product. But Wally saved the day, agreeing to photograph the remaining steps and the completed rifle. If he could do that I would have a complete photographic record of a craftsman's procedures of hand-making a birds-eye maple gunstock in record time. Wally completed the stock by late afternoon. Take away coffee and lunch time, the entire job from barreling the action, blueing it, checkering and finishing the stock took just under 20 hours. "I got a real good 'do' on this one, yes sir, a real good 'do.' But it was a bugger, I'm glad its finished."

The next day Wally took the completed rifle with mounted Leupold scope to the firing range. It wasn't a gilt-edged weapon but it shot a very respectable group. He was satisfied. He had hand-crafted another beautiful shooting piece. Complete with scope and sling it sold for around $550. Considering the quality of workmanship and the possibility that a Wally Springer custommade firearm may someday be a collector's item, it may have been a good deal at twice the price.

North Dakota OUTDOORS, May, 1977

Postscript

Riflesmith Wallace A. Springer, 78, is still at it matching the finest steel barrels he can find to his hand-shaped walnut and maple stocks. Wally says, "the demand for good rifles throughout America is good - always good! Some go to Canada, Alaska and numerous other areas." Lately Wally has been making rifles for the big cowboys of Oklahoma and Texas. "Can you imagine," Wally querries, "a pull of 17½ to 18½ inches. These are really big men. Hands twice the size of my own and standing a little under seven feet (pull is the distance between the trigger and the butt plate). Wally expects to continue making rifles for big and small people for a long time. "A supply of suitable walnut for a stockmaker like myself runs between 200 and 400 blanks." And that's about the supply of excellent walnut he has on hand right now. Do you want a fine, homecrafted rifle, beautiful wood, Douglas barrel steel or better, all shaped around the sturdy mauser action? Look no further - call Wally. That's Wally Springer - out of Hettinger, N.D. - still gunmaker extraordinaire.

Spring, 1988 H.T.U.

MILLER BEDFORD:
FALL IS JUST AROUND THE CORNER

I hope Miller's still around.

Why? Because it's fall again — it's his time of year. But I don't really know Miller, I never met the man, so why should I care? The only reason I even know of him is because a friend once gave me a bottle of his Bedford Gunjuice, Miller's that is, hardly reason to have any feelings about the man.

Several years ago I wrote a piece about preparations for fall's golden hours afield and in that article I referred to the gunjuice that I had regularly used. Even then, only a few drops remained in the plain patent-medicine-like bottle. So, the following fall, when the last of the keen-scented gun liniment was wiped across the worn receiver of my Model 12 sixteen, I wrote for more, to the rather obscure address just barely visible on the oil soaked label: THE BEDFORD CO. NEW LONDON, OHIO. With the letter I included a copy of the article that made mention of the uncommon gun oil. I don't think I really expected a response.

Pleasantly surprised I was, though, when one finally came. Thus our introduction by way of correspondence—me to request another bottle of pungent gun lubricant—he to write back about the dissolution of his gunjuice business with a liberal sprinkling of endearing testimony about his love for gunpowder, fields, and water spaniels and his special fondness for fall days. His response, typed on green onionskin paper, front and back, was barely legible. It seemed an unnecessary exercise in frugality, unless that piece of paper was the lone one in his household.

He started out: "Mighty good friends, Ted: You brought joy to yer ole friend. Liked your article, liked the monument you have left me re: the gunjuice. Sat on the sunny side of the house and read and reminisced. Too wet early and too dry now and hot which I like, but those beautiful fall days, when you can toast in the sun and freeze in the shade are starting and those are the days that make Norma and me excited!"

What about the gunjuice, I thought, when's he going to get to what I wrote him for?

"Used to get her studying game laws out west . . . the west is the place. Your place—North Dakota, South Dakota. Once I thought I'd go 'spite of hell or hot weather. Oh well, we ain't suffering and I intend to shuffle off with more than I can use."

"Oh, how I used to love this kind of weather out there. Before my water spaniel learned about jackrabbits he almost got one. Those jacks knew no dog would chase them but they did not know he didn't know it and he being big and fast nearly got the jack. Before my pal got wise his tongue was out a foot and no water. We searched and maybe found a slough. The old dog knew the minute I changed from pheasants to ducks and acted accordingly. What a nose he had. Time and time again he trailed on the driest ground . . . when the highly touted dogs lost the smell.

"After a successful hunt I might end up 75 miles from good old Starr's place [a South Dakota muzzle loading shotgun expert]. I would head for home with the radio on and the old Buick Roadmaster hitting those rough roads 75 miles an hour. The dog and I would go into a restaurant and I would buy him regular people hamburger sandwiches and ice cream cones. God, how he loved it! Had a trunk in the back and after the hunt and eats he would look out as though he owned the world or was at least the boss and smile all over all the way home then strut his stuff when he got there. Just like me. Starr was then in the middle of his career—like I and the gunjuice."

What an unusual man, out of the blue, sharing with me his life and times, laid out on flimsy tissue almost impossible to read. He wrote longingly. He seemed without a cause, perhaps the gun-juice business was dead and his ambition eroded. It seemed as if my note and the enclosed article had given him something or someone with whom to talk. But, in the next line the tempo picked up as he wrote about hunting.

"Norma and I shot the first two deer they thought had been shot on the Deer Corral in Wyoming in 30 years. Starr was there. With modern guns. We hunted antelope on the prairies and hence knew long running shots . . . 30/06, 150 grain Jordan bullets. In those days Jordan made the tough jacketed bullets and we used them."

He was happily into his subject, communicating it more with each touch of his typewriter key, spilling information over the page like gravy on hot spuds.

"We now recommend the 125 grain bullet in the '06, scoop loaded and pounded in with the fastest powder you can use and it ain't 4350. I could write a book on true ballistics instead of the mythology supposedly knowledgeable writers put out and are wrong. They copy the previous mistakes and most tables are intelligent guesses. I wildcatted several big game caliber magnums . . . the light bullet that will hold together drops the game dead before the knees buckle. And does not spoil the meat. Hydraulic action. Tiny exit hole. I have a helluva time getting these fellows away from thinking in terms of the old lead bullets."

He knew more than the gunjuice business. He'd been around, had some firearms instruction and a lot of experience.

"Starr once said gunjuice did half his gun repairs for him. You know, that South Dakota loam goes to finest black dust and mixes with household oils to lock up actions, particularly the model 12s."

I liked him. Didn't know him beyond this confusing communication. But I liked him. He had other friends, too, and the list read like a Who's Who of the gun world.

"We were good young friends of Pop Neidner, who taught me a lot and how to learn ballistics. Were friends of Gen. Thatcher. Knew old man Crossman, Col. Whelan, Harry Pope, top gun officials and experimenters, Elmer Keith, Phil Sharpe, Major Slim Ackerman, the real fun folks of the world. Oh, and Jack O'Connor, who once told a bellyacher: 'If Miller Bedford doesn't know who does?' Col. Whelan got me in the gunjuice business. I must add Herbert Hilton, the engraver, who used to be with me at Camp Perry, an old time record army man with the Krag when younger, moved to Arizona . . . and is still engraving [1973]

26

and must be crowding 90."

A few more words, a final fact or two thrown in for authority's sake and the letter ended: "Yrs., Miller."

Miller Bedford. I'll be danged! Shooter, gun collector, sportsman, dog lover, Starr's attendant, and founder of Bedford Gunjuice, the best gun cleaner in America. You're alright! But why did you stop making the gunjuice? I liked it. Maybe Hoppe didn't, but I liked it. I must have, because my one-and-only bottle lasted many years — I dispensed it in very small doses, like an expensive perfume.

Last week I went to my closet to prepare my guns for fall. There on the top shelf was an empty bottle I have carried with me since its content disappeared several years ago. I reached for the dusty-shouldered container, held it in the palm of my hand and read:

8 Fluid Ounces

B E D F O R D

G U N J U I C E

Best Gun Cleaner

in America

Use in EVERYTHING on or in a GUN. Metal, wood, inside, outside. Better than water, oil gunks, grease, other effuviums. Contains no coal oil, fuel oil, diesel oil, vinegar, soap water, or weird ingredients dreamed up by some ancient alchemist on his way home from the local dead toad rubbing society in the light of a low moon long after midnight, on Friday, the 13th of January 23rd. THE BEDFORD CO., NEW LONDON, OHIO. Not Guaranteed.

I hope Miller's still around.

Why? Because it's fall again — it's his time of year. The gunjuice vats are empty, the bottles are dry, but I've got a place in my heart for you, Miller Bedford. But I don't really know you, so why should I care? Because you made a mighty fine product and now I think there had to be a little of you in each and every drop.

Hey Miller, go ahead, crack the cap on that last bottle you've been saving. Steal a sniff. Now feel your mood change, the season brighten. It's fall again, Miller, and that empty bottle on my shelf reminds me of it and you and other exciting falls when the bottle was still half full.

North Dakota OUTDOORS, September, 1977

Gunjuice Epilog, November, 1977

Miller Bedford, 74, is gone. In a personal letter received earlier this month from his widow Mrs. Norma Bedford she stated, "My sad, sad news to you is I lost my Miller May 29, 1977."

An article in the September, 1977, issue of **North Dakota OUTDOORS** titled "Miller Bedford: Fall is Just Around the Corner," addressed itself to Miller Bedford and the Bedford Gunjuice product he once manufactured in Ohio. I was unsure that he had passed away.

A number of people have commented on the article. A letter from a Bedford advocate came from Ohio with a monetary memorial which we put into the North Dakota Prairie Chicken Fund. He said, "Miller . . . was a man of great intelligence in so many areas of life the layman had to be on his toes to keep up, most just listened when Miller talked. I have a bottle of gunjuice I cherish."

A letter from a man in Anchorage, Alaska, included some other thoughts. "I too miss Bedford's Gunjuice. I think I bought the last bottle . . . Log Cabin Sport Shop, Lodi, Ohio, had in stock. I met Miller in the early '50s. He used that tissue-like paper in all of his correspondence. Bedford used to tout the juice as being good for everything. I alas, now believe him."

I only became acquainted with the man through our correspondence, hence, comments like these added a little bit more to my understanding of Miller.

A day after I received Norma Bedford's letter, a package, also from her, was delivered to my desk. I could smell what it was before I removed the heavy wrapping. Inside was a full bottle of Bedford Gunjuice.

Postscript

Miller Bedford's wife, Norma, and the author have corresponded annually for several years. They have never met, yet there is some identification, like that which the author felt in reading Miller's onionskin letter. Now 86, Norma still drives her own car "everywhere I can afford gasoline." The author still has a bottle of Bedford Gunjuice. It must be the last of all of it.

Spring, 1988 H.T.U.

NANCY...GRAND LADY OF THE HEART

The scene is tranquil. A variety of farm buildings stand unemployed in a grassy yard, some shaded by the narrow ribbon of forest that flanks the Heart River on its way to meet the big Missouri. Barnyard livestock are absent. Machinery is gone, except for a line of rusty steel wheels that rest against a weathered board fence.

Few human sounds survive the trip to this remote valley hideaway. Other sounds are natural. The wind through the trees, melodious bird songs, and the drone of insects replace urban cacophony; sounds perhaps little different than those heard by saddle-sore 7th Cavalrymen who crossed the Heart just north of here on their way to the 1876 Battle of the Little Bighorn, or by brave freighters that used the Keogh Trail to carry mail and supplies from Bismarck to Miles City and back.

In 1882 the Northern Pacific Railroad reached Miles City and Keogh Trail traffic ended shortly thereafter. In the same year Swedish immigrant Sone Christenson came to this valley and filed on a homestead. This farmstead—this tranquil place. He lived here for a short time, but long enough to put up a cottonwood-log claim shack and stake some boundaries. Then he returned to Sweden, auctioned all but his essential possessions, packed up his wife Christina, three sons and two daughters and returned to the homestead in May, 1884. On February 26, 1886, a third daughter, a sixth and final child, was born to the Christensons in their drafty, one-room frame home. They named her Nancy.

Today Nancy is 91 years old. It isn't her age alone, however, that makes her special. It's not that she managed to survive nearly a century nor that she has outlived her brothers and sisters and two husbands that brands her unique.

Her specialty is lifestyle. Though she herself may not be conscious of it, others are. Her unbending loyalty to her Heart River valley heritage, her mockery of Father Time and her rather successful avoidance of the "developed establishment" over the years, first with her family and now alone, is her adopted way. But she's not a recluse, even though solitude is her most frequent companion. She loves people and enjoys visits from friends and children. The telephone gets a daily workout. She makes and takes scheduled calls from friends along the valley and from Mandan and Bismarck.

Like her father Sone did when he first filed his claim in '82, Nancy lives alone now, unwilling to turn her back on the peaceful valley that has been her whole life and move to the city where some say she would be "so much more comfortable." But there's no question in her mind that the city would have been the death of her years ago. Except for twelve days in 1933 when she was in Chicago she has never been off the place for more than a day. For the last several years she has ventured off the farm only once each year, usually in September. She has no car so friends take her to Mandan for her annual medical checkup, flu shot, and eye examination.

She uses this opportunity to stock up on provisions for the winter. The generally unimproved trail winding down to the valley from the plain above is periodically blocked. Sometimes, during especially snowy and stormy periods, the mailman may not reach her for a week or so and the telephone is her only link with neighboring families.

Living in the kitchen area in which she was born and the front room in which she was schooled and where few excessively modern changes have occurred, save for electricity and telephone, Nancy has watched the surrounding countryside change to accommodate 20th century America. An old black and white television, a radio and numerous periodicals, magazines, and newspapers have been her public information servants because of her reluctance to travel away from the valley.

At first glance she doesn't seem physically up to living alone in such independent fashion. She stands barely over five feet tall, and must weigh less than one hundred pounds. But seeing her in action, in her joy of hosting visitors, suggests her capability. Her black and gray hair is braided and pinned delicately across the top of her head and wisps of it float away from her temples as her brisk pace takes her flitting around her home.

She has some hearing loss and her eyesight is slipping a bit. Each September her original wire-rimmed glasses are adjusted a little bit more. She's petite. But she's also rugged. Her energy seems boundless and her mind is alert and sharp like someone's fifty years her junior.

School for Nancy began when she was six years old, in 1892 up to about 1900. In those days school was held only three months every other year during December, January, and February. The farm home was the school house and about ten kids attended. They walked or rode horseback up to four miles to get there. The teacher was paid $25 per month but was charged $8 per month for room and board. Reading, writing, and arithmetic were required courses and electives were few. Pump-pump-pull-away and last-couple-out were favorite recess games. The Christensons were a family of great readers. They subscribed to nearly 20 magazines, periodicals, and newspapers and the children continued their educations with exposure to this and other literature. Nancy became a local news correspondent for the Mandan Pioneer.

One of the main reasons the family tried to get at least one representative to Mandan each week was because of the mail. During one winter period Nancy remembers that heavy snow prevented travel even by horses. But the family was so anxious to get the mail that her brothers made a pair of skis and retrieved the Mandan mail soon after.

Nancy didn't get into Mandan until she was nine years old. Probably her favorite childhood memory is that day in 1895 when she finally got to town and bought a colorful ribbon for her hair. Shortly after that she got her own horse, a white gelding she named Two-Bits, and rode him to town frequently for several years. She kept that horse for 22 years. Around 1915 she graduated to a motorcycle for farm to market transportation. Gardens were big in those days and they weren't grown so much for fun or hobby as for providing essential food stuffs. Nancy had a three-acre nursery garden on a quarter she homesteaded. One year, she recalls that it was 1914, she grew a bonanza strawberry crop. The family had all they could eat fresh and they canned until the jars ran out. There was still plenty so she sold picking rights to neighbors and made the garden pay off in cash too.

The garden provided for much of the Christenson's vegetable and fruit diet. What about protein? Wildlife provided a lot of that need. In the valley woods and surrounding prairie, "chickens" and sharp-tailed grouse were abundant as was venison on the hoof. But the buffalo was gone even before the homestead was filed in 1882. The family loved cottontails and also found the lanky jackrabbit fit for their table.

One day in the late '90s a pair of pigeons arrived and took up housekeeping in the barn. They became firmly established and the family began depending on them for food. For years the family ate squab, boiled, fried and in pigeon pie. Nancy recalls using at least a hundred a year. Then in the late 1960s, just before her late husband's death they captured 102, butchered 100 and released a pair. The two disappeared, descendents of birds that were a part of the Christenson farmstead for over 70 years.

Early in life Nancy discovered her talent for drawing and sketching animals from the pages of magazines. She called it copy work. But the likenesses weren't tracings — they were her own freehand replicas. She got ahold of a camera and soon became a serious photographer of farm animals, most of which she dressed up to resemble people by using doll-size clothing and using miniature props. Before she was done she had gained national attention and many of her photographs were carried on postcards. With this and a small commercial film developing and printing room situated in a small corner of the cramped farm home, she did quite a business in the 1920s and early 1930s.

She married Herman Apenes, a Mandan storekeeper in 1927. Together they lived on the farm with Nancy's family sharing the hard times of those years. Mr. Apenes died in 1934. In 1935 Nancy married Carl Hendrickson and he too moved onto the farm. In 1970 he passed away, leaving Nancy alone.

Since then she has remained by herself on the picturesque homeplace. At 91 years old she displays a commendable perseverance, a strong will to live her final years in her childhood home. Why does she stay? "I have everything here," she replied. "Why should I move away from this nice place. I want to be here until I'm called home."

North Dakota OUTDOORS, November, 1977

Postscript

Nancy Hendrickson believed life in the city would be the death of her. And so it was. In July of 1978 she fell and broke her hip and for the first time in her life, according to nephew Ernest Blaich of Bismarck, "we had to take her out of her beloved home where she was born and lived all her life." Nursing home life was not Nancy's way. Blaich says, "She just sort of gave up." She died November 20, 1978 at 92 years of age. A resourceful pioneer was gone. Her photographic successes, which began for her before 1920, included animal photos in the New York Times, displays in the State Historical Society and appearances in **Morton County Roots.**

Spring, 1988 H.T.U.

BILL BURNS
– A BIOLOGIST'S ENGINEER –

$\mathbf{D}$riving through what Bill Burns calls the "north-forty" on Amoco Oil Company's Mandan refinery site is like touring a professionally managed wildlife area. Really a 320-plus acre tract, it is principally a treatment ground for the refinery's water effluent. The excellent quality of this industrial discharge is in itself a noteworthy accomplishment. An impressive byproduct, however, is some 100 acres of undisturbed vegetative cover, 15 acres of woody plantings, 90 acres of leased alfalfa, some 20 acres of wildlife food patches (sunflowers and corn), and even 3-4 acres of back-eyed peas (which the deer have finally found) that surround the eight-pond, 100-acre, gravity-flow water course.

Pheasants, sharptails, Huns, wood ducks, giant Canada geese, a variety of other waterfowl and shore birds, deer, mink and muskrat are all represented on the area. Most wildlife is here voluntarily in response to the developed vegetative diversity. Burns raised some pheasants and released wood ducks at one time, but today most species are self-sustaining. Last winter over 40 antelope tuned in on this "Amoco Oasis" and utilized available food and cover.

If there is anything disappointing about the area it's that no hunting is allowed. As interested in hunting as Burns is, the tempting tract must necessarily remain off limits to hunters because of commerical and residential development surrounding it. "I've thought long and hard to come up with some way to allow some hunting," pines Burns, "but I see no way to do it."

Still, it's all somewhat of a mystery, at least at first glance. Why such a vegetatively and wildlife-rich acreage within bounds of an imposing oil industrial complex?

Stetson-hatted Burns, Amoco's head man at the Mandan refinery says, "It's a challenge and it's good to combine what we have to do in the water treatment area with conservation of wildlife. Before we started on this system of water treatment the area was sort of a barren place—no game, no cover."

Significantly, healthy wildlife exists here and is used as an environmental barometer. "If animal life can exist and flourish here," Burns claims, "then we have a pretty good idea that refinery impacts in the area of water quality will have little effect on humans."

That pretty much ends the mystery. There is a legitimate and sincere effort at Mandan's oil refinery to treat the plant's waste water in the best way they know how. Eight years ago Burns came to Mandan to manage the refinery, but he accepted a new challenge in water treatment. This and conservation planning on refinery lands have been his pet projects ever since.

You don't listen to Bill Burns long before you realize that he's a southerner. A slow, deliberate speech accented with a Texas drawl, though somewhat quieted by eight years of northern yankee living, gives him away.

Interest in wildlife and natural resource conservation is probably an outgrowth of his boyhood in West-central Texas. Here, as a grade-schooler, amid towering derricks and the pungent odors of a burgeoning oil industry, he bird-dogged doves for his physician father, uncle and his mother, a nurse and outdoor lover. Soon he graduated to the .410 gauge shotgun and at age 12 inherited his deceased father's 12-gauge Model 11 Remington, which is still shoots today.

His father's death didn't slow the family's interest in hunting. Supervised by Mrs. Burns, numerous trips were taken in the old

Nash touring car for quail and doves. Dove hunting remains his first love. Shooting, though, was but a part of the experience. A love of the outdoors was cultivated and a thirst for knowledge about the natural community, its plants and animals, probably began in Bill Burns in his impressionable boyhood days of the 1920s and '30s.

Yet the ubiquitous Texas oil fever was contagious and it captured his fancy. After graduating from the University of Texas at Austin with a degree in chemical engineering, he began his career in the petroleum industry with Amoco Oil (then known as Standard Oil), the company to which he has devoted most of his working days. He began work at the Texas City refinery in 1943. Ten years later he moved to Savannah, Georgia to work at the company's asphalt refinery and ten years after that he journeyed to their Neodesha, Kansas refinery.

It was at Neodesha that Burns became interested in new ways to treat plant effluent. It was also during this period, the late 1960s, when various environmental groups clamored for a new responsible environmental ethic in government and industry. In general, industries across the country were being scrutinized for air emissions and water effluent quality, among other things. Already inspired, this new impetus perhaps encouraged Burns to pull down his Texas Stetson thinking hat. Fortunately, Amoco Oil had in Bill Burns not only a cracker-jack chemical engineer, but also a man with an environmental conscience.

In 1970 Burns moved to Mandan to head-up the 175-man Amoco light oils refinery. On the plant's 1,000-acre site Burns began some low-key water experiments involving routing chemically-laced lagoon water through ponds for purification. He proceeded intently, but cautiously, aware that his Chicago-based supervisors were keeping a questioning eye on his progress.

In 1974 the Environmental Protection Agency (EPA) issued Amoco a permit to run more extensive water quality studies in cooperation with Bismarck's municipal water plant. New surface water quality standards for the Heart River meant that Amoco's lagoon discharge, via a two-mile ditch south from the plant to the Heart, must come to an end and the company was forced to further treat lagoon water for discharge elsewhere. The Missouri River, immediately east of the plant-site, was the next choice. First, though, water effluent quality had to be measureably improved, and, it had to pose no problem when discharged upstream of Bismarck's municipal water intake.

And why is there a water quality problem to begin with? The oil refining process takes water, and substantial amounts of it daily. Approximately 1,000,000 gallons are pumped from the Missouri River each day to replace water that is evaporated and discharged into the plant lagoon for routing through the treatment system. River water quality changes for the worse as it moves through the plant system because of chemical treatment to make it acceptable for plant use.

The accommodating Burns can turn out a technical recitation on Amoco's water processing that can dizzy his listener. Before he's finished he takes on a professorial attitude that transports one back to college chemistry days. But he clearly summarizes: "We have three main water quality problems: 1) cooling water, 2) water made into steam, and 3) water and steam that contact oil surfaces. The big contaminants that result are phenols, ammonia nitrogen, BOD (biological oxygen demand) compounds, and chromium, which in some forms is very poisonous to plant and animal life." (Toxic forms of chromium are converted to acceptable forms before being released to the plant lagoon.)

For many years this material was discharged from the plant lagoon into the ditch down which it flowed into the Heart River. No more. Today lagoon surplus water is pumped to a high point on the southwest corner of the plant site and there it begins its several-week trip through Burns' sophisticated pond system that will cleanse it of all but trace amounts of contaminants. Contaminants are "processed out" while moving through the man-made marsh system by infiltration, bacterial action, absorption by aquatic plants that metabolize some compounds, and by oxygenation by movement over pond outlets.

At Dam 4 (named in order of construction), the final pond before discharge into the Missouri River, Burns confidently drinks the "naturally repurified" water. Pollutants are at such dilute concentrations that the water poses no currently identifiable threat to human health. Discharge into the river effects further dilution and the Bismarck municipal water plant "can't detect us in their intake water," says Burns. "Our coliform bacteria (a bacteria associated with human sewage. The plant lagoon also handles plant sewage) count is low . . . that's why I can afford to taste and drink it."

How efficient is the pond treatment system? Manager Burns reports that their effluent quality already is better than self-imposed 1978 plant standards. Impressively, discharge at Dam 4 meets and surpasses proposed 1983 EPA limits. But Burns is practical. He continues to refine and develop the treatment process—soon a ninth pond will be tied into the system. He knows full well that future limits will be even higher. He says, ". . . it may even come to the point where no discharges at all will be allowed." Irrigation studies have begun to meet that eventuality.

Dollars? Burns estimates that an alternative mechanical/chemical water treatment process known as activated carbon sludge process would have cost the company $3,000,000 to start, not counting labor, chemicals, and upkeep. Burns' biological pond processing system has done the job as well for a cost of, at the outside, $250,000.

As quickly as the unassuming oil executive goes into the technical explanation of water chemistry he's out and admits, "I'm not a biologist, so I hired an environmental consulting firm to evaluate our pond system and water treatment efficiency." Burns has also utilized advise from Dale Henegar, fisheries chief with the North Dakota Game and Fish Department who has pronounced Burns' efforts in water treatment as "exemplary." Burns has also consulted with the federal Fish and Wildlife Service. Bob Randall, Bismarck, a retired wildlife biologist, has been contracted to document game bird and nongame bird representation and densities on the area.

Mort Johnson, an Amoco employee, was so impressed with his superior's progress that he encouraged waterfowl biologist Chuck Schroeder of the State Game and Fish Department to visit the area and suggest what could be done to attract waterfowl. But even then the area had matured. In October, 1976, Burns observed a flock of giant Canada geese on the treatment ponds. In April, 1977, he reported what he thought was a nesting pair of giant Canadas. He was correct. By late summer seven young reached flight stage at Amoco. In May, 1977, the Game and Fish Department released 35 yearling giant Canada geese. In spring, 1978, numerous geese stopped at the "north-forty." Five pair nested and subsequently reared 17 young to flight stage. The area is now established as a production site for the giant Canada goose, a species which, under intensive management, is staging an impressive come-back in North Dakota. The Amoco contribution is no small part of this effort.

Indeed, Bill Burns has done wonders with his "north-forty." "It helps to have a man like 'Red' Hager (Bismarck). He's a good man — he can really move earth." Hagar is Burns' right-hand man on construction and management.

Staff engineers like Les Helm, Mandan, have become infected with Burns' enthusiasm for the entire project. "At first I wasn't sure it was going to work," confessed Helm, "but it has worked out just fantastic . . . water quality is way better than we thought we'd get. And the wildlife . . . everybody around here, including many townspeople, are amazed at what's out here."

Results have also impressed top Amoco officials in Chicago and elsewhere. Burns' system compares favorably in water quality to other Amoco refineries across the country. Company representatives visiting the plantsite this past September were very pleased and are convinced the pond system is practical, efficient, and importantly, economical.

The bottom line to this entire account, however, is that Bill Burns looked for and found a better way to do a job. Someone else may have chosen other less environmentally sound options to solve the plant's water quality problem and been less concerned with the integrity of land and water acres under company control. Burns has demonstrated his and Amoco's concern for maintaining quality water and land use standards. Traditionally, rivalry has existed between engineers and biologists, particularly at the university level. When Bill Burns wants to cross the frothy waters that separate these two disciplines, he can do it with immunity. He talks two languages. He's a biologist's engineer!

And what about those black-eyed peas? Well, when the Burns family came North they reluctantly left a warm climate and excellent dove shooting, but they managed. What they couldn't handle was life without black-eyed peas. In his typically orderly style Burns outlined his interest in black-eyed peas, a dish as southern as Texas Tea. "Number one," he said tugging at his index finger, "deer can't stay out of them. If you want to shoot a deer in East Texas you go to a pea field."

"Number two," he continued about to divulge a bit of his inherent philosophy, "they're a legume and therefore fix nitrogen and benefit the soil."

A smile spread across his face and a chesty chuckle followed that seemed to relax this serious, southern gentleman. "Number three . . . I like them . . . my wife likes them . . . we just love to eat them!"

Ten years from now 58-year-old Burns will be retired. It's a pleasant thought but he's afraid he won't see the maturation of his plans for the "north-forty." Maybe he'll stay up here in yankee country, but if he's enticed to retire in Texas, lazy-afternoon dove shooting and black-eyed peas will have figured big in his decision. For now though, he'll continue to keep on top of refinery water problems and continue looking for ways to make Amoco's "north-forty" a hospitable home for wildlife.

North Dakota OUTDOORS, November, 1978

POSTSCRIPT

Today Bill Burns is 67 years old and living in Austin, Texas. After this *article originally appeared and others showed up in the **Amoco Torch** magazine, Burns has been widely recognized for his environmental management. In 1979 Governor Arthur Link presented him the Water Conservation Award of the North Dakota Wildlife Federation. The Environmental Protection Agency, in 1980, awarded him their Citizen Participation Award for "care of this planet and protection of its life." In 1986, the Greater North Dakota Association presented Burns with their Natural Resources Award as an expression of gratitude for continuing a leadership role in the development and conservation of natural resources in North Dakota. Then in 1987 Burns journeyed to Washington, D.C. to accept an Environmental Achievement Award from the Corporate Conservation Council of the National Wildlife Federation. All this because of his innovative work on the "north-forty."*

Bill says, "I have hunted my last hunt, and that was in North Dakota, fittingly." Burns' health has deteriorated over the years from a head injury he suffered while swimming in his youth. He misses working: "I had the best job in the world and for the best company . . . I had planned to improve the "north-forty" in many ways . . ." Now this is left to his successors. It will be easier for them to pay attention, mainly because of the bridges Bill Burns crossed and the alternatives he advanced in corporate environmental stewardship.

Spring, 1988 H.T.U.

OSCAR NELSON: PROFILE OF A TRAPPER

Seems like everybody is doing it. From school kids to senior citizens, farmers to businessmen, a lot of people are laying a lot of steel next to the fencelines, field borders, marshes and streams of North Dakota's outdoors. Trapping, my friends, has become one of the most exciting fall pastimes to hit the outdoor scene in years.

Some do it for fun, for sport. Most, however, are probably out to see what part of the nearly two million dollar North Dakota fur harvest they can take home. The promise of a big greenback return makes it a competitive undertaking. Lately a good, prime, trapped fox has been worth a $50 bill. Could that be why 25,000 licenses were sold last year, but only 7,000 were sold in 1970 when ol' red's hide was worth only $6?

Oscar Nelson, Sharon, N.D., is a trapper. He runs a trap line and has done it for years for both fun and profit. For over 60 years he's been at it and most of them were years when big dollars weren't around. The 72-year-old Nelson is adaptable—knows the mink, muskrat, skunk, and badger sets as well as the fox set. So he isn't out of the trapping business when one pelt price slacks off. He's no Johnny-come-lately. His wide experience enables him to shift his efforts to pay-off species and during the 1970s, the price of long-haired furs, like fox, has brought him a tidy bundle.

But saturation trapping hasn't been the key to his success. You can skim the top off the fox crop with this method but you can't consistently be successful when the youngsters are gone and you're dealing with older more wary critters. Nelson's method is skilled technique—reading sign, habitat, recognizing good set sites, and improving on materials and methods. His best year was 1973 when he caught a record 90 fox in ten days and 212 for the season. In addition he trapped mink, raccoon, badger, and skunk.

In 60 years Nelson has come onto some good trapping ideas and has put them into practice. And you might guess that he must have collected a few stories in that time, too. He recognized that his life experiences on the trap line might interest others and be worth something to future generations. So, with the help of writer, Steve Sylvester of Grand Forks, Nelson produced a 64-page booklet entitled **Oscar Nelson: 60 Years a North Dakota Trapper**. This is available for $5.00 by writing Nelson at Sharon, N.D., 58277.

Little did I know I was heading into the season's first mean blizzard when I left Bismarck early on November 8 to visit with Nelson and hopefully spend a day with him on his trap line. The day before temperatures were high. In downtown Bismarck I'd had the car air conditioner on. Now I proceeded northeast in a rain that was changing to snow and ice. Strong winds prompted a radio announcer to broadcast November's first wind chill factor. I pulled into Sharon after lunch. There was two inches of snow on the ground and more was coming.

I found Mr. Nelson in his shop out behind the house, lighting the oil stove. The familiar smell of hide and carcass of a skinning shack greeted me as I entered. On the west wall hung a couple dozen skunk hides stretched inside-out waiting for the final fleshing job. I introduced myself, shook his strong sinewy hand and mentally sized up this trapper. About five foot eight inches tall, wiry frame, weathered leathery face, quick of movement, a certain vitality. He's no 72 years old, I thought to myself—he looks like 55!

"Isn't this something," Oscar stressed in a slight Norwegian brogue. "This will shut me down pretty good . . . have to reset now."

True enough the wet snow fall would ruin his sets — he had about 60 out — and each would have to be redone. The storm had kept him from the field. He didn't like it either, because checking traps daily was part of his trapping credo.

With no fresh furs to work on Oscar had little to do in the shop except scrape the skunk hides after they warmed a bit. All he could do now was wait out the weather. We headed to the house where Oscar's wife, Cora, made coffee and served homemade bread and jelly. We talked for several hours about his trapping career. All the time the snow came on, the wind whipped it about, beginning the drifts that would block roads across much of eastern North Dakota by morning. I made plans to stay overnight in Finley, ten miles to the south.

"Oscar," I asked, "where did you get your start trapping, how'd you become so interested?"

"Started when I was 11, about 1918. Really had no background, I must've been born a trapper — I think that's the only way I can put it."

"Was your father a trapper, any of the neighbors?"

"No, not much. Got started trapping jackrabbits which we used for food then. We weren't rich and jackrabbits helped a lot then to feed the ten of us. That's probably where I got my start. Guess this was fun for me, but it provided food, too."

"Seems like the need continued. Like the depression — 1932 to about 1936 — I trapped skunk and weasel. Got 85 cents for large and 65 cents for medium weasel. Skunks brought me about $2.50, if I recall. On Thanksgiving one of those years money from the furs helped us celebrate the holiday more than most people could. I remember I was skinnin' weasel in the kitchen and Cora was sewing baby clothes."

Oh, we were so happy for the furs," added Mrs. Nelson.

"I think it was that year I trapped around $300 worth of skunks and weasels and that was a lot of money then. We had enough to buy a battery-operated radio . . . neighbors came to listen to it."

"I suppose you've got special memories about skunks then," I asked.

"You bet, fond memories. Also used to pull skunks out from under granaries and rock piles. Think it was in '29 that Cora helped me. She was a little worried about getting sprayed, but it didn't happen. We used a long pole and a wire noose at the end. You hooked one carefully and pulled him out quietly and without any fast movements. Then you put him in a holding box.

We caught 'em this way early in the fall, then held 'em 'til they primed."

Times have changed and Oscar's the first to admit that. Time was when hardly anybody trapped. The country was wide open and for years mink was the big money pelt. But to make a trap line pay you had to be adaptable—be able to set for all kinds of furbearers and be able to process furs. There wasn't much competition from other trappers a few years back either.

"Nowadays a fella spends as much or more time looking for a place to hide his traps from others as he does looking for the best trap site. And that's too bad 'cause 75 percent of your luck is where you set."

"Have you had problems with theft?"

"Last year I lost one trap and two foxes—that's because I concealed them. Couple years back I lost eight sets in one week. I decided I'd have to be more careful where I set. In snow though it's pretty hard—you leave tracks. I don't like to trap in snow."

"How about the new permission law," I asked, "do you agree with it?"

"Good. It's good. You know where you're going to trap and you just feel better about it. Once in awhile there is some confusion like with a tenant and landowner giving different people sole rights. I carry my written permission slips right in the pickup."

Our discussion told me that Oscar Nelson lived by some rules—trapper ethics, if you will. There were certain things he avoided. I was pleased to discover, for example, that he had no time for the carcass set.

"No, that's a waste of time and good bait. I cut off a little piece of skunk, my favorite bait, and wire it onto the stake. I cover it with dirt so birds, like magpies, aren't attracted."

I found he doesn't trap closer than one-half mile from farms because of the chance of getting a dog or cat in the trap. He checks traps daily if at all possible. In his book he suggests trappers must "treat the land you are working like you own it."

But in spite of his efforts to stay "straight" Oscar says, "the big trapper, the professional, gets a lot of blame for what the amateurs do wrong." The novice may be hurting the future of trapping by not being properly instructed in field responsibilities and humane trapping techniques. As far as the anti-trapper sentiment, Oscar says defensively, "I have put some money into that."

This year Oscar delayed getting all his sets out on opening weekend. He figured it was a bit early. But since then he has worked hard with his 60 sets and it's clear to him that fox numbers

44

are way down from last year.

"Didn't the Game and Fish Department forecast about a 40 percent drop over last year," Oscar queried.

"That's correct," I said, "and you're not alone in noting that fox numbers are way down. I've heard others say they figured a solid 50 percent down from last year might be more reasonable."

"What do you owe the change to, Oscar?"

"Lots of trappers and hunters and some snowmobilers, too. I wonder if the coyote showing up again has anything to do with it. I know of some people up near Hatton, about 25 miles southwest of Grand Forks, that dug out a coyote den last spring."

"So, I've spent more time with skunks this year. I've got over 60 now and with them all being stretched and dried I expect to do better than five bucks apiece. Maybe go out west for coyotes. Looks like if I get a couple dozen foxes here I'll be doing good. But I'll do some good on mink, and rats too, if I can find decent water nearby. You gotta be able to trap all kinds."

Techniques? Ya, we talked techniques for quite awhile. Why he uses wood stakes instead of steel; a level dirt set rather that a dirt hole set; skunk fat for bait rather than the commercial stuff; single sets instead of doubles; problems with snow and rain; badger and pocket gopher mounds for ideal set sites; right-of-way sets; trap preparations; spring tension for different critters; chain length and how it affects animal escape; best methods to humanely kill trapped animals; avoiding skunk smell and a variety of other things. But they're all in his book and well worth looking at.

Oscar Nelson must be a pretty good trapper. Of course that hasn't been his only endeavor. During his life he's been a finish carpenter, poultry man, and a farmer. But I get the feeling that he would like to be remembered first as a trapper.

He's done it for fun, for love of the outdoors. Sure, he's made money, too. In fact just recently part of his trapping return helped pay for a new four-wheeler. "Thought I might as well get it — always wanted one. Money isn't going to do me any good when I'm dead." Mrs. Nelson agreed, "ya can't take it with you — ever seen a U-haul behind a hearse?"

The storm continued. Dusk was upon this quiet little community and if I was going to get to Finley I had to get going. Before I left the phone rang. Oscar answered.

"Who's this?" Oscar quizzed, "Spins you say? Hey Cora, it's that Spins program — that T.V. program — they want to come up here and go on the trap line with me."

Reckon Cal Olson's prairie television program "Spins" also

figured Oscar Nelson, 60 years a North Dakota trapper, is worth talking to.

North Dakota OUTDOORS, December, 1977

Postscript

Oscar Nelson is 82 years old. "Yes, I am still trapping," writes Oscar, "this past year was my 72nd year . . . I got 21 fox, 14 coons, one mink and 14 muskrats . . . I run 60 to 70 traps." In the summer Oscar raises lots of strawberries and raspberries. He says, "I plant 100 strawberries every year, so I have some income from the garden." Oscar looks forward to spring when he drives a big 4-wheel drive tractor and helps a neighbor put in the crop. Even so, he still has time for a little spring beaver trapping. Cora, his wife, passed away November 1, 1987.

Spring, 1988 H.T.U.

A LOOK AT
THE STUART YEARS

CONSERVATIONIST OF THE YEAR – 1977

R ussell Stuart is going to hang it up! Eighteen years the commissioner of the North Dakota Game and Fish Department, ranking senior administrative head of all state game and fish agencies, this crew-cut, trim 65-year-old North Dakota native will turn over the reins on May 31 of the agency he has been associated with since the early 1940s.

Over the years Stuart has marked up significant achievement for the Department and for himself. His professionalism and integrity have been witnessed on local, state, national, and international fronts. He has served on innumerable committees, boards, and councils and some of the most prestigious of those include: on two separate dates he was chairman of the Central Flyway Council; served on the legislative committee of the International Association of Fish and Wildlife Agencies, was a member of its executive committee, became its vice-president and finally its president in 1977; served as vice-president of the Midwest Game and Fish Commissioner's Association.

He has presented a number of papers to various organizations, and one of them given to the 1964 Convention of the National Wildlife Federation in Las Vegas on Public Law 566 pointed out the environmental problems of that law. Since then Stuart has vigorously opposed channelization projects. Politically popular they are, so he often risked his job with his objections. He is especially proud of presenting two papers, at different times, to the International Waterfowl Symposium.

He has held membership in a number of professional organizations, and the North Dakota Chapter of the Wildlife Society, of which he is a charter member, bestowed their North Dakota Award on Stuart in 1971. In 1977 he won the North Dakota Conservationist of the Year Award from the North Dakota Wildlife Federation.

All of the above he accomplished while commissioner since 1961. Yet his fish and wildlife experience prior to that time provided the solid foundation for these and many other achievements. In 1961, Russ Stuart was no tenderfoot to the natural resource profession. He began in this business years before.

In 1940 he hired on with the North Dakota Game and Fish Department as a biologist. He was one of the first professional people hired by the Department. With time out for service with the U.S. Army Air Corps radio school in World War II he returned to the Department in 1946 as assistant coordinator and research director working there until 1953 when he resigned to enter private business.

From the days of his youth on the farm near Bucyrus, where he was born and raised, Russ had an interest in natural science. When he left for the Agricultural College in '34 he enrolled in soils and chemistry but wound up with a strong botany background. Financial conditions of the '30s squelched his plans to go West for forestry training. Hard times and few jobs suggested he remain at school and complete his M.S. When the North Dakota job came along Russ said, "I grabbed it right away!"

Several days ago I sat with Russ and his long-loyal deputy commissioner, Wilbur Boldt, collecting material for this article. Stacks of paperwork were being whittled away as Stuart cleared out files and flipped through reports, manuals, and memoranda that were the hot issues (some still burning) of other days. The reality of retirement had finally struck home. Relaxation was obvious, the smiles came easier. Russ Stuart knew that the demanding schedule of public service would disappear, almost overnight, in just a matter of weeks.

Major achievements were accomplished by the Department under Stuart's guidance since 1961. Russ says his greatest satisfaction ". . . would be the acquisition of the Killdeer Mountain Wildlife Management Area." This 2,600 acre area was acquired in 1973. Stuart persevered in the face of considerable political and legislative opposition and saved for the people of North Dakota, *ad infinitum*, an area of rich floral and faunal diversity and cultural history. Acquisition of other lands also received his special attention. The native woodlands of the Turtle Mountains have been threatened for years and cleared for agricultural production. Stuart, working with Bob Rollings, wildlife resource management biologist from Devils Lake, aggressively sought acquisition of these increasingly rare aspen/oak woodlands.

In 1961, the year Stuart assumed the commissionership, the Department managed 57 game management areas totalling just over 50,000 acres (this includes leased Army Corps of Engineer lands associated with Lake Sakakawea). By 1979 the Department owned or leased 147 separate wildlife management areas scattered throughout 47 of the state's 53 counties and containing 148,431 acres of land and water (68,550 acres are in fee title and the balance are leased acres). Also during this time Stuart committed the Department to cooperative development of no fewer than 24 small watershed dams that today support fisheries. A few of the more noteworthy include Crown Butte, Sweet Briar, Davis Dam, McGregor Dam, Mt. Carmel, Buffalo Lake, Clausen Spring, Brewer Lake, and others. It is important to note that these areas are all open to public use, benefiting boaters, campers, photographers, and hikers, not just hunters and fishermen.

Stuart also feels good about being able to add two big game species to the huntable list. He placed continued emphasis on a program begun in 1956 to establish the California bighorn sheep in the North Dakota badlands. In 1975 the first modern-day bighorn sheep season in North Dakota was held. Through legislative work, mostly, he was able to secure a limited moose season for the state, the first one beginning in 1977.

Stuart served North Dakota during a transitional time in wildlife management. He saw the end of an era when nonprofessionals were gradually replaced by trained biologists. "That, too," he says, "has been satisfying—to see the general upgrading of personnel and the scientific approach to wildlife management."

At times when other Department programs were under fire, Stuart seldom heard any public criticism of the Department's official publication, **North Dakota Outdoors**. "One of the things I'm most proud of is the prestige and stature of 'Outdoors' and this, of course, is due primarily to the editor (Ed Bry)."

And there have been disappointments. Since land acquisition was a high priority objective of Stuart's administration, he is saddened to see the great opposition to further acquisition. "This has been a major disappointment and it is going to be felt in the years to come in a negative way."

"Another disappointment is that we have made little or no progress in working with agriculture, primarily in Congress, to come up with a stabilized program to provide certain benefits to wildlife . . . but until we get a national farm program that consciously looks to benefit agriculture, the consumer, and wildlife at the same time, it's going to be a hit and miss proposition."

The North Dakota Game and Fish Commissioner is appointed by the Governor, so it is generally considered a political post. Yet over the last 18 years the Department has remained strikingly nonpolitical.

I asked Russ if he had any idea that this job would run to 18 years. "No," he insisted, "when I took it I figured it would be for two years (length of term)."

"Do you have any idea," I queried, "what led administrators over the years to keep you on as commissoner?"

"First of all, I'd have to attribute most of it to luck," he chuckled, "that's the honest answer. I feel that one of the reasons I was able to weather storms from time to time was that I did everything in my power to keep the Department nonpolitical. In no case did I hire people due to political affiliation . . . in a Department of this kind I think this is vital to the continuity of our work. I made a real attempt to play no favorites with anyone—with employees or the public. Unfortunately, a nonpolitical stance does not make many friends for an individual."

A classic example of Stuart's dedication to the people and natural resources of the state and not to the "political machine" involved the proposed Kindred Dam to be constructed on the lower Sheyenne River for flood control for Fargo and vicinity. The dam would inundate the beautiful Sheyenne River valley, destroying unique plant life, and significantly reduce wildlife, especially white-tailed deer. In addition, dam building did not address the real source of flood problems—extensive wetland drainage within the watershed. Stuart laid his job on the line (late

1960s) and his future as commissioner when he traveled to Washington, D.C. to testify in opposition to the dam. On the same plane was Governor William Guy, a proponent of the project. The Governor and Stuart had earlier discussed their differing views and Governor Guy somewhat reluctantly gave Stuart his okay to make the trip providing Stuart confined his testimony to the fish and wildlife aspects of the project.

"I think it was extremely broadminded of him (Governor Guy) that he approved my travel request. I feel a credit should be given him . . . he could have easily knocked out my personal testimony by simply disapproving my travel." The Kindred Dam has still not been built.

Fun times? Humorous incidents? Over many, many years crazy things happen. But they're funny or maddening depending on where you stand — a subordinate or top administrator. Stuart's got a favorite employee (current employee) about who he loves to tell hilarious stories. But in order to print any of those this particular employee would also have to retire. "These must be held in abeyance," Stuart urged.

Once in 1940, his first year of employment with the Department and working under Commissioner William Lowe, Stuart was told to go to the Turtle Mountains to investigate intensive and widespread cutting of highbush cranberry by the Indian people of the Turtle Mountain Reservation. Apparently there was national demand for the bark of this species which was used in the preparation of drugs for the treatment of certain female disorders. The Department was concerned because of the possible impact to wildlife in the area and had no concern whatever about the economics of the mushrooming industry. During his investigation Stuart met with a "bark-buyer" who had in his home, and as a result of his prosperous business, all the period comforts (including an electric refrigerator). The man was living high-on-the-hog and he loved it. But he became suspicious of Stuart and thought his presence was to stop the lucrative cranberry bark business.

"If you're here to stop my business," the man yelled, "I can have a thousand Indians in town before sundown and there will be another Indian uprising in North Dakota!" Somehow understanding prevailed and Russ escaped. The bark issue finally ended up in Congress. Stuart's biological conclusion was that the cutting was probably good, not bad, for the highbush cranberry trees, because cutting promoted vigorous regrowth.

Roy Bach is a name that continually surfaces when Stuart recollects the old days. Bach was a biologist that worked with

Stuart in the '40s and was a man many say was 25 years ahead of his time in terms of biological and population dynamics savvy. Bach and Stuart pioneered aerial survey techniques for big game and some furbearers and the basis of their early work is used by state agencies around the country today. But, it is funny either Bach or Stuart survived those early evaluation flights as each—although licensed for piloting small aircraft (J-5s, Luscombes, etc.)—had little flying logged and precious little low-flying experience.

One day returning from Dawson the pair realized at Menoken that they would have to make a night landing. Bach was pilot. He yelled back to Stuart in the tandem cabin, "I've never made a night landing."

Stuart returned, "You've got nothing on me, I'm not even licensed to try!" Somehow Bach got out of the front seat and changed places with Stuart, hoping that Russ could make a safe landing. He did, but not without some sweat and tears.

Another time Stuart and Bach were returning from Pierre, S.D. from a meeting. At about 1,500 feet over Mobridge and the Missouri River, Bach got sick (he was flying) and roused Stuart who was asleep in the backseat and told him he'd have to fly. This time in a less stable aircraft the seat exchange was nothing but elbows and knees in trying to get a sick Bach out of his seat, keep the plane level and for Stuart to take command in the front seat. But in the process the plane went into a dive. Miraculously, "musical chairs" ended just in time. Stuart pulled back on the stick to level out only 150 feet above the Missouri.

Sometime in the mid-'40s marauding pheasants were doing in corn supplies on private land. Again with Bach in tow, Stuart decided to use some "duck bombs" (used by Fish and Wildlife Service people at Lower Souris National Wildlife Refuge to scare depredating waterfowl) to put the run on huge flocks of pheasants. From the air the pair harassed pheasants (moving them away from cornfields with about as much success as today's efforts to move blackbirds from sunflowers) until one of the "grenades" chose to detonate just as it left Stuart's hand and not far from Bach's head. "That was the end of that," Stuart nodded. "Well, for the time being anyway . . ."

Several months later the two biologists planned for a trip across the state. In the trunk of Bach's car they found this gunny sack full of duck bombs. They discussed how to safely discard them and finally Stuart suggested incineration would work because they would very likely fizzle, like firecrackers often do when put in fire. Much to their surprise, however, several massive detonations followed (they were in east Bismarck at Bach's home) and a thick pall of smoke enveloped the neighborhood. Neighbors buzzed with concern; Stuart and Bach left town pronto to avoid an embarrassing confrontation with police. Several hours later they returned quietly, packed their bags and slipped out of Bismarck unnoticed.

Perhaps one of the reasons that the Game and Fish Department no longer occupies space in the Capitol building is because of a slight error in preservation of some biological materials. Stuart told of a cohort who had collected dozens of pheasant gizzards for later work but stored them in a one-half gallon fruit jar containing a very weak formalin solution. They were left in the janitor's closet (best in lab facilities at that time) in the Game and Fish office in the balcony behind the senate chambers. You guessed it! By the following Monday morning after a warm September weekend Stuart arrived at work at about 7:30 a.m. in advance of most capitol employees and discovered merely by smell the "crawling gizzards" in the fruit jar. The stench was gut-wrenching. Stuart finally got the mess wrapped in paper and removed from the building. But the stench was out of control and soon it had traveled through the elevator shaft and stairways to the 17th floor—not, however, before it had infiltrated Governor Norman Brunsdale's office. He sent out a search team. Evidence suggested that the problem area was somewhere near the senate chambers, but they never did completely indict Game and Fish. ". . .'course, we don't have offices there anymore either."

Stuart was schooled and went to work with the Game and Fish Department during the terrible drought and depression years of the '30s and the recovery years after World War II. From the standpoint of attitudes about land, natural resources and conservation he has witnessed drastic change. Prior to the depression, poaching, for instance, was very common. Few played by the rules. But after the drought Stuart said, "It was just not fashionable to do that. In 1940 when I started, we were just coming out of very bad times and as a nation were assessing just where we had gone wrong. This was the beginning of the Soil Conservation Service and there was a national feeling for soil, wildlife, and water conservation."

This national concern continued for several years and independently of it and the Game and Fish Department, wildlife populations flourished because of the vast acreage of idle ground covered by rank weeds and a lot of sweet clover. Pheasant numbers boomed and large flocks became almost uncountable. White-tailed deer numbers also erupted. The land was alive with wildlife. The nation was recovering. It began to look healthy and so did fish and game agencies across the country. Stuart says, ". . . so the climate was very favorable for biologists, for stride-making in season setting." Wildlife, in places, was a real nuisance: seasons helped reduce numbers and relieve crop losses.

But in the 1950s land values began to climb and grain production started moving as modern mechanization hit the tough sodbuster who had withstood the drought and depression. Habitat acreage shrunk—wildlife numbers tailed off. Attitudes changed. Fewer and fewer acres were available for wildlife production.

"And this is one reason I think it is all important that there be land acquired primarily to maintain at least limited populations of species," Stuart seriously stated. "Today the game is economics. Wildlife has to compete with other land uses and whether we like it or not it has to be on a dollar basis . . . we're going to have to pay for it."

"The only way I see this coming about is the hunter . . . he is going to have to pay for it . . . yes, the birdwatcher, photographer, hikers, etc. benefit and should pay too, but most of the burden will fall on the hunter. This is a traditional thing, and it will take more time to erase it, but a good many people here, and across the nation, still have the idea that hunting privileges should be virtually a free ride—buy a license and duck stamp and expect (if not demand) to be entitled to 'x' number of days of hunting recreation."

"My biggest hope for the Department is also my biggest fear; land acquisition is being endangered by attitudes of people by recent controversy over small wetlands acquisition and the confusion over mitigation acres involved with Garrison Diversion. Hopefully, in the next few months and years these problems can be resolved, but I think it is going to be a tough row to hoe . . . a lot of work to get understanding in various segments of our society."

A recently organized, nonpolitical, nonprofit group known as the North Dakota Landowner-Sportsman Council was encouraged by Stuart to formally organize. "This group can do a lot to put things in proper perspective, clear up inconsistencies, and promote better human relations between the landowner and sportsman and among special interest factions in the wide, natural resources arena."

So, an unusual career has ended. Russell Stuart, a man who served North Dakotans well and stood strong in their behalf fighting for the welfare of North Dakota wildlife and the people's right to behold, will retire. He'll sit back to become an observer and from time to time he'll have to bite his tongue. It's hard to give up command, to let others make the decisions.

Stuart has no earth-shaking retirement plans, no rabid fascination for seeing the rest of the world in 80 days. He'll be happy and content to stay in North Dakota and continue to live in Bismarck. He and his wife, Iris, will travel some, but North Dakota will be home base. "I've been here all my life—why leave now?"

His hobbies will not be much different than his life's work. Experimenting with habitat, manipulating plants to produce wildlife on small acreages will occupy many hours on land he owns in the country. He is a beekeeper now and will probably expand that area. He also likes to dabble in pioneer and early North Dakota military history, so he may be outdoors following trails looking for artifacts. Ironically, a game and fish commissioner has little time for the outdoor sports he promotes and Stuart confidently says, "I'm definitely going to spend more time hunting and fishing!"

North Dakota OUTDOORS, May, 1979

Postscript

Russ Stuart, 74, has found it impossible to give up public service, despite his claim that retirement would mean more hunting and fishing. Today, and for several years since his retirement from the North Dakota Game and Fish Department, Russ has been a Burleigh County Commissioner. In addition, he serves on the Game and Fish Department's Interest Money Committee. He's an avid gardener and raises honeybees on his rural Apple Creek property.

Spring, 1988 H.T.U.

S.W. MELZER, M.D.

—An Original Hunting Country Doctor—

I was astonished! Out of the driver's seat of the pickup he rushed. Down the steep highway ditch, across the freshly mowed yard, moving his short legs and stocky frame in a rapid shuffle. His right arm waved urgently above his straw hat.

"Hey!" he yelled. "Hey . . . Hey you!" The man he was yelling at on the lawnmower could not hear. Finally the workman stopped, not because of the old man's cries, but because the mower was about to run Doc over.

S.W. "Doc" Melzer, 92 years old, as fit of mind and limb as any near-centenarian could ever dream of being, simply wanted the key to his old office building that the Woodworth city fathers were refurbishing in his name.

56

Whatever is that kind of bold ambition it's probably what carried Doc successfully through over 50 years of country doctoring on horseback, sleigh, skinny-tired horseless carriages, and newfangled autos.

It also allowed him to jealously pursue a hunting vocation on the broad Stutsman and Kidder county alkali lakes that attracted his favorite quarry, the canvasback duck. Doc Melzer, over 60 years ago, began a love affair with the North Dakota prairie, its people and wildlife. And today, in the autumn of his years, it is a credit to him and an example to others, that this romance is still alive and well.

Most older Woodworth area people remember Doc for his medical services and less for his love of hunting. But it was hunting Doc first became interested in — not medicine. Back in Wisconsin, in 1900, Doc was 14 years old and began hunting the famous Horicon Marsh area he and his friends hiked several miles to reach from their Mayville home. His first shotgun was a W.W. Greener 12 gauge hammer gun that his merchant father, a nonhunter, traded for a debt.

After high school Doc was still a year too young for medical school, and he was a little short of cash, too. He used his time well teaching readin' and writin' and 'rithmetic at a backwoods school about six miles from his home. He made $40 a month and paid $2 a week for room and board. To add to his savings he trapped mink, raccoons, and muskrats. On the Horicon Marsh he worked as a "pusher" for two wealthy duck hunting clubs and made $2 a day plus room and board pushing millionaire duck hunters through the marsh in duck boats, setting decoys, and retrieving birds.

At 19 Doc entered medical school at Northwestern University in Chicago. Four years later he earned his M.D. and began an 18-month internship at Chicago's Cook County Hospital. There he met a Kansas-born nurse whom he married in 1912.

He first practiced medicine in a Minnesota community of entirely Scandinavian people but had great difficulty communicating. Doc is solid German! In 1915 a friend tipped him off to a possibility in a little town in North Dakota — Woodworth was its name. Doc visited Woodworth, saw the opportunity for a young doctor, liked the people and countryside. "They didn't have a doctor," he said, "and it was a good duck hunting country. I liked what I saw - you bet."

Woodworth was born in 1911 when the Northern Pacific Railroad came in. It was named after a railroad official. When Doc arrived the bustling town already had 450 citizens. "Oh, the town was a boomer . . . two banks, two liveries, two of everything . . . six or seven groceries."

Finally settled, this budding medical practitioner resumed his youthful interest in hunting and was introduced to the canvasback duck, a species he had never hunted or shot in Wisconsin, and a grand bird that would claim his fancy for the rest of his life.

As his family practice grew he found more need to get out, to hunt and let the week's tensions fizzle in pre-dawn skies, inviting fresh enthusiasm to meet another week and the challenges of a busy pioneer country doctor.

Mostly on Sundays Doc and his hunting buddies Albert Hanson, an area farmer, and Jesse Nygaard, a Jamestown banker, took to the field, had the country to themselves and welcomed thick clouds of waterfowl — mallards, teal, pintails, redheads, but especially the cans, to join their wooden decoys on windswept prairie lakes. "We had it all to ourselves . . . right here in Woodworth there weren't three or four hunters." Later, Doc's two boys joined the venturesome outings.

They were usually on the marsh well before daylight, decoys spread and ready to go. Regardless of whether or not Doc's Model 11 Remington got a good workout, at 1:00 p.m., by self-imposed rule, the hunt ended.

Often Doc's services would be needed on Sunday and in the fall someone would know on which marsh to find him. The waving of a white flag or handkerchief alerted Doc to his professional responsibility.

Several times during the fall the women would show up just before the 1:00 p.m. quitting time, and beside a stack of prairie hay (there were few trees then) they would spread a picnic lunch before weary but hungry hunters.

Doc's wife not only helped him with his medical profession, she also picked his ducks. "She wouldn't let me pick any," Doc shrugged hopelessly, as if he'd been denied a complete hunting experience.

Bag limits were usually easily filled, so enroute home Doc often dropped harvested game with area farmers. "They were tickled pink to get it. We had all we could eat . . . I never threw any game away." Doc lived at a time when bag limits were mostly academic. No one paid much attention. He and his crew seldom knowingly exceeded limits, even though by today's standards harvests may have appeared excessive. In those years limits of 15 birds per hunter were common, and they were completely legal.

Doc confessed, however, to a liking for three-quarter-grown prairie chickens, "the real 'chicken' . . . the one with the bare legs." Once in the late "teens" a farmer friend told him of the nice chicken broods he'd been seeing while haying. Doc drooled a few days, could take it no longer, and finally showed up with his shotgun and gingerly removed three birds to be served at suppertime that night.

A week or so later a letter came to Doc from Brown, the game warden, explaining that a complaint had been filed by a farmer living near where Doc shot the birds. Brown warned against any such future activity and then, with tongue-in-cheek wrote, "Next time make sure the wind ain't out of the southeast, then that farmer to the north won't hear your shotgun go off." Doc didn't know exactly how to interpret that letter, but from then on he limited his interest in dinner-table "chicken" to open seasons.

Over the years Doc became keenly interested in canvasbacks. He noted the kinds of lakes they used and when they used them. He checked their stomachs to determine their food habits and recognized the importance of sago pondweed tubers in their diet, and if it was available he maintained, "Cans won't eat anything but sago in this country." He figured sago was not only the key to can welfare, he also discovered that birds feeding on it were the most scrumptious of all.

A politician brother-in-law who worked in Washington enjoyed eating Chesapeake Bay canvasback that fed on wild celery. Then he tasted the Melzer's sago-fed cans and had to admit, "The Chesapeake Bay canvasback isn't in it with this."

Doc used his training in observation to learn as much as he could about canvasbacks. To lure them close to his anxious Remington he bought beautiful $1.50 to $2 hollow-cedar decoys at Herter's Waseca outlet. Behind those bobbing blocks he witnessed cans at their best.

In short, he was an inveterate canvasback hunter and he persisted in his pursuit of them well into January on frozen lakes where reluctant migrants kept small patches of water open. He hunted geese occasionally and some upland game, but the lordly can was his real excitement.

If Doc worked hard as a hunter, he slaved as a medical doctor. In the early years he traveled far and wide visiting and helping the sick. He commonly called on maternity cases; rarely did expectant mothers make office calls and virtually all infants were born in the home. Between 1915 and when he retired in the 1950s he brought over 2,000 babies into the world. In many ways Doc was like the "Doc" on **Gunsmoke** fame, being as much, if not more, a friend and counselor than a doctor.

The 1918 flu kept him moving all hours of the day and night

for weeks. He made calls where the entire family — in one case 11 people — was laid out with the dreaded sickness. In addition to doctoring he often fed livestock and did essential chores that no one else could.

His first office, the same white-framed, false-fronted building now being redone, he first rented for $10 per month. Later he bought it. Through the door of that two-room, 25 foot square "clinic" walked, or in some cases crawled, hundreds of people hopeful of cures. Doc practiced only minor surgery, setting bones, lancing boils, and stitching lacerations. He got $25 for a tonsillectomy, $10 to set a fractured wrist (many hurt by a backfiring Model A engine crank), and 50 cents for a tooth extraction. Later, of course, prices went up.

Doc has seldom been ill. Miraculously he avoided contracting the 1918 flu. He's always had a strong immunity to most everything. A notable exception came in 1936 when he got typhoid fever. "I had a bunch of typhoid in here and the state came up here but they couldn't find out where it came from. I had four or five cases . . . then I got it. Was in the hospital for seven weeks. Before that I had lots of little ills like headaches and some sinus troubles. After I recovered from typhoid, and since, I've never felt better. The old doctor that tended me said that typhoid burned everything out of me. I think he was right."

He was panting only slightly when he returned to the pickup with the key. He started the 1964 crewcab International, his hunting rig, ran us down Woodworth's dusty streets to the near-vacant main avenue and parked in front of his office. Even at mid-day few people were about; Woodworth was no longer a boomer, its population had shrunk to 136 and the nearest practicing doctor was 40 miles away in Jamestown.

Inside the office he pointed out where the isinglass-faced coal stoves stood—one in the reception room and one in his office. Several rows of period medical books stood in an oak case behind the glass. A tall, narrow, steel porcelain cabinet with glass windows contained a variety of his tools. There I saw the tooth forceps. His medical degrees and North Dakota license to practice, all framed in wood, leaned against a wall waiting to be hung. Significantly, among them, in the largest frame of all, stood a watercolor painting of a variety of waterfowl, including the canvasback.

Events surrounding the white office and his practice

are over—gone forever. Some he savored, like the satisfaction of healing wounds and sickness or spending a sunrise with a hundred "bull" cans on a secluded prairie marsh. Some, like the days of the 1918 flu, are happily forgotten.

Doc quit hunting only a couple of years ago when new regulations said no more canvasbacks could be taken east of U.S. Highway 3. "If I could only shoot one canvasback," Doc said longingly, "I'd still go out . . . but that's too far way over there west of No. 3. I'd have to get up at two in the morning to drive there and get set up by sunrise."

He doesn't shoot anymore but that doesn't keep him from the field in October. He drives around, "Just to see how the fellas are doing." Several doctors from Jamestown invite him to their hunting shack near Woodworth each fall and there Doc meets them after the hunt and revels in the unspoken camaraderie of the duck hunter.

It's been awhile since his Horicon Marsh days. Yes sir, a few years have gone by. But he fondly recalls good times in the Wisconsin woods. He gets back there. "For a couple of days I go back . . . then I just can't wait to get back here on the prairie."

The things he loves are here: the prairie, his friends, his memories and fall canvasbacks.

North Dakota OUTDOORS, September, 1978

Postscript

Dr. Simon W. Melzer lived to 97 years of age. He died May 11, 1983. After retirement he moved to Canby, Minnesota, where he lived until his death. He was returned for burial to the prairie that he loved so much at Woodworth, North Dakota.

Spring, 1988 H.T.U.

CHUCK SCHROEDER
AND HIS GIANT GEESE

Then the man sensed other company. He turned slowly. His heart leaped. A separate flight had approached, unannounced. But these were a different kind of geese. There were seven. They were giant Canadas! They were honkers! The most uncommon, but most prized variety of Canada goose, the granddaddies of all geese.

An explosion. Black powder smoke filled the air. Goose talk rose to a clamor. When the smoke cleared, the first group of small Canadas had broken off. To the northeast, six heavy-bodied birds, coursing low over the stubble, retreated. On the ground lay a goose—a giant Canada and next to it knelt an exuberant 12-year-old boy.

—Coleharbor, 1891—

Had there been an endangered species list in 1891, the giant Canada goose probably would have been on it. Few would approach a North Dakota hunter's decoys for nearly 80 years. By 1920, the giant Canada goose was considered extremely rare if not extinct throughout North America.

Charles "Chuck" H. Schroeder, a man who was to become a key figure in the restoration of Canada geese in North Dakota and a North Dakota Department Commander of the American Legion, wasn't around in 1891. He wouldn't be born for another 36 years. Then 41 years would pass before he and other North Dakotans would tackle the giant Canada restoration project — not until 1969, after Schroeder had spent 13 years as a waterfowl biologist with the North Dakota Game and Fish Department.

Today, nine years later, the giant Canada goose has been partially restored as a breeding species on the Dakota high plains. Chuck Schroeder probably made the difference.

"It has a very special meaning to me," Schroeder says, "just the thought of helping bring back a species that was once a breeder in the state's early history . . . first, just to be a part of the overall environment. And now, more importantly, to bring it back as a game species — that's the additional measure. The Canada goose belongs here."

The reestablishment of the giant Canada goose (*Branta canadensis maxima*) in North Dakota is a major achievement of contemporary game management. The bird is the largest of all geese and once nested over much of North America. It went nearly to extinction before it was properly classified. Hunters on the northern plains in the 1880s and '90s periodically reported large extra-heavy birds and some felt they represented a distinct race of Canada geese. Wing spreads in excess of 75 inches and body lengths of 48 inches were measured. Weights commonly ranged over 16 pounds. In North Dakota the last known giant Canada goose nest was reported in Kidder county in 1926.

Then, in 1951, a researcher found in the notes of the late James Moffit a description of the giant Canada goose, a variety Moffit called *maxima*. In 1962, Harold C. Hanson, a noted Canada goose authority from Illinois, Forrest Lee, a waterfowl propagator then with the Minnesota Conservation Department, and others, confirmed the existence of a wild, free-flying flock of giant Canadas among wintering waterfowl at Rochester, Minnesota. The *maxima* had not perished after all.

The 1969 restoration effort began at Slade National Wildlife Refuge in Kidder county, about 50 miles east of Bismarck. It received 142 adult geese, hand-reared at the Fish and Wildlife

Service's Northern Prairie Wildlife Research Center at Jamestown, North Dakota. Forrest Lee supervised the propagation job. From 1969 to 1971 over 300 goslings were produced at Slade and, significantly, two nests in 1971 were found outside refuge boundaries on private land. These represented the first successful nesting in Kidder county of a giant Canada on private land in 45 years.

The geese had done their part. Now, could the program be expanded to establish free-flying flocks at other refuges across North Dakota?

Pen several hundred geese in an enclosure and you're bound to attract attention. Marauding dogs and coons killed over 100 birds in one incident. Goslings, hand-reared from stock in refuges, showed little fear of humans. Released, they congregated in farmyards, unharvested grain fields, even among the decoys of wide-eyed hunters. Furthermore, these newcomers not only had to make it past the guns of North Dakotans and other Central Flyway hunters to the south, they had to survive at least one more spring and fall migration before the females returned to lay their first eggs. Some females wouldn't lay until their third spring.

After two years of suspense, slowly the data trickled in. Leg band returns documented a mortality rate over 26 percent for 1972 releases. Another 1.5 percent were known dead from other causes. Obviously, total mortality from all causes was considerably higher. But known losses from 1973 releases were less. In 1974, nesting studies indicated that the two- and three-year-old birds were reproducing well with nesting success running as high as 70 percent. The giant Canada goose was being reestablished in North Dakota.

"In my opinion," said Forrest Lee, "the giant Canada goose restoration program in North Dakota would never have gotten off the pad had it not been for Chuck Schroeder's leadership and active involvement."

Schroeder "sold" the program to the public — convincing landowners to allow transplants on their lands and impressing upon hunters the need to protect these sites from hunting. He confronted often huffy groups with such success that many suggested closing even larger areas than were recommended.

"It's been a wonderful lesson in human nature . . . to see how much support you can get from people when you go out and explain to them what you are trying to do," says Schroeder. "And, of course, we had a wonderful product in the Canada goose."

Schroeder even got inmates at the North Dakota state prison farm to help raise goslings.

His colleagues voted Schroeder the first secretary-treasurer of the 190-member North Dakota Chapter of The Wildlife Society. Later he became its president. He was awarded the 1977 Professional Award by the seven-state Central Mountains and Plains Section of The Wildlife Society.

Boyd Clemens, past national vice-commander of The American Legion, recalls Schroeder's parallel rise in the North Dakota Legion Department. He and Schroeder competed against each other for post commander one year. Schroeder lost. A few years later, Clemens chose Schroeder for his campaign manager when he ran for department and national vice-commander. Clemens won both.

In the 1930s, Schroeder's dad signed him up in Sons of the American Legion. During World War II Schroeder served as a Navy electronics technician, enlisting just after graduating from high school in May, 1945. He sailed on the USS Iowa and USS Atlanta.

In 1956, after completing his B.S. degree in wildlife management at the University of Minnesota, he came to North Dakota. He became commander of Bismarck's Lloyd Spetz Post No. 1, then fifth district commander and then central region vice-commander. For several years, including this year, he has been director of the department's youth oratorical contest. He is past Chef de Gare of Voiture 291 of the 40 et 8. In 1977, he became North Dakota department commander. Next year he'll have 30 years of continuous service with the American Legion. He also has led the North Dakota State Employee's Association.

"The family is behind him in whatever he decides to do. We all discussed his running for department commander and everyone thought it was good—it was the thing to do," says his wife Cecelia. "He's gone a lot, but he gets a rousing welcome when he returns home!"

The accomplishment that will live well beyond Chuck Schroeder, however, is the return of the giant Canada in North Dakota. By 1980 it is expected to take its place among harvestable waterfowl species.

Epilogue
The sunrise began slowly. The man and boy waited in the cold, dawn stillness. They listened and heard goose talk. The last of night's shadows slipped towards the western horizon. The man and boy flexed with excitement. They hugged the earth, faces flat on dusty fallow, then they reared together and fired. Two giant Canada geese

folded and fell next to 40 frost-washed tin decoys. The year? 1981.

The boy remembered: his father told of his great-grandfather and a large goose, a rare type never seen again, that he shot in 1891 in the "olden times."

The American Legion Magazine, October, 1978

Postscript

Charles H. "Chuck" Schroeder died of cancer March 3, 1988 in Bismarck, North Dakota. He was 60 years of age.

What has been said in the above story rings even truer in Chuck's death. The welfare of the giant Canada goose would have been the less without his unusual determination. Modern harvest management of sandhill cranes and mourning doves would have come much later, if indeed at all, without Chuck's commitment to goals. His pride of membership and service in the North Dakota Game and Fish Department, the Lloyd Spetz Post No. 1 of the American Legion, the North Dakota Chapter of the Wildlife Society and the North Dakota Public Employees Association were fine examples to others, set in unassuming, yet stern conviction. Chuck Schroeder was a servant of humankind — let that be known forever.

Spring, 1988 H.T.U.

OF FATHER, FISHING AND PICKERAL LAKE

By Gerald D. Kobriger as told to Ted Upgren

... Most every son can recall favorite times with a father. But there is always that very special sharing of experience that becomes etched in his juvenile mind and remains forever warm in his aging heart. And when fathers leave us ... well ...

The name was enchanting, mysterious. It rang of far away places and deep clear waters teeming with fish. There were other lakes also, like Red Iron, Clear, Blue Dog, Waubay and Roy. But Pickeral held a special place all its own. I didn't see it at the time, but I now understand why the mere sound of that name has always spelled excitement, from boyhood to adulthood.

I began hearing about Pickeral long before I could spell it. Dad came home to Huron from that romantic fishing lake somewhere far to the north of us and mother and we five kids listened intently as dad told of himself, his fishing buddies, Leo and Bob, and the adventure of late-night trolling for walleyes on the clay banks, pikes point, rock pile and Hyde Park.

Dad always said Pickeral was a beautiful lake. The prettiest, he said, in all of South Dakota - bar none. I heard about it so often, I, too, was positive that it had to be the greatest place in the world. It was my fantasy island.

I lived for the day I would go to Pickeral. More times were ahead, though, when dad and his buddies went and we younger kids could only share those trips through his stories.

So, we pretended. We hiked, thumbed rides and rode bikes down to Ravine Lake close to town. We used cane poles, bobbers and worms and imagined we were at Pickeral Lake with dad, Leo and Bob.

Then finally the long-awaited time arrived. The entire family was to take a summer vacation to Pickeral Lake. We planned and prepared for weeks, it seemed, to insure all was in order. This was a real adventure and one of our first family vacations.

I couldn't imagine how long it would take to travel a "whole hundred miles." Certainly, we would need food for such an extended trip. So we packed a huge picnic lunch and then piled into the jampacked '37 Chevy - five kids and mom and dad. I just knew history was in the making.

We left early in the morning, yet it was a half days travel to Webster. We stopped on the edge of town and spread our picnic lunch beneath a rangy cottonwood and sat about feeling like explorers of some rare region where only daring families, expert fishing fathers and reliable '37 Chevys dared tread.

Then we topped the final prairie hill, the hill dad promised would be coming up soon. And there it was - Pickeral Lake. It was a prairie lake ringed by vagrant woods from nearby Minnesota. It was everything I had imagined, but bigger, wetter, bluer and prettier. Dad was right. Pickeral had to be the prettiest lake around.

We pulled in at Bass Beach and emptied the Chevy, putting the massive pile of bedding, food and fishing gear on the floor of the small primitive cabin we had rented. That done we ran to the lake to swim, immersed in all that Pickeral had to offer until finally we were called for supper.

The brisk prairie wind had feathered to a breath and from dad's earlier stories I guessed he might go night fishing. But I wasn't quite ready when he asked, "Gerald, do you want to go trolling tonight?"

I'll never forget that night. It was very dark, no moon and fairly

68

warm. I had my new rod, saved for Pickeral. My days with cane poles were gone I'd hoped. With dad's help I rigged out a black and white river runt, my substitute for the new red-hot Lazy-Ike that I didn't own. We climbed aboard the wooden resort boat and with a single pull, dad set that little five-horse Johnson to humming.

Now, he pointed out to me what I'd always heard about but had never seen: pikes point, sand bar, rock pile, clay banks and Hyde Park. We trolled down one shore and up the other and I got to know dad's Pickeral Lake.

And then I had a strike. Darkness prevented me seeing what was happening. I tried to keep the line taut, to keep the huge fish from fighting free. Boy, this night fishing was a lot different than drowning worms at twelve noon back home on Ravine Lake, I thought. Finally the great fish succumbed and dad pulled the fighter from the inky waters. It was a northern, a hammer-handle, dad called it. But it was a trophy to me. My first fish from Pickeral Lake - and trolling at night at that.

On another night I had my chance to run the motor and troll at the same time. That was pretty heavy stuff. Here on Pickeral only a few days, and I was already a confident, experienced fisherman and boater. Later that night we pulled alongside the dock at Hyde Park and strolled into the restaurant for coffee. I'd bet that dates my interest in coffee drinking.

Fishing was the highlight of summer days on Pickeral. It was here, though, that dad introduced me to pinochle and checkers. I seldom beat him at either. The family did simple things that weren't interrupted at all by television and seldom by phones. We built sand castles, seined minnows, chased fire flies and swam until waterlogged. Times were never more fun than at Pickeral.

We made several more trips to Pickeral, but after the mid-1950s the family as a whole never did make it there again. Like my family now, ours then began to grow, each person becoming more individual with his own interests and obligations. Yet for a time, two, three or maybe four of us would make it back for a day or so.

Our last trip was in 1978. Dad, my oldest brother, Larry, and my youngest brother, David and I stayed at one of the old cabins at Bass Beach. I think the name of the resort changed, but to us it would always be Bass Beach. We had a super time. We played a lot of pinochle, drank a little beer, did some fishing and barbecued steaks. I laid awake one night listening to the gentle breeze and the waves lapping along the shore. And I heard the familiar sound of the far-away hum of a Johnson - one of those late night trollers still working some secret walleye hold. We decided then that the whole family must return to Pickeral for a reunion. Conflicts were inevitable, though. The family was scattered far and wide - North Dakota, California, Germany. Dad's career with the Soil Conservation Service lasted his lifetime. He was selected as Forest Conservationist of the Year by the South Dakota Wildlife Federation. Soon after, he retired with over 30 years service. He continued his interest in Pickeral but few of his family could share it with him.

After a hip operation his mobility improved and we planned a Pickeral outing. Then dad suffered a stroke, was in serious condition, but rebounded in a remarkable recovery. He was a tough old bird. His other hip was then replaced and following complete recuperation some of us again planned a Pickeral trip for summer, 1980. This time it was all go.

I was there at Bass Beach getting ready to go trolling, waiting for dad and the others to arrive. I was called to the telephone. A voice said, "Hello, Gerald? Pa didn't make it last night."

Stunned, I clumsily repacked for the trip to Huron. Then I hesitated. I walked down to the beach and paused for the longest moment. My mind flashed back 35 years to that first family vacation, and all the times afterwards. I saw, as never before, the pricelessness of that heritage. And in my heartache there was gladness. I had been lucky enough to have shared a special enchantment with father, fishing and Pickeral Lake. And the mere sound of that name still spells excitement.

Gerald Kobriger, a Dickinson resident, has been employed by the North Dakota Game and Fish Department as an upland game research and management biologist since 1964.

South Dakota Conservation Digest, 1982, Vol. 49, No. 4

Postscript

None of the Kobrigers have been back to Pickeral Lake since Phil Kobriger died in 1980. Family maturity scatters its members far and wide. And then there is also some truth in what Gerald Kobriger says: "You can't go back home - guess that's the way I feel." Now new traditions will be established. The times at Pickeral Lake will not be forgotten, though. They will instead be retold to become the heritage of new branches of the Kobriger family tree.

Spring, 1988 H.T.U.

AFFAIRS OF THE PRAIRIE

Lostwood National Wildlife Refuge, all 26,747 coteau prairie acres, is unique in many ways: approximately 70 percent of its rolling grassland and shrub vegetation has never been turned by a plow; it boasts a 1975 U.S. Congress designated Wilderness Area of 5,527 acres; leafy spruge is found on less than 15 acres of the entire complex; and waterfowl die-offs due to botulism rarely occur on Lostwood.

But this story is not about Lostwood NWR per se. It is however, about someone as inherently unique as the Lostwood prairie she calls home. It is about refuge manager Karen Smith and her infatuation with this high plains outpost called Lostwood and the wildlife she is charged to manage.

It's somewhat of an understatement to say that Karen Smith is an interesting study. But, indeed, her credentials are uncommon. She is a wildlife biologist, a "working biologist" she emphasizes, a skilled wildlife artist, and, of course she is a woman. Her inquisitive mind is like that of a scientist yet receptive to the philosophical bent of the artist. She is a dedicated public servant, blessed with the uncommon work ethic of a youthful prairie immigrant. Karen seems distinctly suited for life on Lostwood.

What she does today on the quiet, remote Lostwood NWR, to all appearances somewhere beyond "lands end" on Highway 8, fifteen miles north of Stanley, was once only her fantasy. All of us know of someone who knew exactly what he or she wanted to do with their lives since childhood. Karen Smith is such a person.

As she doodled in wildlife art on 5th grade school paper in Muskegon, Michigan, could she have known through some clairvoyance that one day she and Lostwood would meet? "I was two years old when Dad put me on his shoulders and took me squirrel hunting . . . I was just fascinated," Karen explained to me during a field visit I made to Lostwood last summer.

Tall, slender and wiry, Karen's appetite for long, hard field days keep her in shape to direct and coordinate intensive summer investigations that often begin before sunrise and may run until the late summer sun finally burns itself out on the faraway grassy horizon. Her pretty face, framed by short, dark hair, is wind burned and ruddy. Tanned and weathered hands are working hands with assorted abrasions and chipped fingernails from field labor, hands not unfamiliar with shovels, ax handles, mauls and post-hole diggers.

While accepting of field work, because of her aversion to armchair biology, Karen's active mind works ahead of the moment to consider new study designs to improve prairie habitat. Her work is her hobby, her hobby her work. To visit with Karen is to visit earnestly about Lostwood projects, where she's been with them and her hopes for the future.

For a few moments she rested from cutting a fire trail through an aspen thicket, watered her dry throat, and told me about herself.

At her father's side she learned to be a fisherman on the Michigan waters of the Muskegon, Betsy and Pentwater. "Dad raised me to be a walleye fisherman." Today Karen likes backpacking into Montana's Madison and Gallatin for trout.

As the years went by Karen's parents (outdoor people, but otherwise employed) saw, and Karen felt, a compelling desire to be close to the natural world. "I just became more and more fascinated," until it was understood that Karen's life's work would rest somewhere in the natural resources field - somewhere where her deep belief in the integrity of natural systems could be practically transferred to lands and wildlife management. "For one thing," Karen quipped when I asked her why she had chosen this line of work, "critters don't have a voice in Congress."

And so her course was chartered. She completed her B.S. at Michigan State in 1969 and shortly after landed her first job as a temporary laborer at Seney NWR in Michigan. Later her artistic talents were recognized and she began some interpretive, illustrative and mural work. In 1970 she transferred to the Minneapolis office of the U.S. Fish and Wildlife Service as a public use illustrator, followed by a 1972 move to Sherburne NWR as a public use specialist. In 1974 Crab Orchard NWR in Illinois enjoyed her services and then in the winter of 1974-75 Karen fairly jumped at the opportunity to move to Pierre, S.D. to work in the ecological services section of the Fish and Wildlife Service. It was here that her investigative and managerial talents were developed. Finally, in 1977 the refuge manager's slot opened and Karen packed her bags and two golden retrievers and headed north to meet the Lostwood.

Thousands of grass-rimmed wetlands, twinkling like polished gemstones on an undulating carpet of moving grass, met her excited eyes as she motored into the Lostwood's short and mid-grass prairie. Depending on years, from 2,500 to 3,000 wetland basins dot the Lostwood, and can produce upwards of 40,000 ducks annually, host 45,000 migrating snow geese and provide homes to about 150 pairs of giant Canada geese. Sharp-tailed grouse dancing grounds number close to 40, while numerous white-tailed deer, some fox and several coyotes all run fat in the biological diversity of Lostwood. Heavy nutrient loading of wetlands, common in eastern North Dakota where more intensive agricultural cultivation occurs, is essentially nonexistent on the Lostwood; hence late summer duck die-offs due to botulism are rare.

Now, here she was on the lonesome high plains where, except for summer seasons when field activity was at a peak, she was virtually alone, a companion of wind and solitude. What might have frightened someone else was in fact embraced by Karen. She drank in all the wild landscape provided. On data sheets, film and canvas she recorded the pulse beat of Lostwood. To her dogs she added a horse that minimized impacts of her visits to the most remote corners of the refuge.

Despite the many good things on Lostwood, Karen soon recognized that *all* was not well. Biological observation told her that the prairie was slowly changing from the diverse grassland composed predominantly of native grasses, forbs and low woodies (principally snowberry or buckbrush, a brush species originally found in coulees and draws and occupying about one to three percent of the prairie) to a prairie that had gone to 50-80 percent brush with stands of exotic Kentucky bluegrass and smooth brome invading the natives.

The change had not occurred overnight — it had taken decades. Here was a classic example of native prairie "gone by" because wild fire and massive herds of grazing bison were no longer the architects of grassland maintenance. Karen noted that as man tamed the area, wild fires were contained and eventually stopped altogether, and the great herds of bison were gone by 1880. Vegetational diversity of the original prairie was choking on twentieth century management. Heterogeneity, not uniformity, is a basic ecological tenet that keeps biological communities diverse and healthy. Lostwood was ill.

Karen reviewed the mission of Lostwood NWR. Established in 1935, ". . . as a refuge and breeding grounds for migratory birds and other wildlife . . .," and also to preserve our prairie heritage — the mandate seemed clear. If vigorous wildlife populations were to remain, so must the prairie, and if the prairie was to remain, different grassland management ideas were needed.

Fire was selected as the different management tool with the most potential for controlling and reducing overabundant snowberry and exotic grasses and forbs. But fire was destined to generate other heat far from the flames, even though fire, as a management tool, studied in grasslands elsewhere had been concluded highly beneficial. In addition, techniques had been perfected for its safe application.

Nonetheless, sentiment from adjoining landowners was not in Karen's favor as she reduced livestock numbers on the Lostwood and began "controlled" or "prescribed" burning programs. The public soon became skeptical of her management capabilities that so deviated from long-standing refuge policies.

Prescribed burning was begun with a small 12-acre burn and since 1978 a dozen burns of over 4,400 acres has begun the change. Karen's firm stance, yet open, personable style and commitment to educate has won her some converts. She's conducted field trips and spoken to ranching and other agricultural groups. Her resolve has been admired. Some local ranchers have recognized the possibilities of controlled burning in increasing quality and abundance of forage on their own lands. Karen has even suggested, "why not involve local fire departments to help ranchers with controlled burns . . . the fire departments can chalk it off as training."

In all of this, Karen's excitement about revitalizing Lostwood's prairie has continued to grow since her arrival. Her aggressive work ethic, accountability, documentation and follow-through have encouraged her supervisors in North Dakota and Denver to give her the rein she needs to get the job done. Karen said, "I've been allowed the flexibility to make resource decisions." She is in the process of writing the Lostwood Master Plan that involves an ongoing controlled burning regimen among other things. Even under the wilderness management guidelines for the Lostwood Wilderness Area, natural and controlled fire to maintain and preserve native prairie is fully recognized. Within the US Fish and Wildlife Service, Lostwood is recognized as a refuge of progressive policy. One Denver FWS official said Lostwood is a positive place to be around, and "Karen Smith is one of the Region's real jewels."

Today over 5,000 acres of Lostwood's native prairie is on its way back and in a condition not seen for perhaps 50 years. Even before prescribed burning, Arnold Kruse, of the Northern Prairie Research Center at Jamestown, told Karen that Lostwood is one of the lushest places for native forbs and grasses he's ever seen. Now, in certain tracts, repeated controlled burning is pushing the density of snowberry back to 20-30 percent with improved native grass and forb understory. And native wildlife like Baird's sparrow, LeConte's sparrow, Sprague's pipit, upland sandpiper and others, according to Northern Prairie Wildlife Research data, have increased as a result of fire management. Karen is confident that other indigenous species will increase as the ecology of fire puts the frosting back on the habitat cake.

Where does Karen Smith go from here? Such success is often rewarded with a promotion and move to a supervisory or regional slot—for an armchair view. But Karen doesn't want that. "I'm not a ladder climber," she confesses. "As far as I'm concerned I'm at the top of the ladder . . . I don't need more money." Furthermore, Karen points out, "By 1988, I'll know more than anybody about Lostwood. It seems to me beneficial to let a person stay and accomplish the Master Plan."

Karen Smith had been so busy with her wildlife career she forgot to get married. She had only one love and that was Lostwood. During my visit I asked her when she was getting married and she halfheartedly replied, "When the right person comes along."

Recently her perspective may have changed—the right person

came along. Now she's married, with two loves, Bob Murphy, a naturalist in his own right, and the Lostwood. At sunrise on a fresh April morning this past spring, on a native grassland knoll surrounded by the soft sounds of an awakening prairie, Karen and Bob were married. Colleagues on the prairie in the past, the couple will work hand-in-hand preserving the prairie heritage of the Lostwood National Wildlife Refuge.

Karen has come a long way from Muskegon. Far enough to become as unique as the rare prairie she has dedicated her life to managing.

North Dakota OUTDOORS, February, 1986

Postscript

Karen and her husband Bob Murphy, a dedicated falconer, continue to make their home on the Lostwood. Karen's credentials in art and wildlife biology remain the envy of her peers.

Spring, 1988 H.T.U.

INITIALED GENTLEMEN
OF FALL

When H.J. had the Suburbanite grips put on his blue and gray company car, I knew it was ready to ferry us to faraway hunting grounds never before explored, let along hunted.

It never occurred to me that the knobby lug grips and the blue-gray car served any other purpose than to carry dads and sons to remote prairie sloughs and rose-shouldered drainages to hunt ducks and pheasants. The normal world stopped for me on these occasions, and if it didn't for H.J. and H.T., they never let on.

Now, the H.J. and H.T. association went back a few years. Both of them were, or had been, veteran highwaymen (bus drivers) for the Northland Greyhound Lines, with years of experience shuttling passengers west out of Bismarck across comparatively primitive roadways to the Montana towns from Glendive to Butte. So I never questioned their credentials as wagon masters of my early hunting trips. I'd fall away fast asleep over the whining Suburbanites, insensible to everything but the imagery of hunting prowess, evidence of which usually rode in the trunk of the blue-gray car. I've never been able to sleep while others drive, but I could, securely, when H.J. or H.T. did, for they made their livings doing it right.

H.J. and H.T. had to be called that or otherwise neither one knew who H.G. was calling Harold. The only thing H.G. didn't have in common with H.J. and H.T. was his name. It was Henry, but they called him by his second name, George. He, too, was a Greyhound bus driver and also a hunter; I could also sleep when H.G. was at the wheel. These three initialed gentlemen became the nucleus of reference for some of my earliest hunting memories.

At my youngest awareness of hunting trip planning, I was never quite sure that the planning routine was not in fact anticlimactic ceremony to the final event. I remember answering the phone to hear H.J. ask for H.T. who might in turn say he'd heard from H.G. and that H.G. had a "line" on a good luck slough for the morning shoot and that H.J. should give him a "ring" to confirm stuff. I surely didn't know what having a "line" on anything meant and was at a total loss to explain what getting a piece of jewelry to wear on your finger had to do with going hunting. Let me assure you, these were very early recollections of the hunt. Eventually though, these people and the fall seasons accompanying their heightened association commingled to create delightful memories I recall year after year.

To me these guys were men of the world. They'd been around the block and down a few alleys. They had traveled extensively, escorting passengers to romantic sounding places, steering their precious cargo across the low grade highways of the 1930s and '40s. In those days weather forecasts were inaccurate, wind chill was unknown, snowplows few and far between and most roads were only graveled. In fact, Greyhounds often forged ahead through snow drifts, followed by other autos. Greyhounds were the vanguards of prairie highway travel. Like hunting new country, riding the Greyhounds of that era was adventuresome.

H.T. said when he stuck a bus, he'd simply grab a shovel and resign himself to shoveling it out, then back up for another run. Earlier bus models were never turned off in the winter because they ran without anti-freeze. One time, somewhere between Bismarck and Billings, a furious winter storm closed roads for several days. H.T. hired on with the highway department to stand above and ahead of a huge rotary blower breaking the drifts down into the churning equipment.

H.T.'s hunting instincts were worn on his sleeve, apparently. One night en route from Dickinson to Bismarck, a rangy coyote made a fateful decision to cross the highway in front of the bus. To this day coyotes don't mess with "greyhounds." H.T. stopped the bus, fully loaded with passengers, and with flashlight in hand ran back down the highway to fetch the coyote and throw him into the back of the bus for later sale in Bismarck.

H.T. was never cured of the transportation business. After leaving Greyhound in the late 1940s, he started his own bus line out of Carrington that he named the Honker Lines, for it traveled the goose country from Bottineau to Devils Lake to Carrington. A huge Canada goose was painted on the sides of his buses, another clear statement of his avocational interests. Several times I rode the rumbling Honker Lines through that prime waterfowl country, gripping my ration of a five-cent Pearson Salted Nut Roll. My first dog, a big, male black labrador named Velvet, came home to me when H.T.'s depot agent friend at Devils Lake caught H.T. in a weaker moment and booked the hound's one-way passage to Carrington.

Like H.T., H.J. never shed the bus bug. He stayed on with Greyhound for over 30 years, eventually to drive the monster diesel motor coaches down interstate highways — a piece of cake. H.G. left Greyhound, too, but stayed in the transportation business with Buckingham Company.

But these three friends all trained under similar circumstances. To herd a bus in a snowstorm, you needed a good sense of direction; to get out of difficult situations, you needed resourcefulness; to deal with a bus load of transcontinental travelers — some unbathed for days — you needed a sample of patience and good humor. These attributes served these men well as outdoorsmen, too. For instance, I marveled at what compass-quality could pull them from our dark driveway, fifty miles across the deserted prairie to an equally dark Coteau pothole.

I didn't know what resourcefulness meant, but I gathered there was something darn handy about the way H.G. once recovered a boat anchor stuck in the rocks in 20 feet of cold Canadian waters we were fishing. H.G. hounded and badgered one of our fishing companions, a beefy 250 pound football player from the Canadian Blue Bombers, until the poor guy dove in and wrenched the anchor free. The anchor came aboard more easily than did the shivering football player.

I now know why red fox dens are often located in buckbrush patches on south facing prairie hillsides. Here the wind dies and the fall sun intoxicates anything it touches. No wonder then that these spots were as much the menu for lunch rests, as the contents of the long, narrow red lunch box in the twin thermos bag. Good hunters were patient ones that paced themselves, I was told.

In those days the trio profiled a step-ladder affect. H.J. was tallest and biggest. His thinning, wavy hair was parted down the center of his head. His face was bright and alert, with sincere eyes that always smiled. H.T. is my dad, and except for height, he and H.J. are very much alike. They constantly jabbed at each other over missed birds or spilled coffee. H.G. was a prim, dashing gentleman of the shortest physical stature, but endowed with great social presence. His salt and pepper flat-top was always trimmed precisely, as was his narrow mustache. It was not hard to believe that he fathered a daughter that became a Miss North Dakota (Kitty Page, 1950).

I envied H.T.'s heavy canvas duck hunting coat with the thick corduroy collar. Not because it was new. In fact, it was well-worn with tell-tale stains of birds bagged from other smart trips. It didn't look as if it ever had been in a store—more like it bore some earthly genesis. It *was* the smells and color of fall—as good a definition of that season as I needed. The coat probably entered H.T.'s life at a Minnesota duck hunting camp that he helped run in the late 1920s. It was durable, serviceable and warm like the man who wore it. The pockets were roomy with heavy canvas overflaps. They were gloveless, though, because H.T. seldom wore gloves—they got in his way. A piece of nylon cord was tied to a buttonhold, the other end to an ebony duck call stored in the breast pocket.

H.J.'s footgear impressed me, too. Leather, clear to the upper calf, came with laces to match. The boots were scuffed from many hikes for pheasants through dense rose. Thirty-mile creek got walked on a lot by those boots. Their streamlined appearance, with pants tucked in the tops, reduced drag as H.J. rushed through the rose shouting incantations at Queenie, his black dog of unknown ancestry, to get the pheasants out. As H.J. walked the cover, he made throaty growling noises to scare birds. I don't know if it ever worked, but I sometimes find myself sounding the same raucous tunes today—while walking pheasant cover that is. H.J. wore those boots well.

A plaid red and gray wool shirt was H.G.'s trademark. It wasn't loose and floppy like a lot of hunting clothes. It was a tailored shirt, perhaps a Pendleton. It had a firm, pointed collar and leather-patched elbows. H.G. often took off his outer coat to travel to the sloughs and passes of Tuttle's Lake Josephine, one of our favorite canvasback spots. Cigarette and pipe smoke hung in the fibrous wood thread, and as I leaned forward from the back seat of H.G.'s 1956 Pontiac wagon, the rich smells of smoke and aftershave mixed warm and satisfactorily.

These old bus drivers never let me down. They tried hard for me and the other sons: H.J.'s Jim and H.G.'s little George and Charlie. Seems like we always had some birds to clean, and some days do stand out, like a limit of 21 roosters by 9:30 in the morning. But now, what clearly looms larger than bag limits was the time together. Time spent being different than at the office or at home, time that allowed for special instruction and growth, for ribbing, approval, reinforcement, achievement and laughter: Yes, and slough-side naps the old bus drivers took despite the nagging of restless sons.

This fall I'm 30 years removed from those days. And I wonder, as I suppose other fathers do, if I have created opportunities for my children to capture the mystique of hunting fellowship, whose values far surpass the weight of the bag alone.

One day last fall, I pictured a scene straight out of those favored years that may have answered a part of that question. The sun laid on the cold western horizon as a companion and I and twelve-year-old son Michael began the long trek home from a weekend of hunting. We'd walked our legs weary, shared hot stew and wore flushed faces from camp spirits. We played cards, told jokes and rewrote the day's log where we could get away with it. We may have even talked smart and spit on the floor. Such backwoods brotherhood simply meant we had enjoyed one another.

As another golden hour snuffed to gray and night shadows overtook the prairie, we rode quietly with our private thoughts. At length, I spoke to Michael in the back seat, but there was no answer. Then I turned to see him sprawled against some duffle, asleep. His fingernails weren't clean, and a scratched knee poked through a rip in his pants. Blood from some luckless creature stained his vest and the bill of his cap. Was that me 30 years ago? If so, he too had visited faraway, never before explored hunting grounds. The whining tires sang a lulling tune. His dreams were good. His sleep was sound, steered homeward by a descendent of an old bus driver.

North Dakota OUTDOORS, Sept./Oct., 1986

Postscript
H.T. is the author's father, 82. Retired on Minnesota's Cotton Lake (a stone's throw from his 1920s duck hunting camp) in the 1970s and '80s, he now resides

with his wife, Ismey, in Bismarck. H.J. was the late Harold Himes. He passed away in May, 1988, at age 78, in Greenwood, Missouri where he and his wife, Agnes, have lived for some time. H.W. was the late George Page, Sr. His wife, Peg, lives in Bismarck.

Spring, 1988 H.T.U.

ED BRY
— A MAN AND A CAMERA

I can't for the life of me recall the exact spot, but it was on a hot, dusty road somewhere in the middle of the badlands that I first met Ed Bry. It was 1960 and I was a summer assistant assigned to Jim McKenzie's deer browse crew. We had stopped on the road to talk with Ed Bry. Even then his reputation preceded him somewhat, at least I sensed it. Yet Ed Bry looked like anybody else. He was a game warden, but there was little about him to suggest that status; no badge, no nameplate, and not much of a uniform. Certainly his vehicle gave up no clue; it was a pink, four-door Rambler.

We visited briefly, about deer, maybe the heat, perhaps photography. Ed Bry's reserve, his retiring manner, that's what I recall most. Conversation issued from him in short, quiet staccato bursts, as if all at the same time, he did, and did not, want to talk. So we all stared, for comfort's sake, at the road and kicked little pieces of scoria about. This agreeable, sincere, shy man was the perfect unassuming gentleman. With his khaki pants and worn leather lace boots, I envisioned Ed Bry to have walked from the pages of **Audubon**. He didn't appear cut from the cloth of a west-river warden, although in fact, he was a tenacious adversary for any wildlife violator to tackle.

In those days Ed Bry was paid as a game warden first, though many people across North Dakota knew Ed as a first-rate photographer. Eventually, his superlative black and white photography would stand him apart from others, far and wide. Little did I know, as we stood in the scoria dust on that lonesome road, that someday I would work under this man on **North Dakota OUTDOORS**, and later, supervise him when I became the head of the division that published that magazine. It came to pass — 24 years later. Not long ago I talked with Ed about his career.

Ed Bry was born in Grand Forks on December 13, 1924 to Mr. and Mrs. E.O. Bry of Manvel. He grew up and was educated in the little community of Manvel located some 12 miles north of Grand Forks on the flat, rich Red River Valley plain. At an early age Ed was inquisitive about the outdoors and in the 7th or 8th grade he acquired an Ansco 620 Clipper camera. He took pictures of family, friends and outdoor scenes, then processed the film into 8 x 10 prints in his basement darkroom. His curious nature led him to read a lot . "I had all these bird books . . ." Ed said, "I could identify all the birds and plants pretty much. I didn't know the scientific names but I knew the common names."

In addition to running a grocery and dry goods store, Ed's father also bought and sold cattle, so Ed worked in the store a lot. But he found time to be afield, too. Even though Ed's parents weren't ardent hunters, he and his brothers made up for it, hunting and trapping frequently. Ed first hunted with a single-barrel .410 and then a double-barrel 12 gauge, ". . . a Stevens or something." In his youth the yellow-legs (prairie chickens) were still around. "We had quite a few chickens . . . that was the first thing you went to hunt — upland game, prairie chicken and partridge." Ed says there were very few sharptails around Manvel in his youth. "I hardly knew what a sharptail was . . . it was all prairie chicken" (Ed Bry was a key person in promoting acquisition of prairie chicken habitat. In the 1960s and 1970s the 3,150-acre Prairie Chicken Wildlife Management Area was acquired in several tracts, 7 miles west and 3 miles north of Manvel).

Ed doesn't remember a lot of wildlife in the '40s. "We had more ducks and there were more pheasants in the '40s, of course. But deer were scarce." The Bry boys hunted mostly on the Turtle River and adjacent prairie sloughs and along the Red River although ". . . they were clearing that pretty heavily. I remember when I was a kid, the woods that were there then, are gone now. I remember the first deer I saw, and the second deer I saw. If you saw a deer in those days it was something you talked about." Ed believed year around hunting pressure in earlier years kept deer numbers low.

In 1944 the draft grabbed Ed. He went with the infantry to the Czech border and when the war ended there, he wound up his military career with the U.S. occupation forces in Japan. Back from the war, Ed found that his father had sold the grocery but was still busy as a Grand Forks county commissioner and cattle-buyer. So Ed had time for the 1947 deer season, when he hunted deer for the first time, bagging a buck in the Turtle Mountains with an old Marlin pump shotgun and slug.

His future before him, Ed began thinking about a career. He wrote to colleges for information about wildlife management. In the meantime he farmed for relatives and friends. He wrote a letter to the chief game warden of the North Dakota Game and Fish Department, inquiring about how to become a game warden. Then one day chief warden, Walter Moore, found Ed seeding rye on the prairie and invited him to Bismarck to write the warden exam. On September 20, 1949, at 24 years old (the youngest man at that time to ever become a full-time game warden) Ed Bry became the new district warden stationed at Park River — still toting his Ansco 620 Clipper camera, which, however, he soon replaced with a Busch 2¼ x 3¼ press camera.

Game wardens of the 1940s and '50s were a little different from those of today, especially in the areas of training and equipment. After spending a day in Bismarck for orientation, Ed said, "I came back to Park River a real greenhorn." He didn't even have a car — he'd borrowed a brother's to travel to Bismarck — so he bought himself a used Chevrolet to patrol his 100 x 60 mile district. He had no siren, red light or binoculars. He just had to go out and be a game warden the best way he knew how. They told him, "There's a notebook, a pad and pencil and book of laws . . . and see you later." Chapter 20 of the North Dakota Century Code was Ed's most popular reading for a long time. He finally bought his own binoculars and a red lens for his spotlight. Later, with savings from the service and a couple of years of mink trapping, he had enough money to buy a good set of binoculars and a faster car. Warden pay was only fair, but Ed never complained. The state did pay his mileage, meals and lodging. Ed took to wardening like fish take to water. He loved the freedom and opportunities to make his own decisions about when and how hard to work. A single man, Ed knew no schedule, he always seemed to be at work.

Ed never had much time for girls. In high school, what with basketball, hunting, fishing, photography, skating and skiing on the Turtle River, there wasn't much time left. But he had always liked dogs, (as a kid he had a water spaniel and some collie-like dogs) so he got a weimaraner, named Misty, that became his constant companion. Some nights on stakeout, Ed rigged a board on top and between the front and back seats to rest on. The dog rested on the front seat and they kept each other company through the long nights.

Generally Ed travelled alone, but one companion he welcomed was his "special." Ernest Sarrazin of Walhalla was one of dozens of interested sportsmen across North Dakota at that time that were concerned about wildlife law enforcement and wanted to help. The state issued them special warden badges and they accompanied full-time wardens, or sometimes worked by themselves. "They weren't paid," Ed said, "except if they made an arrest and were paid a small reward, I think $25.00 for small game and $50.00 for a big game case." Ed was involved with only one special. "I was lucky . . . Ernie Sarrazin would go out with me a lot." Most wardens felt better with someone along on nights when they tried to catch shiners. Ed was no exception. "Quite often deer shiners, at least at that time, they'd be in the bar first and get pretty well tanked up before they decided to go and shine deer. So you never knew what you were going to find when you got in the bush." Popularity of deer, because of their relative scarcity, put deer shiners in low esteem, and probably generated more warden response than other wildlife violations. However, poachers for the most part apparently weren't selling the meat. "No, most of them weren't selling, they were just for their own use. It was something new, you know, we hadn't had any deer for a long time, and now they were coming back."

Some of Ed's most eventful game wardening involved deer shiners. One night he and his special were out moving through the countryside with their "blackout" lights on - headlights off. Finally they observed other lights moving in suspicious patterns. A trap was set, sprung, and bingo, the suspected vehicle was stopped. Among the shiners was a respected clergyman. Ed said, "If we had made a list of the area residents that we wouldn't expect to catch shining deer, this man's name would be at the top." But the clergyman went to court, took his licks and paid the fine like anyone else. Many other incidents are reported by Ed in an article entitled, "Hello, I'm a Game Warden" which appeared in the March, 1986 issue of **North Dakota OUTDOORS** magazine.

Perhaps the most dangerous and threatening of all of Ed's warden experiences has never been written anywhere. It occurred up in his Park River district and involved deer shiners again. The details of this night, though they happened over 30 years ago, remain crystal clear in Ed's mind. He recalled that frightening incident:

"While sitting and watching in my car on a hill, I noticed flashing lights in the low clouds of a dark night. It appeared to be a deer shiner several miles away. I drove into the area using only my blackout lights and saw a vehicle shining around a field. The vehicle soon left the field and came my way on the old road I was on. As they came closer, I put on my red light but they speeded up and got by me on the wrong side of the road. The front of my car was hit by the front and side of their car but we both could still drive. I turned around and soon caught up with them but I couldn't get them to stop. The roads were muddy and their car was sending mud over my car. I stuck with them for about seven miles when they drove into a farm and into a narrow shed. They stopped and I had to stop inside the shed. My appeal for them to surrender was answered with, "Bry . . . God-damned you!" As they rushed me from front and behind — there were two of them — one wrestled my long heavy flashlight from me and was swinging it as a club. I pulled out of their grasp and managed to get out of the shed. I pulled my handgun and told them to halt. They came at me again. The fight ended when one poacher was shot in the leg. I later learned they had thrown their guns into a ditch soon after I had first tried to stop them. There was fresh blood and deer hair in their car's trunk and I found a fresh-killed buck at the home of one violator when I later made an early morning search. I drove the violators to Langdon, leaving the wounded man at the hospital and the other with the sheriff."

Ed feels fortunate the violators tossed their guns in a ditch near the beginning of the seven-mile chase. Nonetheless Ed said, ". . . if I hadn't pulled my gun to defend myself I wouldn't be here today."

Ed recalls that North Dakota was one of the first states to get two-way radios. "But when I got mine there was nobody to talk to unless you worked with another warden." His radio was installed in Bismarck in about 1952 or '53 when he was enroute to work the antelope season. "Then they were okay because we could talk to the airplane, we could talk to other wardens . . . then I got back to my own district and there was nobody to talk to because the sheriffs hadn't gotten them yet. When they got radios they worked only a few hours at night . . . so you couldn't talk to them at night." Today's on-duty game warden is never out of reach of communications. State radio or their personal beepers can reach them anywhere, anytime. The advantage of being a lone, free warden was being compromised by newfangled communications. Ed wasn't sure he liked that too much.

Then came a day in 1953 that would change Ed's life dramatically. He agreed to go on a fishing trip with a farmer friend and another man by the name of Alfred Daley. Ed took movies of the trip and planned to show them to the two families upon their return. Mr. Daley's home was chosen the site. When Ed arrived to show the film, he was met at the door by the farmer's daughter, Marilyn Daley, a Grand Forks nurse who happened to be home on leave. "That's where I met her . . . showing that movie . . . and then I didn't see much of her for about a year." Nose-to-the-grindstone Ed heard duty calling and went full bore back into wardening. But he couldn't forget this Marilyn Daley. While in Grand Forks months later Ed called her but there was no answer. Weeks after at Homme Dam Ed found her. Marilyn had moved to take on a new nursing job at Grafton. Rumor had it that during the summer of 1954 the shiners had the run of the hills. Ed and Marilyn were married in October, 1954. "She hardly knew what a game warden was," Ed remembered, "but she accepted it real well."

In the summer of 1955 Ed and Marilyn moved to Belfield and a new warden district. Here they started raising a family, eventually four boys, Don, Tom, Jon and Bob. This new country was a breath of fresh air to Ed. He hunted more, hiked, tented and camped with his family and lugged that old press camera around taking scenic black and whites. Misty, Ed's weimeraner became more a part of the family, a good hunter and loyal companion. "Oh, we enjoyed the badlands very much . . . it's as close as you will get to wilderness without having to drive 3,000 miles."

By now Ed's photography was being frequently acknowledged. It claimed more and more of his interest. And wardening was changing along with Ed's interests. "I was probably tired of being a game warden . . . of arresting people, of always looking for them to do something wrong . . . I guess I didn't like the two-way radio much . . . I didn't like being tied down . . . checking in and checking out."

One day in 1962, Ed was asked if he would consider becoming the new editor of **North Dakota OUTDOORS** (they'd had eight editors in as many years). Ed went to Bismarck and worked a few days. He looked around busy Bismarck and didn't really like what he saw. It probably looked like a lot of "checking in and checking out." He returned to Belfield, discussed it with his family and then called Bismarck and said "no" to the offer. But Bismarck wasn't about to take a "no" that easily. This time Russ Stuart (then Game and Fish Commissioner) and Pershing Carlson (then Chief of Information-Education) drove to Dickinson to see Ed. It wasn't fair! It was two against one! The administrators prevailed. Ed packed up his family along with the promise of a $25 a month raise and moved to Bismarck to accept the challenge. "Although we all hated to leave the badlands . . . a nice home in the cottonwoods south of Bismarck eased the pain." The Missouri River and its meandering haunts became the family's new playground. They fished, camped and hiked the willow sandbars at a time when the Missouri River had few admirers. Ed Bry was one of the river's most early and successful boaters and fishermen. Pepper, a German shorthair and English pointer cross, followed Misty and became an excellent hunter of sharptails and especially of the sly ringnecked pheasants the Bry men pursued in the Oahe bottoms.

Now good wildlife photography began showing up consistently on the pages of **North Dakota OUTDOORS**, especially after Ed retired the battered Busch and purchased his first single-lens reflex camera with telephoto lens. The photo files began to build. Newspapers, magazines, books, wildlife clubs, nature groups, schools, civic clubs and girl and boy scout troops wanted to see Ed Bry photography. And he showed them.

Perhaps sensing his lack of formal education, Ed made it a point to continue to study and accurately observe the plant and animal community. Many department staff people, despite their superior technical training, came to rely on Ed's knowledge of North Dakota bird, animal and plant life, won in the field from hundreds of hours of observation, much of it in cramped photo blinds. He was seldom proved wrong. So his reputation as a naturalist grew along with the admiration people held for him as a photographer.

As time passed, Ed's eye for composition acquired that special vision and his technical ability with the camera and in the darkroom became more and more refined. Editor of **North Dakota OUTDOORS** for 23 years, Ed never missed an issue and never quit showing his readers the wonder of North Dakota wildlife. And that was recognized. In 1968 the North Dakota Wildlife Federation presented Ed with their Conservationist of the Year Award. Ed was also nominated for the prestigious American Motors Professional Award in 1968. Then Game and Fish Commissioner Russell Stuart in his endorsement of Ed said, ". . . in my 25 years as a game and fish administrator I have worked with several hundred persons professionally employed in this work. I know of none who have more successfully combined personal dedication with professional ability than Ed Bry." In 1982 the North Dakota Chapter of the Wildlife Society recognized Ed for professionalism in communicating the story of North Dakota wildlife and presented him with their North Dakota Professional Award. And the Science Teachers' Association of North Dakota understood the contribution Ed made to natural science education when they bestowed on him their 1984 Friend of Science Education Award.

Ed Bry's photography, particularly the black and whites, have been sought after by publishers everywhere. Through this medium, people who have never met him know Ed Bry. Ed's photographs have appeared in **Audubon** magazine, **National Wildlife, Field and Stream, North Dakota Horizons, North Dakota REC Magazine, Dakota Country**, countless newspapers and in (at least) the following books:

Stefferud, Alfred, and Arnold L. Nelson, editors. 1966. **Birds In Our Lives.** U.S. Government Printing Office. 561 pp.

Hyde, Dayton O., editor. 1974. **Raising Wild Ducks In Captivity.** E.P. Dutton and Co., Inc., New York, N.Y. 319 pp.

Stewart, Robert E. 1975. **Breeding Birds Of North Dakota.** Tri-College for Environmental Studies, Fargo, N.D. 295 pp.

Johnsgard, Paul A. 1981. **The Plovers, Sandpipers and Snipes of the World.** University of Nebraska Press. 493 pp.

Johnsgard, Paul A. 1983. **The Grouse Of The World.** University of Nebraska Press. 413 pp.

Grier, James W. 1984. **Biology of Animal Behavior.** Times-Mirror/Mosby College Publishing. St. Louis, Toronto, Santa Clara. 693 pp.

Cadieux, Charles L. 1985. **Wildlife Management On Your**

Land. Stackpole Books. Harrisburg, PA. 310 pp.
Wesley, David E., and William G. Leitch, editors. 1987. **Fireside Waterfowler.** Stackpole Books. Harrisburg, PA. 352 pp.

Ed has also had photos appear in **Audubon Field Guides (Western Birds).** A large book edited by Milton Rugoff and Ann Guilfoyle, entitled **The Wild Places,** called for the collection and review of over 40,000 photographs. Of those, 166 were printed. A classic Ed Bry black and white prairie chicken courtship photo was one of them.

Perhaps Ed's most valued professional commendation was that provided by professional photographers and book editors Ann Guilfoyle and Susan Rayfield (both prior **Audubon** copy and photo editors), when they included an Ed Bry black and white techniques article they prepared as one of ten major sections in their 1987 publication, **Wildlife Photography - The Art and Technique of Ten Masters** (American Photographic Book Publishing. New York, N.Y. 173 pp.). In their introduction to this book the editors said, "The men and women in this book represent the best of wildlife photography today . . . sensitivity to the natural environment . . . fresh insight . . . feelings of the moment. It is the difference between merely looking and truly seeing and feeling that mark them as being among the best in the world. Among the handful of professional nature photographers working in black and white today, Ed Bry is one of the finest craftsmen in the medium."

I don't know if Ed Bry really set out to accomplish all of this. I rather doubt it. It just happened through a love of work. But the fact remains, Edwin O. Bry Jr. has done all of these things, and he has done them with a certain quiet unaffectedness. At a time when egoism seems the fast-track to success, it is refreshing to find a nationally recognized professional with his humility intact. It is likely a thing of genes and heredity — the influence of a resolute Norwegian background. Maybe Ed's relationship to Oskar Omdal lends credence to that notion (Omdal was a cousin of Mrs. E.O. Bry [Nellie Kittleson] of Manvel, mother of Ed Bry Jr. He was a Norwegian polar explorer who spent 32 days near the North Pole with leader Roald Amundsen, see Mason, Theodore K. 1982. **Two Against The Ice.** Dodd, Mead and Co. New York. 192 pp.) No one will ever know that. But to know Ed Bry is to know an uncommon man. Maybe like Omdal . . . maybe better than Omdal.

To know Ed Bry is to know a man suitable for us contemporaries to measure up to.

To know Ed Bry is to know a man of bashful reserve. To the extent (at least to the unaware) that he may appear indifferent. Patient examination, however, shows only that persistant shyness, a trait Ed has always fought, but never fully overcome. Thank goodness, for it is certainly the seedbed of his affability.

To know Ed Bry is to know a husband and father of the finest tradition. A man of Christian example. Youthful in body and spirit throughout his family's years, he played hockey and softball with his sons into his fifties. And always hunted, fished and camped with them. He is their friend and father.

To know Ed Bry is to know a man without ridicule, but with gentility.

To know Ed Bry is to know a man of modest means and natural ways. From 1949 to 1962 he denied himself a modern 35mm camera. An accomplished walleye fisherman, his success is a mental achievement, not due to his old 14-foot Crestliner. His garden provides him fine vegetables, his bee hives golden honey and a successful deer season, venison aplenty.

To know Ed Bry is to know a man we admire for his decisions about what is, and what is not, important. It is more important to suffer five hours in a hot photo blind, capturing on film the exquisite dance of the western grebe, than it is to shop for a new camera. It is more important to leave work to go fishing on a golden October day than it is to stay and grouse over all the work to do. It is more important to carry a light lunch of carrots, an apple or orange, than it is to jeopardize the objective by bringing the kitchen sink. It is more important to know when and where to pick ripe Juneberries than it is to order your jelly from Knotts.

To know Ed Bry is to know a resourceful hunter, fisherman and outdoorsman who loves best, of all wild game, the flesh of the ruffed grouse; who loves duck hunting but would choose first a day of pheasant hunting with his boys and German shorthair, Kari; who thinks walking is the good fun part of hunting; who chooses the lowly jig tipped with a wad of garden angleworms over other tackle; who generally proves, anywhere, that two shells from his Sears (Winchester in disguise) over-and-under is as good as your three shells from any pump or automatic.

To know Ed Bry is to know a man who laughs easily, but loaths Norwegian jokes.

To know Ed Bry is to know a man who has worked where he has wanted to live, rather than lived where he has had to work.

When Ed Bry retired in the fall of 1986 after 37 years of public service, it wasn't necessarily because he wanted to. Lymphoma cancer was the reason. Diagnosed in March of 1984, Ed began chemo treatments soon thereafter. He left work when he felt he was not contributing what he thought he should be contributing. Since retirement Ed continues to fight this aggressive disease. His strong heart and abundant spirit still gives him the strength to aim his camera at birds in the feeders outside his window and to make fishing jigs for family and friends.

Now as I conclude this writing about Ed, I naturally think back to that hot, dusty day in 1960 when I first met him. And, I kind of wonder, now that I have worked myself through this Bry history, if maybe Ed Bry was supposed to have walked from those **Audubon** pages, an emissary sent to show us just how this photography business should be done—and show us good ways to live, too. Since 1960 I have worked for Ed Bry, and he has worked for me. It came to pass. We've never discussed who was the best boss—maybe not important when you know who is the best photographer.

The story of Ed Bry belongs in **Across The Wheatgrass**. Words from Harold Umber, current editor of **North Dakota OUT-DOORS** in "Reflections" (January, 1987 from that magazine) help me say why, simply: ". . . I ponder what there is left to say about a man whose name has become synonymous with **North Dakota OUTDOORS**, except that he is an example of what is right about North Dakota and its people."

Spring, 1988   H.T.U.

ACROSS THE WHEATGRASS

WILDLIFE

HUNS
– AN HISTORICAL SKETCH

The Hungarian partridge has been on the North Dakota scene for the past 50-odd years. Though, to young North Dakota hunters the Hun's presence may be taken for granted, there are many people in the state who out-age partridge history in North Dakota. It seems odd to think that Huns have not always been in North Dakota, for their association with the North Dakota farming community seems as natural to today's younger generation as perhaps the prairie chickens or "yellow-legs" appeared to North Dakota pioneers. But Huns have not always been in North Dakota, Alberta, or any other part of North America. They were introduced here by transplantation from European sources as long ago as the latter part of the 18th century. Let's take a brief look at the status of partridges in Europe prior to North American introductions.

The native range of partridge in Europe is in the northern hemisphere. Within this broad region the most established range lies on the plains of France, Germany, Czechoslovakia, and Hungary. Prime habitat is found on the central European plains or steppes which have been turned into farmland. Fertile, undulating cropland in which large spaces are broken up into numerous fields are best. Birds do not favor large fields planted with one and the same crop, but do well in smaller areas where nonproductive acreages such as strips, paths, tracks, hedgerows, and grassland borders are common.

The European partridge has always been one of Europe's most popular birds. During the reign of Charlemagne (800-814 A.D.), Emperor of the West, the partridge was considered by him to be more of a decorative bird than an economically useful one. However, around the latter part of the 9th century, Frankis Monarchs already included this fowl among the game birds. It is also reported that Charles IV commonly feasted on partridge. During the Middle Ages French Monks relished the partridge so much that they wished it be made sacred to the clergy.

In early centuries firearms for bird hunting had not been fully developed, so other methods were used to harvest the birds. Yarn nets strung across the birds' pre-dusk flyways proved worthwhile. This method of catching partridge was probably used more for commercial purposes than for sport. Although, since partridge flesh was highly prized and brought a very high market price this method may have been most frequently used by poachers. Falconry was another method of reducing birds to the bag, but often this method was merely recreational.

When firearms became available, partridge populations probably suffered greater exploitation. Populations must have been fantastic during the 18th and 19th centuries. Their abundance can be substantiated, in part, from hunting records such as these: ". . . Emperor Francis I and his Court at Oponco in 1758 produced a kill of 63,250 game birds of which no less than 29,545 were partridges" or ". . . on one Bohemian hunt in 1775 twenty-three shooters took 19,543 partridges in 18 days" or records of Frederich William I, who hunting with falcons and firearms took 1,500 partridge in the course of one autumn. Even up to the turn of the 20th century, populations must have been high for in 1904 an American millionaire, James Gordon Bennet, leased the hunting rights of a Czech shoot with the agreement that he could shoot a minimum of 10,000 partridges. In England in 1905, eight guns shot 1,671 birds on one fall day.

Perhaps it was due to the high regard for partridge by

Europeans, their unmistakable sporting value and table quality and amazing reproductive potential that prompted Richard Bach, son-in-law of Benjamin Franklin, to import in 1790 what is believed to be the first introduction of partridges to North America. An unknown number of birds were released near what is now Beverly, New Jersey. This planting is believed to have ended in failure. Records show that few imports were made for almost a hundred years. Then in the late 1800s, Washington, California, and Virginia began importation on a small scale. Apparently success was great enough for interest in the bird to expand almost country-wide. Thousands of birds were purchased by many states with the height of importation occurring in the very early 1900s. Some of these plantings persisted for awhile but the most were doomed from the start as little attention was paid in determining geographical and environmental fitness of the country into which birds were being liberated. Finally, in 1908-09, Calgary, Alberta sportsmen led by Fred Green purchased 70 pair of birds from Hungary. The result was the most impressive establishment of all Hun liberations. Within five years the birds spread from the initial plant east through Alberta and all over the western part of Saskatchewan. In 1913, Alberta opened its first season and allowed a bag limit of five birds per day and 25 for the season.

News spread quickly of the phenomenal success of partridge establishment in Alberta and particularly of the 28-mile-per-year spread into adjacent territory. North Dakota people soon became concerned about Huns and the possibility of birds extending their range into the state. Hence in March, 1909, North Dakota law made it illegal to possess partridge. First reports of Huns in the state came from residents of the northwest counties in 1923.

The 1923 sightings might also be explained by the fact that Montana introduced birds as early as 1921 in the northeastern corner of Montana. Also, a private stocking of Huns in North Dakota was supposed to have occurred in 1915, however, no records on numbers or location can be found.

Finally, in the spring of 1923 the North Dakota State Game and Fish Department purchased 25 pair of Huns from Czechoslovakia for $9.00 per pair. These birds were released near the towns of Bismarck, Red Willow Lake, Velva, Ray, Minto, and Grafton. Additional stocking was done in 1924, 1926, 1928, 1931 and 1932 and some odd trade agreements occurred between Saskatchewan and North Dakota during 1934 and 1936. At the end of a period from 1924 to 1936 the Department had consigned for about 8,000 partridges. By 1931 the Department reported the following: ". . . there are wonderful signs of improvement apparent in the conditions that affect these birds. Reports say that they are to be found in every county in this State with the exception of the Red River Valley . . ." The 1935 Annual Report of the Department said ". . . the Hungarian partridge . . . is second only to the grouse in being able to combat severe winter conditions and find protection from the elements. Observations show that these birds have readily adopted themselves to all sections of the State and are now well on the way to becoming North Dakota's leading game bird." In 1934 the first open season for partridge was held in North Dakota. The bag limit was three and the possession limit was six.

Since the introduction and subsequent establishment of Huns in North Dakota, we have enjoyed some of the highest Hun densities to be found anywhere in the United States. Our best year was probably 1941 when estimates of harvest ranged near 400,000, greater than harvests of any other state advertising a season on Hungarian partridges. Today we still have Huns present in every county of the state. They are exciting to hunt and a joy to watch in all North Dakota seasons.

North Dakota OUTDOORS, March, 1970

SUPER DOG

You gotta admit, coyotes are cool. More than any other species of Great Plains fauna, the clever coyote exemplifies a breed of critter as intrepid as any. He'll be on the heels of mankind to the end. It's an uphill battle, though, and problems are ever-present.

In Oklahoma, coyotes have inferiority complexes. They ain't top critters down there. They're second-rungers. Why? Well, because they've been intimidated for centuries by those cocky, little, stubby-winged roadrunners. Nothing they can do about it either — they've just been out-evolutionized. Trouble is, they won't admit it. So, the race goes on, back and forth across the mesquite plains, over precipitous cliffs and under five-ton rocks suspended by guaranteed Acme skyhooks. Always close, but never quite close enough, our floppy-eared, scraggly friend winds up in a disjointed mass of hide and bones while motor-legs screams by beep-beeping down victory lane. What a deflating experience! Despondency? Why, a gasless balloonist swiftly enroute home from 11,327 feet couldn't feel worse. No way! But somehow this stubborn coyote picks himself up and heads back to the drawing board for another try.

Dakota high plains coyotes, on the other hand, may have superiority complexes. They seem to rule the roost. Up here they're top dogs, and since Oklahoma roadrunners aren't allowed in North Dakota, these comparatively psychologically content critters languish in opulence, stomaches full, and minds courting visions of dominance.

But wait! Lately the tables have turned and the North Dakota gray dog, like the Oklahoma roadrunner, is the chasee not the chaser! Nowadays he's often only a stride or two ahead of a load of hot lead or a step or two from an enticing trapper's set. But never fear, nature's dog is up to the test even though his pressing aggressors are fashionably outfitted with the finest of Acme Sporting Wares (subsidiary of the Tulsa-based, Acme Roadrunner Extermination Co.).

Anybody that's been on the trail of North Dakota coyotes will admit they make few mistakes. But when they do, guess what? Right, the trail boss follows suit and makes a bigger one that allows gray dog's escape. It's the stature of the critter that does it. It brings out the best in him and the worst in you.

I know of times when "turned loose" coyotes, incidentally approached, have ruined otherwise successful fishing outings. I know of trappers who have stood helplessly by, bulletless, while a trapped coyote ran from the scene after a final desperate lunge freed him. Fox trappers say gray dog is smart—has that extra-elusive quality. Government predator control men often have special problems with problem coyotes.

I know of a deer hunter that spoke more braggardly about a wild coyote he missed than he did of a handsome buck he shot the same day. I remember a veteran sportsman who called a coyote to within 50 yards, steadied his custom-perfect firearm on a granite boulder, drew deadly aim through precision, telescopic sights, squeezed a fine-tuned Canjar trigger and then listened to the firing pin fall on an empty chamber. I once witnessed another caller virtually run over when his irresistible call sucked "lobo" headlong into the surprised gunner's hiding place. The coyote escaped, sweeping so near the gunner they both exchanged bad breath.

Humble pie, what a nasty taste! It's tough to confess before friends that ol' gray slipped from your grasp once more. If your friends witness it, you're totally defeated. There's hardly an excuse worth offering. It's simply a deflating experience! Why, a spoonbill hunter who has stalked, shot, and sunk a half-dozen decoys before the startled eyes of a vacationing game warden can't feel worse. No way!

Yup, no question about it, coyotes are neat. You have to admit it, whether Oklahoma or Dakota-born, they possess a certain respectable durability. They've got class. They've got stature. They just won't say "give." Instead they persist, adapt, regroup, and bounce back time and again with uncanny resilience. They've gotta' flair for survival, they've demonstated that. They belong!

What would we do without them? Well, Oklahoma roadrunners might finally find time to grow real wings. Then they could depart aloft to tease eagles. What about North Dakota sportsmen? Well, for sure we'd lose a worthy competitor and our hunting reflexes would corrode even more without the clever coyote to test our mettle.

North Dakota OUTDOORS, February, 1977

GRASSLAND SHAGGIES

*A Selection of Notes on Our
Unforgettable American Bison*

Their immense size and burgeoning numbers contributed to their demise. They competed for space. They needed room and lots of it. So, they were smack-dab on a collision course with progress, whiteman's progress, and to remove them would not only open the plains to settlers—dirt farmers and stockmen—but also quite handily eliminate the staff of life from the plains Indian's civilization.

The American bison, the buffalo, was in the way. Clearly, he was to fairly disappear from this continent in just a matter of years. Even though his existence was prehistoric, his days were numbered.

It was a huge undertaking, endorsed by the War Department and fervently encouraged by many Washington lawmakers. Perhaps no one really believed the seemingly limitless herds could ever be annihilated. But they were—almost to extinction!

Monarch of the plains, largest land mammal in the New World, the great shaggy beasts were cut down, overcome by the unrelenting tide of meat and hide hunters: the military, railroaders, sportsmen, and even the Indians. When the big buffalo guns, like the Sharps, Springfields, Ballards, Henrys, Remingtons, and Maynards, fell silent, a different solitude returned to the plains. Only heavenly thunder remained, none from the "big fifties" and none from the hooves of a thousand stampeding buffalo.

Today there are several thousand buffalo located in a score of state, national, and provincial parks and ranges across North America. They did survive extinction. When we visit these wired reserves and look out upon a contented herd grazing in lush vegetation, we may come away with the notion that they are docile creatures, slow and easy going, like the white-faced cow that usurped their range—lacking in spirited disposition. Such an understanding would help explain the ease with which man seemed to reduce the millions to nearly nothing in so short a time.

But they're not so cordial and submissive as they appear, unharassed in government meadows. On the contrary, their physical stature is awesome and their nature unpredictable. At 300 yards a buffalo bull looks pretty much like any other bovine critter, but at ten feet his massive hulk somehow suggests he can do anything he damn well pleases.

To the Indian warrior the buffalo must have seemed especially frightening. Carried swiftly across the rock-studded plain on a perfect buffalo-runner, badger holes, prairie dog towns, washes and blowouts threatening perilous dismount, the warrior hung on for dear life as his pony instinctively joined the bawling melee of a moving buffalo herd, close enough so his rider could send his flint-tipped shaft on a fatal path to the buffalo's vitals.

Contemporary managers of our remnant herds manipulate these groups with a healthy respect for their contradictory conduct. In the 1500s when Coronado made his way into what is now Kansas, he made a pretty accurate appraisal of them, ". . . 'Crooked Backed Oxen' aren't to be pushed around."

IN STATURE IMPRESSIVE

A Biological Survey of North Dakota published in 1926 by Vernon Bailey, a biologist with the U.S. Department of Agriculture's Biological Survey who spent time in North Dakota in the 1880s, includes this information collected by James Audubon about the measurements of a large buffalo bull shot near Fort Buford (near Williston) in 1843: ". . . measured from top of nose to root of tail, 131 inches, tail vertebrae, 15½ inches, hair on end of tail, 11 inches. When cut into pieces it weighed 1,777 pounds — it was not fat and would have weighed 2,000 pounds if it had been in better condition . . . bulls generally weigh about 2,000 and cows about 1,200 pounds."[1]

Tom McHugh, in his book *The Time of the Buffalo,* states that a full-grown male plains buffalo weighs between 1,400 and 2,200 pounds, and stands between 5½ and 6½ feet at the shoulder and in total length measures from 9 to 11½ feet including about a foot and a half of tail. A buffalo bull weighs more than his closest North American rivals, the moose and Kodiak brown bear, by a thousand pounds. McHugh's figures show that the cow weighs about 750 to 1,100 pounds and stands from 4½ to 5½ feet at the shoulder.

They are of intimidating size and are capable of expressing proportionate rage, especially the bulls. Wayne Gard in his book, *The Great Buffalo Hunt,* quotes an early fur trader, Alexander Ross: "There is perhaps not an animal that roams in this or any other country more fierce and forbidding than a buffalo bull during the rutting season. Neither the polar bear nor the Bengal tiger surpasses that animal in ferocity."[2] And some hunters, Gard says, discovered in a wounded buffalo bull more ferocity than they had guessed.

Even those not wounded, but of a cranky nature when pressed by hunters, could turn in blood-thirsty revenge. A case in point is referred to in a letter written by Father George Antoine Belcourt in 1845, to a friend. Father Belcourt was a missionary accompanying the "halfbreeds" or Metis (pronounced may-tay) on the large annual buffalo hunt (the Metis lived in the Red River country of northeastern North Dakota). Says Father Belcourt: "Thus in order to overtake the cows, one must thrust through a solid phalange of bulls — a most dangerous undertaking. Let me illustrate: Last year one of the Indians, who had been knocked over by a buffalo, was tossed and gored for a quarter of an hour by the infuriated animal. Without slackening its mad career, the brute tossed and retossed the unlucky hunter 15 to 20 feet in the air, catching him each time on its horns."[3]

Father Belcourt further states: "Some idea of the strength of the animals may be obtained from the fact that one of them, when dashing through a line of carts, caught one with its horns and sent it rolling over for two or three turns. These carts, hauled by a horse, usually carry a load of more than a thousand pounds."[3]

The excitement of the hunt and run was contagious, even

though the risks in the hunt itself were often not small. But the Metis seemed to shrug them off easily. Father Belcourt reports: "As I accompanied the hunters, almost always when they left camp to hunt, I witnessed a rather perilous situation in which some of them found themselves during the course of the first chase in this neighborhood. Having dashed off in pursuit of a numerous herd of cows, they were in full career, in the very midst of the herd, when they arrived suddenly at the brink of a steep, rock-strewn cliff. Over they went, pell-mell—hunters, horses, buffalo—in such confusion that it is difficult to explain why some were not killed . . . beneath the hooves of the following horde . . . Only one man was knocked unconscious . . . The hunters who had been unhorsed jumped quickly back into their saddles, with reassuring cries, and took up the chase once more."[3]

And to pursue and keep pace with a moving herd of buffalo meant a highspeed chase. Gard indicates that while buffalo have poor sight, they do possess a keen sense of smell and surprising speed. One Kansas hunter wrote: "They are built for speed, despite their big heads and heavy haunches. Their run is a heavy gallop, and it is not every horse that can come near matching them in speed."[2]

Railroads also had their problems with "track happy" buffalo, and it wasn't singles that gave them fits, rather the herds, which literally swarmed around a train sometimes holding it up for hours. Col. Richard Irving Dodge, quoted by author McHugh, said of frisky herds crossing the tracks, "After having trains thrown off the tracks twice in one week conductors learned to have a very decided respect for the idiosyncrasies of the buffalo."[4]

Wounded bulls were approached cautiously. Occasionally these animals charged hunters, injuring some and killing others. McHugh says, "occasional hunters are dispatched by 'dead' buffalo that rose again to make a last fatal lunge." He records such an incident involving a wounded cow. Charlie Reynolds, who later became Custer's favorite scout, and a partner were walking up to butcher several buffalo just shot when they approached a nervously twitching cow. "As Reynold's partner moved in to cut the animal's throat, she sprang up, charged, horned him with a sudden blow to the chest, and collapsed. Rushing to his companion, Reynolds found him ripped open from belly to throat so cleanly that he was able to view the 'heart still expanding and contracting.'"[4] The man was dead in a short time.

Several references are made by McHugh in his book to the importance of placing shots in vital areas—the heart and lungs and occasionally the spine—for quick dispatch of the buffalo. He says, "the accomplished hunter could bring down the stoutest bull with a single shot aimed at a vital point. If he missed all of these points, however, his shot was practically useless, so tenacious of life was the buffalo."[4]. McHugh also documents a statement by Audubon which describes a victim "which during one of our hunts was shot no less than 24 times before it dropped."[4]

The most impermeable part of a buffalo is his forehead. In one instance McHugh reports a nineteenth century sportsman firing three shots from his Henry rifle against the forehead of a wounded buffalo bull at a distance of only 15 yards which caused no other results than some angry headshaking. The hunter said, "I then took my Spencer carbine and fired twice with it. At each shot the bull sank partly to his knees but immediately recovered . . . I afterwards examined the skull and could detect no fracture."[4]

In a modern-day tale McHugh substantiates the earlier hunter's story about thick-skulled buffalo one day when he was hunting with Crow Indians on the reservation. "Late in the afternoon as our jeep passed near a wounded bull, one of the Indians fired his .30/06 at the animal from the close range of 30 feet. The bullet smashed into the buffalo's head, bounced back and grazed the hand of a rider in the jeep, then landed on the ground nearby, a warped piece of lead and jacket bearing a trace of blood."[4]

IN NUMBERS—NUMBERLESS

And what about the herds, the swarms of buffaloes, just how numerous were they? A number of descriptive estimates were made of buffalo numbers on the North American grasslands. Some from McHugh include ". . . There is such a quantity of them that I do not know what to compare them with, except the fish of the sea . . . Numerous as the locusts of Egypt . . . We could not see their limit either north or west . . . The country was one robe . . . In numbers—numberless."[4]

Alexander Henry, an early Dakota explorer, recorded immense numbers along the Red River Valley in September, 1800, and on January 1, 1801, near the junction of the Park and Red Rivers (east of Grafton). His is a most popular quote in describing buffalo numbers in North Dakota. "At daybreak I was awakened by the bellowing of buffaloes . . . On my right the Plains were black and appeared as if in motion . . . and on my left, to the utmost extent of the reach below us, the river was covered with buffalo moving northward . . . I dressed and climbed my oak for a better view. I had seen almost incredible numbers of buffalo in the fall, but nothing in comparison to what I now beheld. The ground was covered at every point of the compass, as far as the eye could reach and every animal was in motion."[1]

In January, 1803, while riding from Park River in North Dakota to Riding Mountain vicinity of Manitoba, Henry says, "we never marched a day without passing herds of buffaloes, and the men who have lately been up as far as Goose River, tell me the buffalo continue in abundance from this place to that river as far as the eye could reach southward."

Vernon Bailey reports Lewis and Clark in 1803 counted 52 herds from a single point on the Missouri River, 11 miles above Fort Rice (about 30 miles south of Mandan).

At Fort Union on the upper Missouri (near Williston) Audubon in 1843 reported that Mr. Kipp, an employee of the American Fur Company traveling from the Lake Winnipeg area to the Mandan Nation (near Bismarck), "passed through herds of buffalo for six days in succession."

Gard tells of the problems encountered by Captain Grant Marsh who was piloting the steamer *Stockade* on the Missouri River in the summer of 1867: "The buffaloes came so thickly that the boat could not move, and the captain had to stop its engines. Many of the animals became entangled with the wheel, while others beat against the sides and stern, blowing and pawing. It was hours before the whole herd had crossed and the boat was able to continue its voyage."[2]

Nathaniel Langford, first superintendent of Yellowstone National Park, described the swarm of buffalo he and his party saw in 1862 west of the Red River Valley (in eastern North Dakota): "We thought the herds of 5,000, 10,000 or more very large herds, until we got beyond the second crossing of the Cheyenne River, where the herds increased in size. The sky was perfectly clear, when . . . our guide Pierre Botineau exclaimed, 'Buffalo!' . . . Soon we saw a cloud of dust rising in the east, and the rumbling grew louder and I think it was about half an hour when the front of the herd came fairly into view. The edge of the herd nearest to us was one-half to three-quarters of a mile away . . . we judged the herd to be 5 or 6 (some said 8 or 10) miles wide, and the herd was more than an hour passing us at a gallop . . . they were running as rapidly as a horse can at a keen gallop, about 12 miles per hour."[4] Langford multiplied his estimate for the herd's area by the approximate density of the animals and came up with a staggering figure. "I have no doubt that there were one million buffaloes in that herd."[4]

THE FINALE

After the southern herds were wiped out in the late 1870s, the hidemen made their way north. An estimated 5,000 hunters were on the northern range in the early 1880s haunting the last large herds in the country – primarily in western North Dakota, northwestern South Dakota, and western Montana. By 1886 the northern plains buffalo, last of a continental population estimated at from 30 to 40 million only 30 years earlier, probably numbered less than 500.

North Dakota holds the dubious distinction of hosting the last great buffalo hunt near the headwaters of the Cannonball River (some 15 miles west of New England). In June, 1882, 600 Sioux Indians, well mounted and armed, killed 5,000 animals in a two-day hunt. Then, in October, 1883, Chief Sitting Bull led nearly a thousand braves on a final mop-up operation between the Grand and Moreau rivers in northwestern South Dakota (about 50 miles south of Hettinger, North Dakota) where all of a herd of about 1,200 were killed. Minor hunting forays by whites and Indians continued for a few years, but the era of the buffalo had passed. The task was complete.

It seems ironic that the last hunts were affected by the Indians, the people who had lived with and depended on the buffalo for centuries. But by this time the buffalo's fate was abundantly clear to them and perhaps a final, passionate, reenactment of the glorious buffalo-running days was their birthright – before the Indians were subdued forever and quickly forced into such a dramatically different lifestyle, that the change would indignantly suck the lifeblood from their traditional culture.

Now, strewn about the prairies were the spoils. Bones, some bleached white from dozens of summer scorchings, some only recently laid down, still covered with stringy flesh, were maggot-ridden and the stench in some places was overpowering.

Many buffalo hunters turned to the less-than-romantic occupation of bone picker. Others turned cowboy and helped bring in the large cattle herds from Texas. Settlers joined in the picking, clearing the plains of $10-a-ton bones that were railed east and processed for fertilizer and for a product used for filtering and purifying of maple sugar.

The bone trade itself, while it lasted, was a $40,000,000 business, courtesy of the North American grasslands. Penniless farmers and immigrants, many from North Dakota, gathered bones to help pay for the necessities of life that they would need to settle, live and prosper in this new land that once belonged to the buffalo masses and the Indians, both nomads of the plains.

North Dakota OUTDOORS, August, 1977

REFERENCES

[1]Bailey, Vernon. 1926. A Biological Survey of North Dakota. U.S. Dept. of Agri., Bureau of Biological Survey. **North American Fauna**, No. 49.

Barnett, Leroy. 1972. The Buffalo Bone Commerce on the Northern Plains. **North Dakota History**, Vol. 39, No. 1, 49pp.

[3]Belcourt, G.A. Hunting Buffalo on the Northern Plains: A Letter From Father Belcourt. **N.D. History: Journal of the Northern Plains**, Vol, 38, No. 3, (Summer 1971), 334.

[2]Gard, Wayne, 1960. **The Great Buffalo Hunt.** Alfred A. Knopf, New York, 324pp.

[4]McHugh, Tom. 1972. **The Time of the Buffalo.** Alfred A. Knopf, New York, 339pp.

Somehow this unique rodent survived the onslaught of unchecked fur trade exploitation. He is again a rather common inhabitant of North America and North Dakota. Perhaps we should say . . . silk

HATS OFF TO THE BEAVER

A frivolous thing helped save him. Due to an arbitrary change in fashion and to the introduction of silk to the hatter's industry, nature's engineer, that buck-toothed, largest of all North American rodents, the beaver, was saved from complete extirpation.

Incredulously, the silk hat helped save the beaver.

This trinket of man's vanity essentially curtailed the trade of beaver *plus* (beaver skins, pronounced "plews"), as silk succeeded beaver felt in European and American hat fashion.

Morever, the change, which began in the 1830s, came none too soon, for across much of North America, particularly west to the upper Mississippi River valley and north along the Red River to the Hudson Bay, beaver had been systematically removed by adhesive fur trade pressure. World-wide depression in the late

1830s reduced pelt prices drastically and for a time this also stayed the big rodent's execution. But near 1840 when the demand for beaver hats began to fade more quickly, disgruntled trappers, aware their wilderness days were numbered, remarked defensively, "Hell's full of high silk hats."

The Canadian fur trade, which was essentially a trade in beaver pelts, was thought to have begun quite by accident. In 1535, Jacques Cartier, a French navigator, found and began exploring the St. Lawrence River, but presumed he had discovered the long, sought-after Northwest Passage. Near Montreal, formidable river rapids kept the party from pushing west. Undismayed, Cartier began trading with the local Indians. For French knives, kettles, and other metal accessories, the eager Indians offered their furs, even those off their backs—beaver furs! The great North American fur trade had begun.

EUROPEAN NUMBERS

Back in Europe a new hatter's process found the rich beaver *plus* ideal for manufacturing felt hats. The great market demand could not be filled by European beavers as their numbers had already been much reduced by earlier demand for castoreum, the musky glandular secretion from the animal's belly gland which from the time of the Greeks had been regarded as a cure-all for such ailments as colic, epilepsy, frostbite, and hysteria. Castoreum contains salicylic acid, one of the main ingredients of aspirin. In addition castoreum was, and still is, a fixative used in perfume making. Also, in the 17th century beaver teeth were attached to the necks of children during teething in a belief that this would facilitate the cutting of teeth. Demand for castoreum continued into the 1850s so beaver were sought also for this product.

So, the beavers from the New World would provide the bulk of the supply needed by European hatmakers for nearly 300 years.

HEAD GEAR

The "Beaver," what the fine hats came to be called, was not only in demand by the fancified "dandies of the boulevards" and stalwart country gentlemen, they were also wanted by the armies of several nations and this latter demand sucked up the greatest number of these "hairy bank notes," as they were described by trappers and traders who found them as negotiable as any silver coin.

The "Beaver" was made by a process that found it necessary to seemingly destroy these dark, sleek, rich pelts. The first step was to shave both hair and wool from the skin. The bare skin was sold to a gluemaker and the hair was separated from the wool by a blowing process. The soft, loose wool was then wetted with hot water and slowly applied to a perforated, revolving copper cone within which was a suction device that pulled the fur against the cone. Several repetitions plus a good deal of hand working completed the felting process. The developing hat was then removed from the cone and placed in a mold where it was worked by hand into the desired shape. While still warm, shellac was forced into the felt from the inside out. Finally, fine fur was applied to the outside. More hot water and hand work eventually gave the hat a fuzzy appearance, as if it had a growth of fur. This was brushed, sandpapered, and ironed until the surface took on a velvety pile look. Even back in the 1700s, the "Beavers" sold for $10. Out of fashion, indeed, was the New York gentlemen who did not sport one. Today, beaver hatmaking is a lost art and such hats are seldom found except in museum collections.

NEW WORLD NUMBERS

The primitive range of the beaver *Castor canadensis* (24 subspecies are known) covered all of temperate North America wherever there was food and water. In the United States this included all states except the panhandle of Florida and the deserts of western Utah, southern Nevada, and southern California. All of Canada, the Northwest Territories and Alaska save for the arctic North, was beaver country. Best estimates of primitive numbers put the continent population at approximately 60,000,000. The quest for beaver led trappers and traders to almost every part of North America north of latitude 30° 30', long before permanent settlers began to arrive.

In early North Dakota Alexander Henry said, ". . . beaver houses were numerous along the Red and Goose rivers near Grand Forks (then known as a point where the Red Lake River meets the Red River of the North), and more numerous than elsewhere on the upper Sheyenne."[2] In 1804 and 1805 Lewis and Clark found beaver abundant along the Missouri River throughout North Dakota. At the Mandan villages they spoke of French trappers coming into camp with 20 beavers. Trappers were then just beginning to find the Missouri a rich field for the harvest of beavers.

EARLY VOYAGEURS TRADING

During some years of the 1600s it is estimated that 100,000 to 500,000 beaver pelts came out of the St. Lawrence and

Hudson Bay area annually. In 1760 the Hudson's Bay Company exported to England enough beaver pelts to make 576,000 felt hats, and other companies were shipping, too. In these earlier days it was the Frenchmen, paddling crude log canoes deep into the new America's interior and the Canadian wilderness, who became the pioneers of the North American fur trade. These tough, raw-boned men became the backbone of the early fur trade and often spent more than a year at a time paddling remote lakes, settled pristinely along the inter-connecting river system of the north known as the *Voyageurs Highway*. In 1763 the British conquered Canada and to exploit the great wilderness they opened more Hudson's Bay posts (Hudson's Bay Company originally chartered in 1670) in the East and founded the North West Company which established outposts along the route of westward moving trappers and traders.

Trading posts in what became northeastern North Dakota began with the first Hudson's Bay post at Pembina in 1797 and with the North West Company's Fort Pembinats in the same year. A number of posts were operated along the Red River of the North and its many tributaries during the early 1800s, initially for beaver trade and later for trade in buffalo robes and hides.

At the Park River Post, Alexander Henry's first post in North Dakota, he traded for 643 beaver in 1800. In 1801 and 1802 Henry's Hair Hills post, located in what is now Walhalla's city park, traded for 24 packs of furs each weighing about 90 pounds (there were about 75 skins per pack). The Turtle River post built by John Cameron and located about seven miles north of Manvel, North Dakota, traded 16, 90-pound packs of furs (not all beaver) in 1802. In 1803 Henry traded in the Pembina vicinity for 1,801 beavers, 195 black bears, one grizzly and a number of other furbearers now extremely rare in North Dakota including wolves, fishers, marten, otters, wolverines, and black bears.

On the Salt River posts C. Hesse in charge of these posts experienced only fair returns. He did 14 bales, but only 160 beaver pelts. Henry notes that there was a "certain epidemic disease" which killed off most of the beaver. John Tanner, famous for his narrative of his captive life among the Indians says of beaver on the upper Red River in about 1800,: "Some kind of distemper was prevailing among these animals, which destroyed them in vast numbers . . . Since that year the Beaver have never been as plentiful in the country of the Red River and Hudson Bay as they used formerly to be."[2] On January 1, 1805, Alexander Henry abandoned his post at Pembina River because the country was "almost destitute of beaver."

MOUNTAIN MAN TRAPPERS

In 1803 President Thomas Jefferson purchased the Louisiana Territory from France, an area of over 827,000 square miles for which the United States paid $15,000,000 or $18.33 per square mile (2.9¢ per acre). Later, the "Purchase" contained all or parts of 15 states. More trapping pressure west of the Missouri and Yellowstone rivers came after Lewis and Clark completed their epic journey through the continents mid-section by following the Missouri River from St. Louis north to the northern plains, and across the Rockies to the Pacific during the period 1804-1806. It was the expedition's mission to locate and secure a trade route to the Pacific as well as to determine the degree of international competition for this vast area's commerce, at that time the beaver and other fur trade. There was particular concern about the northern section of the territory where continued British encroachment increased the chances of a border dispute. For whomever settled this wilderness would also likely control commerce.

Because of this it has been said that the beaver is the most important fact in American history — and indirectly, perhaps, the felt hat. The beaver was abundant; its pelt was excellent for the current demand; it is gregarious and relatively easily trapped; and it attracted men from all creeds and nations. The beaver was an object of incalculable economic worth and political struggle among the French, British, and Americans. It was clear that the nation in command of the fur trade might also command the surrounding territory.

The War of 1812 postponed immediate plans of several new American fur companies to ascend the Missouri and enter into the fur trade. Finally, in 1822, William H. Ashley, Missouri's first Lt. Governor placed an ad in a St. Louis newspaper asking for 100 "enterprising young men" to ascend the Missouri and there be employed as free trappers for the Rocky Mountain Fur Company. The kind of men that signed on with Ashley and other company traders like him, became known as the "mountain men." Names like Jedediah Smith, Jim Bridger, Moses "Black" Harris, Edward Rose, John Colter, Christopher "Kit" Carson, Joshua Pilcher, Hugh Glass, John Potts, James O. Pattie, Jim Beckwourth, Joe Walker, and others, would become synonomous with the fur trade, simple means and courageous character. The era of the mountain man roughly paralleled the period of greatest beaver exploitation west of the Missouri and covered the decades of the 1830s, '40s, '50s, and '60s.

Along the upper Missouri and the trade area around Fort Union (near Williston), Maximilian reported 25,000 beaver pelts bought during 1833. Because of decreasing beaver numbers, however, mountain men pushed westward. In 1843, Audubon visited Fort Union and noted that beavers were "once so plentiful, but now are very scarce."

One Rufus Sage, himself a trapper during the 1830s, described a typical mountain man: "His skin, from constant exposure assumes a hue almost as dark as that of the Aborigine, and his features and physical structure attain a rough and hardy cast. His hair, through inattention, becomes long, coarse, and bushy, and loosely dangles upon his shoulders. His head is surmounted by a low crowned wool-hat . . . His clothes are of buckskin, gaily fringed at the seams . . . The deer and buffalo furnish him the required covering for his feet . . . His waist is encircled with a belt of leather, holding encased his butcher-knife, and pistols . . . from his neck is suspended a bullet-pouch . . . from his shoulder . . . strap . . . are affixed his bullet-mould, ball-screw, wiper awl, etc."[3]

The mountain man usually carried several knives, pipe, and tobacco and often some reading matter which popularly included the Bible, Shakespeare, and books of poetry. He carried spare locks and flints, some 25 pounds of powder and a hundred pounds of lead and his gun which was usually a heavy .40 to .60 caliber rifle preferably a work of the Hawken brothers of St. Louis. Save for some coffee, flour, tea and salt, the mountain man carried very little food. He lived from day to day from the land and he may have often feasted on the object of his endeavor — beaver — for the flesh was quite acceptable as was the tail which was considered a delicacy by many including Lewis and Clark. His most important possessions, next to his guns, were the four to six beaver traps, weighing about five pounds each and which cost him from $12 to $16 apiece.

His trapping seasons were two; one in the fall which lasted until ice and snow made travel and trapping impossible, the second in the spring when the ice began to break up. The spring season lasted until the fur quality deteriorated.

Trapping success varied per individual and group. In 1825, James O. Pattie caught 250 beavers in two weeks on an Arizona river. Alexander Ross and his 20 trappers working the Bitteroots in 1823-24 took 95 beavers in one morning and 60 more the same day. The group took 5,000 beaver out of the Snake River country that year, exclusive of other peltries and despite constant Indian trouble. In all of 1824 some 80,000 pelts were taken from the Snake River country, mostly by British trappers.

Audubon and Backman wrote of Rocky Mountain trapping

that in 1850 "A good trapper used to catch about 80 beavers in the autumn, 60 to 70 in the spring, and upwards of 300 in the summer in the mountains; taking occasionally as many as 500 in one year." In the 1860s George P. Beldon lived with the Sioux and said, "A trap weighs about five pounds, and it is considered a good load to carry 12. It will require a walk of 10 to 12 miles, and all of the day, to set a dozen traps properly . . . three catches each night for 12 sets is good."[2]

The western trappers, the mountain men, were less traders and more free trappers. They faced a lethal wilderness for 11 months and then came to summer rendezvous, usually located in the Utah, Idaho, or Wyoming mountains, where they sold their furs and where for a solid month they bragged, fought, ate, and drank themselves to excess. Then they resupplied for another year and, usually alone, returned to the wilderness to tackle new challenges. Trapper James O. Pattie estimated that of the 116 men who left Santa Fe in the summer of 1826, only 16 survived until the next summer.

John Colter, a survivor of many campaigns, faced one especially frightening confrontation. A private attached to the Lewis and Clark expedition, Colter was granted early separation by his leaders when on the upper Missouri (in North Dakota) during the party's return to St. Louis. Two men, Joseph Dickson and Forrest Hancock met the returning party on August 15, 1806, and invited Colter with them to trap beaver. The two men barely lasted the year, but Colter remained in the bush for four years and became established as the precursor of the mountain man. In 1808 Colter found himself with John Potts, also an old Lewis and Clark member, enroute into Blackfoot country to trap beaver to bring back to Manual Lisa's trading post on the Big Horn fork of the Yellowstone. In a fracus with the Indians, Potts was killed and Colter captured. He was stripped of his clothing, allowed a 75-yard headstart and then pursued by dozens of Blackfeet. His salvation was found in the security of a beaver lodge that he was able to enter from underwater. He waited there several hours, exhausted, bleeding from nose, mouth and cactus-punctured feet. He heard the Blackfeet nearby but they finally gave up. A week and 200 miles later Colter showed up at Manuel Lisa's post. He had survived, thanks to the beaver and his own familiarity with their lodges.

HAIRY BANK NOTES

In Canada in the 1600s a beaver skin sold for 32 shillings (in colonial America a shilling was worth 12 to 16 cents). In 1801, in North Dakota, Henry profited to the extent of $7,000 for approximately 1800 skins, most of which were beaver. Average price paid for a beaver pelt in 1801 was $3.50. This compared to other furs sold in 1801 as follows: otters up to $6.40, fishers $1.60, wildcat and wolverine about $2.40 each, and the kit fox at only 40 cents. Beaver, though, in its wide distribution, great abundance, and trapping vulnerability was the hottest fur trade pelt.

In 1828 William H. Ashley paid $3.00 per pound or $5.00 per skin to his free trappers. In the 1820s and 1830s pelts ranged from $5.00 to $6.00 each. In 1843 at Fort Union (near Williston) James Audubon said "It takes about 70 beaver skins to make a pack of 100 pounds; in a good market this pack is worth $500, and in fortunate seasons a trapper sometimes made a large sum of $4,000 (pelt price would be about $7.00 each)." It has been reported that some trappers earned several thousand dollars more than that per year and that one trapper earned $50,000 in a single year. At $5.00 apiece, that amounts to 10,000 beaver *plus*, somewhat unbelievable. It's likely that this trapper did some fast trading, probably with Indians for alcohol, where he may have turned a several-thousand percent profit by exchanging watered-down rum for progressively more and better peltries.

Besides money, the sleek beaver pelts could be exchanged for a variety of other commodities. In 1670 one beaver skin would buy: one pound of tobacco or a one-pound kettle or four pounds of shot or one large and one small hatchet. It took six skins to buy a lace coat and 12 nice pelts to acquire a long rifle. In the early 1800s one gun was worth 14 beaver skins. One blanket was worth six skins and an ax, kettle, beaver trap, or length of cloth was worth two skins. A nine-gallon keg of "spirits" (often diluted) brought 30 beaver skins.

Traders in small posts known as *Bourgeois*, or managers, would bargain with Indians, or any interested prospect, and for their furs exchange gunpowder, lead, blankets, cloth, butcher knives, tin kettles, axes, sugar, coffee, tobacco, thread, rings, hawk bells, bracelets, large brass wire, assorted beads and, of course, liquor.

After the 1830s the buffalo robe started to replace the beaver pelt as a unit of value and was equal to: two beaver skins, four deer skins, three wolf skins, one bear skin, and two elk hides. A fairly good horse was worth five buffalo robes, but a good buffalo pony would bring from 50-100 robes, or, an equivalent of 100-200 beaver pelts worth $500 to $1000, local prices.

BEAVER DESTINY

By 1840 beavers had become scarce in the eastern part of the continent and the big companies shifted their trade more to buffalo robes. Yet the period from 1860 to 1870 is described as the peak of the fur trade and an estimated average of 153,000 skins annually were handled by both American companies and Hudson's Bay Company. During the period 1853 to 1877, Hudson's Bay Company sold almost three million pelts on the London market. But then the all of North America had been penetrated and, notwithstanding the completeness of the eastern beaver harvest, the final effort, continentwide, brought the total take up to what some think should be more like 500,000 per year for the period of peak fur trade.

By 1895 the trade in beaver pelts was down to nothing and the year 1900 was called the "blackest of all." In that year 8,000 beaver skins were produced in the United States and only 66,000 in the entire world.

Ah-misk', the Cree's name for the beaver, was rather suddenly a stranger in a land where he was once abundantly common. *Tsa*, the Chipewyan's name for the beaver, had found no safe place to step. *Ah-mik'*, the Ojibway's name for the beaver, was rarely seen along streams, instead only deteriorating dams and lodges. *Chan-pah*, the Ogallala Sioux's name for the beaver, faired similarly, except along the big Missouri and other permanently deep, fast-moving waters where his use of bank dens lent him less susceptible to trappers.

In North Dakota, Audubon reported the beginnings of reduced numbers at Fort Union by 1843. David Thompson, an explorer of the Canadian fur trade, noted that by 1848 beaver were scarce on the Red River near the mouth of the Park River. In 1887 no trace of beaver could be found along the Red River nor were any colonies heard of in the Pembina vicinity. In the Turtle Mountains in 1912 only one colony could be found. But all through the mountains old traces of former abundance of beavers were found and it is reported that the best of the meadows in the area are all old beaver ponds that have since filled with silt. Elsewhere in the state beavers were not reported numerous, but they were not uncommon either. Areas along the Missouri, Cannonball, and Little Missouri rivers and their associated drainages were reported to have some beavers.

In 1917 there was no legal protection for beavers in 20 states — perhaps because there were no beavers. By 1927 there was a closed season in 26 states. Based on an annual report of the Forester, U.S. Department of Agriculture in 1926, total beavers in the United States and Alaska numbered approximately 252,000. Alaska had about 50,000. Colorado was estimated to have 47,000 and at the low end was the Virginias, estimated to have about 10 live beavers in each state. North Dakota was thought to be supporting about 2,000 beavers.

From 1931 to 1951 North Dakota had a special permit system for beaver harvest that allowed the removal of principally problem animals. In 1952 the season was opened statewide and open seasons have been held since then. Beaver populations across North Dakota responded well to protection of the early 1900s and today good populations of beaver can be found across the state, of course, not in the numbers that Lewis and Clark or Alexander Henry found them.

But they're not gone, totally extirpated. They're far from that, and perhaps we owe that to the silk hat!

North Dakota OUTDOORS, March, 1978

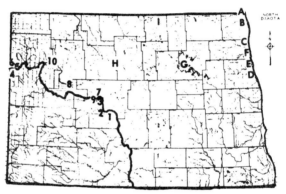

North Dakota played no small part in hosting the beaver men. There were several fur posts and fur forts located in North Dakota in the early 1800s. As early as 1797, Hudson's Bay Company had a post at Pembina. Jesseaume's Post on the Missouri was built by an illiterate French-Canadian in 1794. The map above presents a sampling of these fur posts and forts. There were many others which lasted for varying lengths of time, some only a season or so.

RED RIVER POSTS	MISSOURI RIVER POSTS
A) Hudson's Bay Post at Pembina (1797)	1) Jesseaume's Post (1794)
B) Fort Pembinats (1797)	2) Fort Mandan (1804)
C) Park River Post (1800)	3) Fort Manual Lisa (1809-10)
D) Grand Forks Posts (several posts operating as early as 1796, but most in first decade of 1800s.)	4) Ashley and Henry's Post (1823)
	5) Fort Union (1828)
	6) Fort William (1833)
E) Turtle River Posts (1802)	7) Fort Berthold (1845)
F) Salt River Posts (1804)	8) Fort Manevry (1870)
G) Duncan Graham's Post (1814)	9) Fort Atkinson (1859)
H) Minot Post (1820-21)	10) Hall's Trading Post (1855)
I) St. John (1853)	

Taken from **Fur Trade in North Dakota.**[4]

REFERENCES*

Adams, Ramon F., et al. 1963. **The Book of the American West.** Julian Messner, Inc., New York.

[1]Bailey, Vernon. 1926. A biological survey of North Dakota. **North American Fauna** No. 49, U.S. Dept. of Agric.

Barlett, Jen, and Des Bartlett. Beavers. **National Geographic.** Vol. 145, No. 5, May 1974.

Collins, Babney Otis. 1977. Blackfeet vs. barefeet. **Colorado Outdoors**, December, 1977.

[3]Gilbert, Bil. 1973. **The Trailblazers.** Time-Life Books, Inc., New York.

Hall, Raymond E., and Keith R. Kelson. 1959. **Economic Mammalogy.** Charles C. Thomas, Springfield, Ill., and Baltimore.

[4]Killie, E.S. 1969. The fur trade in North Dakota. **Official Newsletter, North Dakota Historical Society, Inc.**, Vol. 3, No. 3.

[2]Seton, Ernest Thompson, 1953. **Lives of Game Animals.** Vol. IV - Part III. Charles T. Brandord and Co., Boston.

Tanner, Ogden. 1977. **The Canadians.** Time-Life Books Inc., New York.

*The fur trade in North Dakota was an extremely colorful period of our heritage. A more specific bibliography co-authored by E.S. Killie and Rev. Robert Williams is available in **Project North Dakota**, a reference resource inventory obtainable from the North Dakota Department of Public Instruction, State Capital Bldg., Bismarck, N.D. 58505.*

WOODLAND DRUMMERS

Drumming grouse?

Nearly 20 years ago I pondered that riddle myself. As a student at NDSU - Bottineau Branch (then N.D. School of Forestry) I solved it after applying for and landing a spring job with the Game and Fish Department conducting ruffed grouse drumming surveys in the aspen woodlands of the Turtle Mountains. The surveys provide indices to population trends.

"What do you mean, 'drumming grouse?'" I asked Morris (Moe) Johnson, then Department upland game biologist, on hand at Bottineau to ready me for a trial run the next morning. I had earlier concocted a hysterical fantasy of a portly male ruffed grouse setting up a solo snare drum performance on the drumming stage of his favorite aspen log, there to grandstand before the fairer sex as well as to defend his territory against other males. Well, the latter part of this impression is true, but his "drum" was hardly transported through the dense hazel brush to "Carnegie Hall" in a canvas case slung over his shoulder.

Johnson confessed he'd suffered similar absurd illusions, but he was seasoned now and knew the truth. He offered that the unusual sound could be audibly interpreted as drum-like. A better analogy, he said, is the engine sound of an old one-lunger John Deere tractor operating a mile away. I could make my own interpretation early the next day.

Many wildlife surveys begin in the dark — that is, very early in the morning — and the drumming of ruffed grouse is best heard near dawn when males are most active and when the wind is most apt to be calm. On that long-ago morning at 4:30 a.m. I stood quietly next to Johnson absorbed in the shakedown run, ostensibly recording drums during the standard four-minute listening period.

Finally Johnson spoke. "O.K., how many did you tally?"

"I heard three, possibly four, but one was incomplete and it's best to disregard those," he said.

I thought he was putting me on. I allowed that I wasn't putting *him* on. "I heard nothing," I apologized, "nothing I would have counted as a John Deere tractor or anything else making a boom-boom sound!"

Johnson put the pressure on. "Well, if you can't hear the drums you can't do the work . . . we'll just have to get someone else."

We drove to the next stop, two miles down the road on the 20-mile route. Again Johnson recorded several drums. Most, he said, were far off, like those on the first stop.

I was becoming concerned. How come I can't hear them? I remember thinking perhaps I'm trying too hard.

On the third stop I thought I sensed a far-away "throb." I needed confirmation. "Moe! Moe! I blurted out into the sacred silence of the listening period, "was that one?"

"Shhhh!" Johnson gestured, finger to lips.

Finally the period ended. "How many did you get," I asked excitedly. I was sure I had finally identified a drum.

"Got four. What'd you get?"

"One . . . I think. My drum was faint . . . like a heart throb . . . like a pulse inside my head . . . like an inner vibration."

"Ah, ha," Johnson concurred, "when you interrupted, that's the one I was picking up too. You may land this job yet!"

On the next stop, about two minutes into the silent vigil, I turned to Johnson, smiling, nodding and pointing off to my right into the forest. A close bird, probably within a couple hundred yards, drummed a most perfect love-lilt that drifted confidently to my ears through calm, dawn air. Thump . . . thump . . . thump . . . thump . . .thump.thump.thump.thump.thump.thump . . . thump—the final sound ended in a rapid drum roll. In my mind I saw that young amorous male ruffed grouse, chest puffed out, and primary feathers holding the drumsticks of love. Gotcha!

A second morning with Johnson and I felt like a veteran surveyer—like I could hear and identify a sound mysterious, if not unheard by many others. When Johnson left to return to Bismarck, leaving me with several 20-mile routes to run three times each, I was recording results very similar to his—the close and the faint. I had me a job, and an odd one at that.

Now, 19 years later the sight and the sound was immediately before me—hardly ten feet away. This was as close as I had ever been to a drumming ruffed. With the aid of a canvas blind, I was able to eavesdrop on the very private world of a male bird in prime breeding condition. Despite late snows, below-freezing temperatures and a season that still seemed like winter, this bird played a storybook performance. Daylength (photoperiod) was the key that triggered the beginning of the primordial drumming display ritual.

I arrived near the blind at 5:45 a.m. on May 10. The forest was silent, but as I approached the blind, some 200 yards from the road, I heard the woodland drummers' faint sounds. Crystallized snow banks, some still over a foot deep, blotched the gray forest in the overcast morning. It was light already, about 18 °F., windless, and a trace of new snow dusted the leafless forest vegetation.

A drum, loud and clear, went off up ahead. Sure enough, my friend was already at work announcing his ambitions forest-wide. I thought he might flush, but my careful approach, though suspiciously eyed, was somewhat tolerated. Twenty feet away, with the blind separating us, ol' ruff indignantly hopped from the log and moved several yards away. I took the opportunity to move myself, camera, and tripod inside the small 4x4x4 foot fabric cubicle.

Scarcely situated, I peered out the slit in the canvas and there he was, right back up on the drumming stage (spot on log religiously chosen over others) 8-10 feet away, preparing to drum his heart out. And he did. For 90 minutes, roughly every 3-5 minutes, he gladdened the woods with his personal territorial beat, cocking his head from side to side in studious determination to explain the like sounds of his competitors. I had intruded on a primitive courtship drama. Drumming is a behaviorial adaptation that evolved over time, lots of time. This personality trait is a critical link in the survival of this king of gamebirds. The male before me was apparently in peak reproductive condition. He was totally preoccupied by neighboring drummers (of which I heard at least three others) and unwittingly driven by physiological and behavioral commands to do what springtime dictates male ruffed grouse to do. He appeared oblivious to the blind (which had been erected only a night before) and to me and the sound I made grunting and groaning, trying to find a comfortable position.

Now I could see in raw detail this cock bird's total execution of his drumming display. As one drum followed another, I noted that the loudness did not seem proprotionally greater with closeness to the bird. I remembered the first loud drum I had identified with Moe Johnson 19 years ago. This one sounded as loud, yet the former seemed more than a hundred yards away.

Early listeners claimed that the unusual muffled drum sound was the result of the bird's wings beating against its body. Indians called the ruffed grouse the "carpenter bird" because they were of the opinion the drum sound was produced by the bird beating its wings upon a log. In fact, the sound is a result of rapidly compressed air from lightning-fast, forward and upward wing strokes.

I was pleased with my luck — my proximity and the fearless drummer. My 200mm telephoto lens was almost too much. Any closer and the bird would have overflowed the frame. I tried the 200mm with a teleconverter which produced a 400mm telephoto and half the bird filled the entire frame.

Finally the male grouse tired of his morning workout, left the log on foot to disappear into the gray of the spring forest. I had run out of film at the right time. He was tired and so was I — cold too, from remaining as motionless as possible for an hour and a half.

Another cold and cloudy day had begun. But this experience with a woodland drummer was the perfect way to add a little sunshine.

North Dakota OUTDOORS, June, 1979
The Drummer, August, 1979

THANKS B.C.

Sleep tempted the truck driver. He cracked the window letting November's fresh dawn air gush through the slit. Bill Hickling, big-game biologist for the North Dakota Game and Fish Department, stretched his large frame as best he could within the cab of the snub-nosed Ford truck. Next to him department maintenance man, Balzer Vetter, having just completed a six-hour driving stint, slept soundly, his limp body bouncing with the road rhythm. Two other department personnel followed the truck in a second vehicle.

The non-stop trip was into its thirty-ninth hour. November 5, 1956 dawned crisp and clear over the eastern Montana horizon. Two, perhaps three more hours would put the team and their precious cargo at Magpie Creek enclosure, some 18½ miles west of sleepy-eyed Grassy Butte, a cowtown on the eastern fringe of

North Dakota's Little Missouri badlands. Their cargo was 18 California bighorn sheep (*Ovis canadensis californiana*), live-trapped on November 2 in the Williams Lake country of British Columbia.

In the second vehicle Arthur Brazda, biologist in charge, welcomed the sunrise. Daylight at least suggested an awakening. Somewhat over 1,000 miles long, this bighorn transplant journey had gone well. Icy roads in the mountain passes had been the only obstacle. And the sheep, well, they were traveling like veterans and were apt to come through the ordeal better than the haggard crew transporting them. Customized stalls, fresh water and alfalfa were comforts provided each animal.

In a few hours this phase of Operation Bighorn would be complete, and with Dennis Shearer his partner at the wheel, Brazda relaxed and drifted euphorically in reminiscence.

It had been nearly seven years since North Dakota began researching the feasibility of a bighorn transplant. Now those years of planning, dashed hopes, renewed hopes and the historic significance of this frosty November day flashed before his mind's eye.

From the beautiful B.C. mountains and fish-rich Fraser River country, east across the plains to the North Dakota prairie, this short, olive-drab caravan carried the California bighorn, a race of sheep to be released on the native range of the now extinct Audubon bighorn (*Ovis canadensis auduboni*). Operation Bighorn was more than just another transplant project. It strongly implied a reconciliation with the past, with the time of the Audubon. A sincere gesture of "righting a wrong," however ostentatious it might appear.

Historically the Audubon mountain sheep occurred east of the Great Divide in the arid, broken plains of western North Dakota, South Dakota, northwestern Nebraska and eastern Wyoming and Montana. Lewis and Clark (1805), Maximilian Prince of Weid (1833) and James Audubon (1843), all early explorers of the upper Missouri in North Dakota, found bighorns common along the breaks of the Big Muddy (Missouri River). Indians reported them some 50 miles west to the Little Missouri badlands. But early pressure from both Indians and white hunters seeking the bighorn's savory flesh, desirable hides and magnificent trophy heads severely depleted numbers by the 1880s.

Senior cowpuncher Chris Rasmussen out of Medora in 1960 said, "The last bighorn was an old buck that was living at Hells Hole in approximately 1907-08. He later moved over to Elk Creek northwest of Medora and was killed by Charlie Will . . ."

So, only a century after Lewis and Clark sighted their first bighorn, and some 66 years after James Audubon named it, the era of the Audubon bighorn ended — forever.

Brazda remembered it was 1949 when the North Dakota Game and Fish Department conceived of an Operation Bighorn. In that year the Colorado Game and Fish (now Colorado Division of Wildlife) was contacted to determine if they might be able to supply Rocky Mountain bighorns for North Dakota. Details were worked out and finally Colorado agreed to the proposal. Yet before the transplant could take place a series of unfortunate circumstances negated the deal.

The effort continued. Other states were contacted, but in every case no spare sheep of a suitable race could be located. For a couple of years the project was temporarily postponed, but it was not scuppered. The idea remained a viable dream of several North Dakota biologists. Enter British Columbia.

In 1955 word filtered south from Canada that B.C. might be in a position to provide suitable transplant stock in its native California bighorn. Biologists Brazda and Hickling snapped to attention at the prospect and began communicating with Dr. James Hatter, then chief game biologist for the British Columbia Game Commission (now B.C. Fish and Wildlife Branch). The commission was supplied with written and pictorial materials describing a host of environmental factors and land use patterns in the badlands as well as a history of extinct Audubon sheep.

Late in 1955 the answer came. Dr. Hatter and his staff reported that a thorough review suggested that major ecological requirements of B.C. California bighorns could, in all likelihood, be met in western North Dakota and that the sheep stood a good chance of adapting to the badlands' rugged terrain. Operation Bighorn was on the front burner again!

Dr. Hatter's decision was progressive and far-sighted. At the time, California bighorns in B.C., even though the province represented the sheeps' primary continental range, had generally been on the decline since 1900. Any sheep removed would be a threat, yet Hatter reasoned that transplants into new areas might result in establishment of new populations and thereby safeguard the future of the race *californiana*.

Native California bighorn range once included much of the Sierra Nevadas in California, north through the Cascades of eastern Oregon and Washington and southern British Columbia, and on the eastern slope of the Coast Mountains between 50° and 52° north latitude. By the early 1900s California bighorns were confined mostly to British Columbia, with only a remnant population in California. By the 1950s B.C. bighorns were only holding their own and in some areas declining.

Encroachment on range by cattle and domestic sheep and other agriculture was perhaps most responsible for reduced populations. Hunting, uncontrolled before 1900, also contributed to the decline of the bighorn, but since 1910 has not been an important factor in sheet status. In 1952 the British Columbia Game Commission estimated a province-wide California bighorn population of some 1,200 head. The largest bands were found at Churn and Riske creeks west of the Fraser River. Vaseux Lake and the Ashnola River country, east of the Fraser River, accounted for the rest.

Norman Brunsdale, governor of North Dakota, moved swiftly after being informed of B.C.'s decision and submitted a formal request for breeding stock to British Columbia Game Commissioner Frank R. Butler. Butler advised he would be only too glad to co-operate in the venture and offered to supply not more than 20 sheep. There were few strings attached to the deal. All North Dakota had to do was provide help in the trapping operation, arrange for international border clearance, provide transportation and provide an enclosure at the release site. The last stipulation was to help insure herd acclimatization without herd scattering.

During the spring and summer of 1956 a 198-acre, approximately six-and-a-half-foot-high enclosure fence was erected in the rugged heart of the Little Missouri badlands within the U.S. Forest Service's 1,976,837-acre National Grasslands. In mid-October the word came that preparations were complete for trapping to begin.

On October 20, 1956, the North Dakota team arrived at Williams Lake. There they met their hospitable hosts, Lawson Sugden, a range management biologist and warden, Joe Givault. Approximately 28 miles west of Williams Lake on Riske Creek and on the Jack Moon ranch, a drop-gate enclosure had been erected and baited with raw cabbage and dairy feed. A detonator, positioned some 546 yards away, would fire dynamite caps that would in turn cut the ropes holding the drop-gates.

At times nearly a hundred sheep were in the vicinity, but seldom would the required number enter the trap. Finally on November 2, after a dozen days of work, several frigid nights in sleeping bags, patience and constant observation of the enclosure, the drop-gates were detonated and 18 California bighorns were captured. The animals were held overnight in the enclosure for processing and then loaded into the truck on November 3. Custom details had been worked out and a Canadian veterinarian inspected the sheep at Williams Lake and supplied a Certificate of Health for U.S. Department of Agriculture inspection of the sheep at Oroville, their Port of Entry.

By noon on November 5, the 18 sheep (three adult rams, three yearling rams, six adult ewes, one yearling ewe, three male lambs and two female lambs) had been ear-tagged, inoculated for black leg, brucellosis and hemorrhagic septicemia and released in the Magpie Creek enclosure. Understandably, sleep was the only celebration invited by the proud transplant team.

That first winter two rams, an adult ewe and two lambs died. However, in April, 1957, six lambs were born. The winter of 1957-58 was uneventful, but the 1958 lambing season was historic. Four lambs were born, the first to be bred in North Dakota in well over 50 years.

In 1960 an enclosure of 180 acres was erected in the South Unit of Theodore National Park to handle excess numbers from Magpie Creek. In 1961 eight more sheep were moved to Dutchman's Barn enclosure, a third holding area built south of Medora. Six years had passed and now the enclosures held over 50 animals. The time for a fertile, wild release was approaching.

In the fall of 1962, 12 bighorns were trapped from the Magpie Creek and South Unit enclosures. They were released on an especially craggy site known as Devils Slide, some 19 miles south of Belfield. Another chapter in the saga of Operation Bighorn was complete with this wild release.

Over the next five years more releases were made and by 1967 the enclosures at Magpie Creek and the South Unit were removed. By 1970 an estimated 200 to 250 California bighorn sheep were free-roaming, most associated with their original release sites.

In November, 1975, a limited hunting season (12 permits) was held to allow for the removal of large rams (3/4 curl or better) to adjust the sex ratio with fewer males, thus promoting better lamb production. Similarly, limited seasons were held in 1976, 1977 and 1978.

In 1979-80 a lungworm parasite (*Protostrongylus stilesi*) was suspected of reducing lamb survival. This problem is not unique to North Dakota but is common throughout the continent. Certain population factors and cold, wet lambing periods, however, can make newborn lambs very vulnerable and at times heavy mortality can occur. Transplacental migtation of lungworm larvae puts newborn lambs at an immediate disadvantage.

Ongoing research involves several recaptured sheep transplanted to the renovated Dutchman's Barn enclosure. Three ewes are presently in the Dutchman's Barn enclosure where they have undergone chemical "systemic" flushing of the digestive tract to eliminate the lungworm parasites. Experimental results of this treatment have been encouraging to date — perhaps over ninety per cent effective.

Future plans call for trapping other sheep, holding them in enclosures for treatment and breeding and then making transplants of "clean" off-spring into unoccupied ranges. A major limitation is successful live-trapping of wild sheep. Winter trapping using apple pulp for bait shows the most promise. However, good snow depths restricting availability of normal food are needed. For two years now, snow cover across North Dakota and particularly in southwestern North Dakota has been virtually non-existent.

Everyone involved in the project is optimistic. It's been nearly 25 years and North Dakota's British Columbia bighorns continue an admittedly slow growth, but at least a tenacious foothold on this relatively new ground has been made. North Dakotans are thankful for the chance to have thus far successfully propagated the magnificent California bighorn in the Audubon's historic range. The success of this program ranks as a classic big game management achievement and it stands as a striking testament to international co-operation. Credit first and foremost goes to the generous and forward thinking B.C. Fish and Wildlife Branch and the people of B.C.

North Dakotans say, thanks, B.C.!

British Columbia Wildlife Review, September, 1981

Postscript

North Dakota's California bighorn sheep population is still estimated at between 200 and 300 animals in several herds in the badlands north and south of Interstate 94. New state legislation has allowed for the auction sale of a single sheep permit that the Game and Fish Department has processed through the Foundation for North American Wild Sheep. Gross sale prices for the last three years have been $17,000, $21,000 and $15,000. Ninety percent of these proceeds, grants from the Foundation and federal matching dollars has generated nearly $200,000 for stepped up research and management activities; improved sheep production and some range extension is anticipated within the next few years with the ultimate goal of providing additional harvestable sheep. The Game and Fish Department has allowed the harvest of about six sheep annually in recent years. It is interesting to note that 1988 disagreements between the Game and Fish Department and Enron Oil Company, about the siting of a drilling rig on a bighorn sheep lambing area, centered around the Magpie Creek habitat, the general location of the original 1956 British Columbia bighorn transplant.

Spring, 1988 H.T.U.

ACROSS THE WHEATGRASS

DAYS
AFIELD

WELCOME TO
YOUR FALL

The fun summer is about over, that is, if you measure its length against a school kid's vacation or the passing of July. Late summer days are here. They are quiet, it's too hot to play ball. Fishing is slow. Many other activities that occupied us on fresh June days have become entertainingly stale. Most, it seems a time that is just tolerated. Summer doldrums make the mind wander to new seasons and new experiences.

For thousands of North Dakota sportsmen this signals the beginning of a strange metamorphosis — a frame-of-mind change. It may start with mildly pleasant thoughts of fall colors, but the change progresses until complete and we find ourselves participating in the year's first hunting season.

It is interesting to watch this change occur in people one has a year-round relationship with. It's exciting to see nonchalant behavior turn to child-like fascination as hunting seasons approach. Overall enthusiasm increases as days grow shorter and nights cooler. Casual conversations with friends spur discussions of up-coming seasons that help kindle the fires which generate the interest which begins the change in attitude. Perhaps this is what summer dog days are for, they may serve a purpose after all.

Not long ago, in late July, I spent an evening with a friend who was well aware that fall was drawing nigh. Now, this is a bit early to get the feeling, nonetheless, in him I could see the process had begun. It wasn't a cold evening, in fact the night was muggy and my garage shop was quite close. The fire box in my woodburner was still. So, wood smoke or crisp temperatures could not be held accountable for his mood. He was, however, handling his prized Model 12 Winchester and as he rubbed oil into its weathered stock I saw that he was reliving a hundred experiences he'd had with that gun.

"My God," he finally exploded, "I don't think I'm gonna be able to sleep tonight . . . I really get restless around 'fall things' . . . the more I look and touch the worse it gets."

This individual is a very light smoker, the type that buys a pack and forgets about them for a week. That night he sucked up half a pack. We exchanged tales for several hours, each trying to outdo the other and each trying to separate fact from fiction. It was 12:30 a.m. We walked out into the quiet summer night half expecting to feel a frosty October breeze and hear the sounds of geese on a distant marsh.

Within a few days I was again reminded that fall seasons are just around the corner. This turned out to be a striking example of prejudgement.

I met a man this past spring, but had occasion to visit with him only a few times during the following months. In no way, from our brief visits, did he strike me as the type who cared much about hunting. His outward appearance indicated, at least to me, that he had other interests. He is an excessively mod dresser and I quickly pegged him as an aggressive socializer who played late and slept late. This impression plus the fact he made no reference to outdoor activities led me to assume what interests he did have were indoor related. An amiable chap he was, but not one to talk ballistics with.

Recently I met this man again — it was late summer. He walked into the office and quickly dispensed with business matters before rushing into an exhaustive review of his past hunting experiences. I was taken completely by surprise, and my reaction to laugh had to be tactfully snuffed by a faky coughing jag. This I accomplished and he was none the wiser. He continued, and when he finally touched on the subject of 1973 hunting seasons and the prospects they held for him, his face lit up like a small child's about to see his first circus. This guy was in the midst of his fall metamorphosis. And, it appeared to me the change was near complete, yet it was only late July.

The excitement of fall is not a thing reserved only for the youngsters and middle-aged sportsmen. When it comes to bountiful harvest time, neither can some of our senior citizens deny the calling of this magical season.

I know a man in his middle 60s who has been loyal to his feelings for over 40 years and has religiously shared the stubble with late season mallards. On a spring day when his fancy had turned to fishing I heard him say, seriously enough so I believed him, that it was time to do more fishing than hunting. More sitting, less walking.

Late summer arrived and one evening while I was weeding my cucumber bed he came down the alley to announced he had found nine boxes of shotgun shells left from last year. "That's too many to give away or let rot," he said. I chuckled to myself and thought, we won't lose him this year. A week later he was showing his shotgun to a friend who had offered to buy it. But the would-be buyer knew he was only being teased as the elderly sportsman explained its lightning-fast action and extolled the excellence of North Dakota small game hunting.

You can't argue, late summer is a time of change for the North Dakota sportsman. A metamorphosis does begin. Like the butterflies morphological change, the hunter undergoes a change of spirit, a change of heart that prepares him for a few days of soothing mental therapy. Warm recollections of previous autumns set the mood and from there on the sights, smells, and sounds of the changing season guides the transformation onward.

Season priorities must be chosen. Limited time and money is a reality that shatters the fantasy. What shall it be, a long deer hunt or two extra trips for sharptails? Or, should one sacrifice everything for a solid week of goose hunting?

The search for that new piece of sporting equipment can be put off no longer. Shell reloading occupies evenings. Waders are patched and decoys untangled. Dry leather becomes supple once more with a new oil treatment. Bedford gunjuice shines on firearm receivers. Phone calls and letters arrange dates and places. The dog kennel sparkles for the first time in months and its occupant is reintroduced to the retrieving dummy and the freedom of open fields. Hour after hour is invested in the preparation, but oddly, the job is refreshing, not exhausting. An early frost quickens the pace even more.

Suddenly, time is gone, fall is here. You know it because you can feel it, almost taste it, and more absolutely, the calendar spells out — S-E-P-T-E-M-B-E-R. All things, real and imagined, that make a fall your own private adventure have played on the senses to create a high the likes of marijuana could never produce. This is your fall! Good hunting!

North Dakota OUTDOORS, September, 1973

FLAGGIN' DOWN SNOW GEESE

A wisp of wind tickled my two-day beard and sent rivulets of goose bumps, of all things, down my sides as I watched the lighting of another October sunrise in north-central North Dakota. Dug into the stout grain stubble nearby lay Frank Martz, grade school principal at Rugby, and one of the most persistent waterfowl hunters I've known. We had been field companions for seven years, ever since I moved to Rugby to assume a position of upland game biologist for the North Dakota Game and Fish Department. We'd had some good shoots.

Today was special though. We were both excited to see if our new decoy spread, consisting of nearly 300 cloth and plastic flags attached to dowel pins, would prove as inviting to snow and blue geese as the full-bodied decoys costing $45 per dozen ($1,125 for 300).

Located on a diagonal line between the well-known J. Clark Salyer National Wildlife Refuge (formerly Lower Souris) and Lords Lake, a small easement refuge but significant goose rest and staging area, we knew a shortage of geese would not be a problem. A conservative estimate by Federal officials put the number near 20,000.

We waited patiently at first, but less so as sunrise passed. Predawn shadows ebbed and we were exposed to a high bright sky. I got up to stretch, refreshed from a 40-wink nap, then walked over to Frank's shallow body pit. He was snuggled in tight, head buried in the crook of his arm sleeping.

"Frank," I yelled, knowing full well what was going to happen next. I wasn't surprised. He snapped awake.

"O.K., ya, what 'cha got."

"Caught ya didn't I," I challenged. He slumped back, yawned, and resumed his original posture. I walked back to my spot. We were both tired after two previous mornings of goose hunting. Another short nap wouldn't hurt.

By 10:00 a.m. restlessness overcame us and we broke open the last thermos of coffee. "Can't figure these guys out," Frank said as he considered the empty skies. "Yesterday they were moving almost before sunrise, now today they probably won't get off their downy butts 'til after shooting time."

I shrugged, "That's snows and blues for ya." "They're inconsiderate I know, but if they were too predictable they wouldn't have the following they do."

Coffee finished, we went back to our respective spots and continued to wait. It looked useless. We both knew, though, that patience will always be the goose hunter's greatest virtue. So we loitered some more, until our constant fidgetiness made our earthern pits look like buffalo wallows.

A half hour passed and a light wind swirled the powdered soil of my pit into the last of my coffee. A haze seemed to appear in the southeast and took away some of the brightness. I could see a dark cloud line developing. I continued to study in that direction. Suddenly, I flattened out, like a pancake on a griddle, afraid to even reach up and remove a stem of wheat stubbled that had rammed into my nostril.

Frank had detected my excitement and tuned in on the action. Out ahead, 300 yards or so, about a dozen snows moved ahead of the incoming front. They were on an intercept course with our spread. The wavy line came on in its characteristic ripple and swell motion, working east then west on a sloppy heading apparently snooping for just the right place to settle.

139

Tension mounted. Patience had won out. I laid with my head flat to the ground. I heard their calls now, sweet notes indeed. It was time to carefully judge the situation. I craned my head slowly and as far to the east as I could until my vision blurred. My head swung back, bobbed momentarily, then craned to the west trying to locate that thin line. Where were they? I lost them!

"Frank," I yelled in a hushed voice, "did they sit down?" His dusty face peaked over a dirt clod and he gestured unknowingly. I raised up more and there . . . there they were on our blind side coming in just as proper as could be to a spread of stuck-up diapers and Glad Bags.

"Frank!" He saw them now. I flipped over on my back, one instant their wings set, the next they flared to the outside of the spread. Shotguns roared. Two snows dropped to the ground just beyond the decoys. A survivor retracted his landing gear and struggled for altitude finally joining his bewildered friends. The dust settled, the field regained its solitude, and with dusty smiles we acknowledged our special success without a single word.

Good distribution and concentrations of geese in recent years in North Dakota have certainly provided the opportunity for increased goose hunting and harvests. More geese, however, doesn't necessarily mean better hunting. You still have to entice them within shotgun range and the most effective way of doing that has been decoying — a durable tradition of waterfowlers. But decoys do cost money, no question about it — lots of money for a big, nice spread.

That was the problem me and my hunting cronies faced in 1972. There wasn't a rich man amongst us. Nobody was about to fork over several hundred dollars for what one wife harshly referred to as "daddy's plastic toys." That would be a sure way to end a romance with the outdoors that presently was at least tolerated.

I began looking around at what others were using for decoys. I found a lot of other guys had been similarily forced to improvise. One of the most common substitutes for a factory-made goose decoy turned out to be the large white plastic Hilex or Chlorox jug. I scrounged from friends, neighbors, and some rural dump grounds (excuse me, sanitary landfills) and finally located a couple dozen jugs.

In order to carry them easily I ran a long piece of clothes line rope through the handle of each jug, then threw them in the back of the station wagon. I used them one day. Over these and another dozen of Frank's we did manage to harvest a couple of geese. But we agreed, they clearly were not what we were looking for. They were bulky and a few took up lots of space. They got tangled on the line and knotted up in crazy ways. They blew around easily, although a little sand or dirt in each one helped anchor them. Mostly, without a big grain truck, you'd never haul enough to make a decent spread.

I also recall some good goose shooting that's been had over squares of white rags. This is a common Texas method. A similar but less fashionable and probably cheaper approach is attained with the use of large white bakery sacks. I once witnessed two men achieve almost instant success using bakery sacks while only 300 yards away a large spread of commercial decoys pulled in only an occasional straggler. They may work well, but neither of these methods are really that convenient. And the material soils, mildews or disintegrates way too soon.

Finally we came up with the idea of using white rags attached to sticks. I'm not even sure now whose idea it was, but we glommed onto the thought and gave it a try. I came up with a few worn-out diapers my wife agreed to sacrifice from the rag box. When she wasn't looking I borrowed a few more good ones and left my little man, Michael, so short-suited that he had no other choice than to progress to training pants.

The other guys did the same, scrounging anything white they could find that could be attached to a stick of wood. We cut the cloth into about 18-inch square pieces. Then we purchased 150, three-eighth inch, three-foot dowel pins, cut them in half and sharpened one end. A square cloth was draped over a pin and a two or three inch tuft was pulled out over the end of the pin. This arrangement was secured with a rubber band and a light paper staple. The tuft resembled the head and the balance of the cloth fluffed out around the pin and suggested the body.

In no time we had a hundred decoys, prototype par excellence. But we ran out of rags. We had to have more white stuff to hang on the remaining 200 dowel pins. Someone suggested we use white plastic garbage bags. He turned out to be pretty smart at that. We attached the rest of the pins to the five-gallon size white Glad Bag, a perfect substitute for the rare and endangered white rag. As we used these over several seasons, we found that they were far and away superior to cloth. They don't soil, mildew, rot or disintegrate. They're cheaper and more can be put in a smaller space.

By midnight the night before examination Glad Bag, we'd completed decoy construction. We had to laugh. The humor of our labor, of this revolution in plastic decoying finally hit home. Were we naive enough to think that the noble, deceptive snow goose would respond to this madness?

At 4:30 a.m. the next morning my wife jabbed me in the ribs when I didn't react to the alarm. She muttered something about being late. Another jab startled me into an upright position. I drug my legs over the bedside, teetered on the edge and finally sorted out a few basics — who I was, where I was, and why jockey shorts don't fit right over hunting pants. Somehow I got dressed and coffee fixed just as Frank appeared in the doorway, bubbling with excitement over the great experiment.

We traveled 40 miles to Bottineau and had breakfast at the Country Kitchen where we found stools and booths jammed with men in brown canvas clothes. We left with plenty of time to find our way another 10 miles west and locate the field we'd spotted at sunset the previous day.

Our first experience with our flagged sticks was very pleasant. As tired as we were, the unpacking and set up of 300 commerical decoys would have meant our ruin. Instead, we set up our experimental spread in less than 15 minutes, moved the car, returned and were in position with yet 20 minutes left before shooting time. Ah . . . it was nap time.

The new day approached quietly with the sunrise. Light, not noise awoke me. On this day we would sit apprehensively, perhaps a little embarrassed and for darn sure well aware of the ragged spread we sat with. But the spread did work. It did pay off. The visit from that first, tardy line of snows and the convincing evidence of the two silent white forms resting before us was proof enough.

"You don't s'pose this set-up will work again do you?" Frank questioned. He wanted to believe it, believe that our simple spread costing a mere fraction of the price of store-bought decoys could somehow do the same job.

We were both made believers in the next few hours. By 10:30 clear skies were replaced by cloud cover. A stiff breeze, on which is often carried the promise of a wildfowler's dream brought our unlikely decoy spread to action. By 1:00 p.m., closing time in North Dakota's Unit II goose area, we'd shot six more geese, two short of our limit.

Since that day in 1972 our simple, inexpensive, white decoys have flagged down a hundred other snows, blues, and Canadas. With them we have consistently decoyed and consistently shot geese. I have since given up the notion that commercial goose decoys are a must for field shooting geese. Nonsense! If you don't mind the company of an acre of diapers and garbage bags, your goose shooting success can be as real as the law will allow.

North Dakota OUTDOORS, October, 1976

FISHING IS GOING TO BE GREAT!

The opening of the 1978-79 fishing season is just an ice cake or two away. Everyone is talking about how wonderful it's going to be to shake old man winter, find that special, warm grassy slope next to a favorite prairie lake and then proceed to hook into the latest edition of 1978 fishing action. Fishing is going to be great! Great you say? Now that's a daring prediction. How are you so sure?

I remember a friend telling me about his father who manages several public hunting and fishing areas in Missouri. He used to get calls all hours of the day and night, his son told me, from people wanting to know if the fishing was any good. At first he sincerely tried to recall recent observations and discussions he'd had with fishermen about their success. The callers wanted to know where the hot spots were, if the walleyes were biting, if the panfish were of any size, if the northern pike were hitting on silver, red, plain or baby spoons, if *he* thought it would be worth it for *them* to drive a hundred miles to sample the fishing. All of these questions he tried to answer to the best of his knowledge. If he didn't know for sure, he offered an educated guess. He tried his darndest to advise them on the wherewithal of fishing success — shy only of baiting their hooks.

As you might have guessed, seldom did he satisfy many anglers. In his zeal to provide good information he was accused of keeping the good information for himself or friends. If he was right about what species was biting, he was wrong about the time of day or the bait they were taking. If he was right about how the fish were biting yesterday, he lied, because they sure weren't biting that way today. He couldn't win. Furthermore, he began to see that people were judging a successful fishing outing by the weight of their stringers, and if they didn't "limit out" or come close to the number of fish they could legally take as provided by the conservation department, they weren't very good fishermen — hardly successful outdoorsmen.

Finally he saw he would have to change his ways. Mum would be the word. Even if the sweetest feminine telephone voice caressed his ear, he vowed no longer to be the fisherman's "guide to success."

Shortly after he'd made that resolution the phone rang and a fisherman caller wanted to know, like always just e-x-a-c-t-l-y what he might expect for success if he made the trip.

"It's been great," the manager reassuringly offered, "fishing is really good . . . yes sir, it's *really* been good!" Fired with enthusiasm by the manager's glowing report the caller's surprised voice thanked him and the line promptly went dead.

Late that evening a man approached the manager's quarters. He was a fisherman and his deliberate manner suggested he had something to say. Called to the door by a number of sharp raps on the screen door, the manager was about to greet the visitor when the fisherman burst out, "I thought you said the fishing was great? You told me on the phone that fishing was really good up here!"

Quickly the manager seized his chance to speak. "That's right, I did in fact say those things. You bet, fishing is great, still is as far as I'm concerned and it'll remain that way all summer!"

"What the heck are you talking about?" screamed the fisherman, on the verge of snapping his rod to kindling. "I spent four hours out there and caught one lousy fish! You call that great?"

"Depends how you look at it. I think the fishing is good —

period," the manager countered. "I didn't say anything about the catchin', did I? I just told you the fishing was good . . . lots of fine recreation out there. Sometimes you catch'em, sometimes you don't. So you didn't get many fish. Didn't you enjoy the time spent trying? Did you see the wood ducks in the tree hollow just a few yards from where you anchored? How about the muskrats in the shallow bay—didn't they amuse you at all? How about the two gals sunbathing on the beach—didn't you even notice them? Did you see the kid on shore with the cane pole and his excited face when he pulled in that bullhead? How about the quiet, did you appreciate that. Didn't you feel the warm, sun, the breeze. Didn't you find the afternoon to be a peaceful, restorative experience? How long did it take you to catch that one lousy fish? Two minutes, three minutes? What'd you do the other three hours and fifty some minutes? Ya must have had *some* fun!"

By this time the fisherman was totally perplexed. He turned, bedeviled and frustrated, body bent in submission and walked off shaking his head mumbling unmentionables about the over-throw of the conservation department.

And here in North Dakota the fishing is going to be great too. That is, if we let it. If we can learn to measure the success of our fishing outings more by the total enjoyment of the overall experience and less by the creel weight alone, we can have great fishing anytime.

Everyone likes to catch fish and contemplate the possibility of pulling in that all-time whopper. This must never change. But let's not make a production out of the catchin' and find we've never been fishin'. Relax, fishing is going to be great!

North Dakota OUTDOORS, April, 1978

NIGHT-TRACKERS

Steve Allen, coyote specialist for the North Dakota Game and Fish Department nudged me on the shoulder. "Hey, you awake, no fair sleeping on the job." It was somewhere on the bad side of "dark:thirty"—say, after 3:00 a.m. I had indeed drifted, unable to fend off the drowsiness that comes after several hours of pickup riding. Moreover, it was an hour or two past my bedtime.

I grabbed for a thermos of coffee and poured another round. Allen stopped the rig on a knoll for more effective reception, turned up the speaker volume on the telemetry receiver and settled back with a cup of steaming brew. The nighttime air was cool now and a long-sleeved shirt felt good even though the previous August afternoon saw temperatures reach into the high 90s.

Only a very healthy imagination could make out the faintest

of faint dawning, far and flat against the eastern horizon. "Come on sun, anytime now!" I mumbled, "sooner you're up the sooner Allen will call it a day and take me home." Then the data sheets would be filled with another sample of raw information that when analyzed will tell him more about the life and times of coyotes in North Dakota. The sooner then, I can head to bed. But the light was only starlight — dawn and fresh sheets were hours away.

For fifty nights Allen had been out here somewhere on this 200-odd square-mile study area gleaning movement data from coyotes he and others captured back in May (see **North Dakota OUTDOORS**, June, 1978) and outfitted with radio transmitting collars. Rarely on these nights did he have any human companionship — except for tonight, for me, one of the unwise. Mostly he spent the night with study subjects he has affectionately named Sparkplug, Leroy or Sweetie. Tonight the schedule found us in Crankshaft's and Petunia's home range, an area of some 20 square miles southeast of Bismarck. But these "friends" he seldom saw. Rather he heard from them, as the telltale intermittent radio signal beep-beeped locations through the telemetry equipment.

This was the third and final summer of the tracking phase of the study titled "Spring Interfamily and Intrafamily Characteristics of Coyotes," which is a pretty fancy handle for saying you want to find out what a coyote family is and how it might be annually surveyed, accurately. That may be a bit more of a simpler statement of objective, but fancy footwork will be needed to achieve it.

Coyotes are most active at night. Therefore at night was when the data collection had to occur. So, Allen's days turned into nights. Starting about sunset he climbed into his antenna-doned pickup, hung a set of earphones over his head and set out to record half-hourly radio fixes on the particular male and female scheduled for tracking.

Several miles to the north where coyote range changes to fox range, Jim Hastings, another night-tracker employed by the U.S. Fish and Wildlife Service, was keeping tabs on some of the 15 radioed red foxes serving as part of another study, aspects of which are tied to the coyote study. He, too, seldom had company during the dark prairie nights save for the signals of his wired canines and what creatures would appear in the shadow of his headlight beams. Generally Allen and Hastings would rendezvous for coffee somewhere near midnight, then for the rest of the night busy themselves with recording azimuths; they seldom met again. Their CBs were tuned to the same channel, however, and once in awhile came in handy when a vehicle broke down, got stuck or whatever.

This time it wasn't my imagination. Clearly I could detect a lightening eastern sky. Suddenly, Crankshaft began to move as evidenced by several new radio fixes each farther apart than the previous. He had been relatively disinterested in covering most of his territory up until now. "Guess what?" Allen quipped, "Ol' Crank just realized sunrise is only fifteen minutes away and he's got ten miles yet to cover."

And sunrise has got to mean something special to these night-trackers. It did to me. I was tired, not conditioned to this living on the wrong side of the clock. They were conditioned, but I got the idea, nonetheless, that sunrise meant another night gone, bringing them closer to when this segment of the project would end and they would be able to resume schedules like most of the rest of us enjoy all year.

North Dakota OUTDOORS, October, 1978

"FRY" FISHING 1979

Winter fishing is finished for another year. And so, too, is the "brotherhood of the fish house." An ice angler's euphoria, it is heightened by glowing wood heaters, bulging lunch sacks, good friends and, perhaps, a dash of snowshoe spirits.

Levon Grinde, warden supervisor out of Cando, once told me his most cherished leisure hours were spent hidden inside some smokey fish house jealously guarding what free time a judicious game warden might have, doing for a few hours, what many sportsmen fill entire days and weeks with. In his confession, though, I easily gathered that the perfect sweetness of his moments there, were brought home in the culinary delight of fresh-caught, pan-fried perch.

Out of the water, deftly filleted, floured, sprinkled with salt and pepper, and into a cast-iron frying pan, its sizzling oil heated on a woodfired tin heater, went the tiny fillets. "Winter fishing," Grinde lectured, "can be darn fattening! All you need," he says, "is a frying pan, bread and butter, salt and pepper, flour and oil — and, of course, some willing perch, but that's hardly ever a problem."

It's true, perhaps the finest thing about fishin' is the eatin'. But just because the "brotherhood of the fish house" has evaporated for another year, like the snowbanks of April, don't put that frying pan away just yet. Heck, it's just getting broke in with a good carbon crust — nature's non-stick surface. Yes, there's more fishing and more eating right up ahead.

In just a few more weeks you'll be able to stretch out, unfold from cramped winter fishing quarters, and travel across the state to tackle bluegills, trout, walleyes and northern pike — some so big they must be cut in half to fit the skillet. They scrap furiously for the right to remain bathed in North Dakota's prairie lakes and wetlands — over 150 such places now managed by the Fisheries Division of the North Dakota Game and Fish Department. And, you'll industriously flail the water with wonder lures and baits. Everything from Eager Ed's Shallow Spoondangle to the Jolly Green Giant's lowly canned pea, you'll use in your zeal to bring these fish to creel, and then, soon, ceremoniously, to the warming camp kitchen skillet.

Wood fires, of course, are most desirable. They smoke our food as well as our imaginations. To the food combine a zesty smell and taste of natural spices. Crackling grease leaves browning fillets to fall on the fire's chalky ashes sending them airborne — some to land uninvited within the skillet to flavor its contents. Fishing is a scrumptious pastime!

And infected imaginations. What is it that happens to us when we kindle a cook fire with aboriginal fuel — wood — and add hand-caught prey — fish — in a kitchen wildly appointed with rock chairs and a carpet of green living fibers. Ah, this is the original bar-b-que. Maybe the equation is really uncomplicated: heat + food + quiet simplicity = contentment. To the fishing camp atmosphere append place names like Bear Den Bay, Wolf Creek, Buffalo Lodge, Devils Lake, Badger Bay and the Missouri River. With your front side hot, your back cold, circled about dusk's cook fire, mix the evening's first coyote howl with historical contemplativeness and let the medley of notions further spice your banquet.

It seems to me, these are the best conditions for spring and summer fish eating.

Who likes fish? Well, just about everyone. For some reason

fish generally go over better than wild game, maybe because fresh fish don't taste gamey and are way more palatable than the finest supermarket offerings.

I knew a guy, call him Epsibah, who darn near quit hunting because his harvests, though expertly cleaned and stored, were seldom used. His wife barely tolerated the time and money he spent in pursuit of things clad in feathers and fuzz. But about fishing she had the utmost acclaim! On the chance Epsibah would return home with a half-dozen "sunnies," his wife would bless a 10-day trip to the uttermost haunts of Sweet Briar Dam. Oh . . . and when Fish Creek Dam was on Epsibah's itinerary she just knew she'd be in piscatorial heaven — for why, unless creel limits were easily achieved, would such a dam be so named? She always was optimistic about this success, unless, of course, he fished "Frettum Lake."

Each spring wanderlust especially affects fishermen. Those who consistently manage transcontinental junkets must have wives like Epsibah's, that urge them to throw in with the first fish-bound expedition and bring home pounds of heavy, silver fillets. Yes, everyone, but mostly mothers and wives, like fish.

Winter fishing is done. Now another season with over six months of uncommon fishing opportunities is staring you right in the eye. To prove I'm right, 100,000 or more fishing licenses will be sold this year to people from all walks of life.

Fun to these people, however, means back to work for game wardens like Levon Grinde. In the upcoming months he'll talk to thousands of fisherpeople. You may even be the one to offer him a sample of your shoreline lunch — fried fillet from a blackened skillet. The taste will transport him back, back to a raw January day in a snug and smokey fish house . . . then onward to winter 1979-80 to the "brotherhood of the fish house" and his most cherished leisure hours: jealous hours that he will again share with good friends, bread and butter and panfried fish.

And me, what will I be doing? Heck, I haven't been able to eat a thimble-full of fresh water fish for years — developed a respiratory allergy. Maddening! This one I grew into, not out of. But I plan on doing some fishing for sure — gotta wife that loves fish. Out there at the camp kitchen over wood coals, though, there'll be two skillets — one sporting lovely *fillet* of walleye and another, *patti* of hamburger!

North Dakota Outdoors, April, 1979

WISDOM OF A CRANE HUNT

One shot . . . two shots . . . another. Mouth agape, I felt a final, fourth shot delivered with thin-steel precision. My throat went dry and my jaws numbed.

The shot charges strangled my nerve endings until either side of my face felt like someone else's. . . *deer spotlight survey with Roger Johnson tonight.*

It was 10:00 a.m. when I left the dental chair. Sweaty, shaken and unsteady I rode the elevator . . . to the first floor from the second. My mouth was packed with a dozen gauze pads. A stained tissue in my hand held four grotesque wisdom teeth, moist war medals that one must carry for days for show-and-tell, at work, at home and on-the-way. Badges of courage overwhelmed at eight bucks apiece. . . *crane season opens sunrise tomorrow.*

Another minor interruption in a busy day was put to bed. Back at the office I went through a stack of mail, edited an article, corresponded with a third grader who wanted to know why horned toads are horny; and then I ruined two rolls of Ed Bry's film when I flicked on the darkroom lights. I finally decided on a coffee break, but found no humor, as did some of my colleagues, in trying to wrap numb lips, like some foreign prehensile appendage, around the rim of a coffee cup.

By noon the swelling and puffy numbness diminished. But in its place wandered the tell-tale throb of pain. I threw down some aspirin.

I dozed through lunch hour and dutifully returned to work to help handle the normal barrage of Friday afternoon phone calls placed by sportsmen across the state in quest of all forms of hunting and fishing information.

By 4:00 p.m. I began to realize that perhaps I had better find a replacement to help Johnson with the deer survey. I could find no replacement. I could find no Roger Johnson. All I had was a place and time—Dawson WMA, 7:00 p.m.

I was tired. My head hurt. I was hungry, but I was nauseous, too. . . *crane season opens at sunrise.*

Johnson was depending on me to ride the night road with him, aiming a bank of intense spotlights across the night prairie while he recorded deer in an effort to evaluate a deer survey technique. Who was I to interrupt the march of science. . . *crane season in the a.m.*

It was September. Early in the month but still summer hot and humid. Sure enough, 7:00 p.m. south of Dawson, Roger stood by the small camper trailer . . . waiting . . . just for me. Too darn dependable, those Norwegian biologists.

There was only one way to explain. Out of my pocket came the garish evidence. Four "smart teeth" rolled in the palm of my hand turning Roger's face temporarily colorless as I pointed proudly at my wordless mouth and sickly countenance.

It was time to deadhead to the survey starting point. The night hung breathless and sultry at 80 degrees plus. By now I saw the whole ordeal as a test, a challenge in memory-making. To move ahead and endure would make it lasting—to submit would make it fleeting. The pickup bounced and the lights flashed crazily across the dark plain, periodically exposing things about the nocturnal nature of critters great and small . . . and we tallied deer.

Roger said Jerry Gulke (presently data processor for Game and Fish) was going to spot sandhill crane feeding sites and arrange for a place to set up for the morning shoot. I nodded with mocked enthusiasm. That's all I needed was a 12-gauge three-inch going off against the side of my face.

We finished the route and were back at the trailer just after 1:00 a.m. It was still warm and muggy. Gulke was about in the closeness of the camper, sweat beading on his brow as he wiped an oil rag across the receiver of his shotgun. He was excited. He'd found a perfect field with hundreds of cranes. Roger's face brightened. Mine remained nondescript, eyelids at halfmast. Gulke's quizzical look led me to demonstrate my plight. Again from my pocket came the uncomely wisdom teeth. Gulke gulped, then nodded in understanding. . . *crane season should open next week.*

We reclined on sticky bed clothes and listened to the drone of insects and then rested. But sunrise in September still comes early. I felt better, though I'd slept only a few hours. I was hungry. A bread heel and a bit of chunky peanut butter was the best around.

We proceeded in darkness to the field Gulke had spotted and began setting up several large, homemade crane decoys. Scary things in the shadowy dawn light, they resembled prehistoric creatures in childrens' books. Man's passion to fool wild things seems more alive than ever, I thought. I stumbled through the heavy fenceline grass swatting at mosquitoes with each step I took. Fowl hunting in North Dakota in the heat of summer? I found my spot and made my nest quickly.

The hurting had subsided, my headache was gone and I seemed back to normal save for hunger and drowsiness. I knelt for a while watching for specks in the sky, for these little brown cranes. It was lighter now. I was still warm so I waited for what all waterfowlers know as the coldest time of day—sunrise. But on this close September morning I welcomed it.

I resisted for a time but at last the soft grass of my nest whispered its invitation. Somehow I was on my back and off in solid slumber . . . *crane season opens in just a few minutes.*

One shot . . . two shots . . . another. Mouth agape, I heard a final fourth shot. I arose confused from my grass bed. Cranes had fallen to my comrades while I had slept.

I moved toward them embarrassed, unconsciously juggling in my pocket $32 worth of wisdom teeth that would always figure prominently in the memory of my first North Dakota sandhill crane hunt.

North Dakota OUTDOORS, September, 1981

THE "DEBUT"

Father and son were traveling alone to a sharptail hunting area in the windy, rolling grasslands of central North Dakota.

The man carried the eleven-year-old's first hunting license but had yet to tell the eager lad that this day he would carry more than the "stringer." The decision to let the boy carry the .410 had been made only after watching him handle the gun in many practice sessions. The two were alone this day for a reason; father concluded that his son was ready to begin, and these beginnings were private matters.

Off the pavement and onto a gravel road, father finally dug for his wallet, removed the license and handed it to his boy. The youngster was momentarily confused by the gesture, but slowly his expression brightened as he understood the significance of the blue paper with his name spelled in the square spaces.

In sharptail country now, father watched intently for good habitat to hunt and a spot just right for his son's first hunting experience. Then a sign caught his eye. He stopped the vehicle, backed up and read: "Walking Hunters Welcome." Surprised, he read it again, then looked beyond at the land, then back again at the sign to confirm its intent.

Rolling grassland looked good; some mowed, some tall and waving against the edges of silverberry and chokecherry clumps. It looked like a spot just right.

By now the boy was ecstatic. Yet the adult-like responsibility of the moment shone through as he readied the .410, his father's own first gun, then looked up for approval and the signal to begin walking.

Northwest winds were gusting to 30 mph and the air temperature was unseasonably cool. Memories of falls from dozens of years set father's mood as he readied himself and now this small loved-one to sample one of man's great traditions.

They moved out directly into the gale, spaced several yards apart and bent forward into the pushy wind. Hand signals spoke clearer than words and the boy responded to adjustments father wanted.

The first cover was thick and the wind made songs as it whistled through the chokecherry branches, some still heavy with wrinkled fruit. No sign. Another cover and then some grassland produced no action. The wind had quickened more until it teared the hunters' eyes and pushed cold, moist rivulets back against their temples. Summer had skipped the country, that was sure, but would fall be whisked away too soon?

Now the pair moved upward to the leeside of the grassy hill, and then, just as if they had stepped indoors, it was quiet. At the same instant a lone sharptail flushed from the grass across and in front of the boy. Father was out of position and helpless to shoot. The bird was up out of the calm and into the wind abruptly.

The boy raised the .410, cocked it and for a brief moment swung, like a skeet master, on the windswept bird. The small report was an insult to the hungry wind as the gale rushed the sound elsewhere. The tiny lead shot charge was not to be denied. The sharptail folded and hit the hilltop downwind.

The boy broke the single-shot, ejecting the spent shell as father broke into a run to retrieve the bird he feared might escape.

Limp and gray, the feathered form was silently studied, then excitedly acclaimed on top of the prairie hill. The man and the boy yelled their accolades while the wild, screaming wind spread the happy news across the lonesome coteau.

The ceremony continued until the son saw the bird as a shining medal of the "hunterman." To father, the harvest was tangible evidence of more important achievements and the basis for more rightness in his son's hunting future.

Now the "stringer" hung heavy with the boy's own prize. He had won a new freedom and begun the long journey to responsible hunting.

More wind was faced and uplands walked that day, but not another bird was seen. The singular experience stood alone and perfect.

North Dakota OUTDOORS, September/October, 1985

A GOBLIN DAY IN OCTOBER

Stubble mulch mud oozed into the fine leather grain of the dress western boots. He muttered unmentionables. Again he resumed a crouched, staggered approach, resembling the halting gait of a barnyard chicken. His companion, 30 yards to the right, likewise, was in sneak position. So subscribed was he to this primordial mission, that he hadn't noticed the mud gathering on the butt of his polyester casuals that drooped down into the wetted loam. He waddled forward.

Part of the Halloween sun touched the top of a multi-row tree belt a mile to the west. Only a few rays penetrated the soggy cloud cover. Golden hour was gray and in its final minutes. The quarry was almost within range. What pulled these salesmen from the velour comfort of their vocational world to this cold and muddy field? Had errant genes finally surfaced. Usually they answered nature's call at highway rest areas. But this . . .

Mud balls, ten pounds apiece, hung from each fine leather boot. Then, suddenly, out of balance, the wearer pitched forward landing on all fours squarely in the gooey mulch. His companion covered his mouth to keep for expelling hilarious laughter and alerting their quarry. He paused, finally realizing that his own center of gravity had been severely altered by the accumulating mud ball on his polyester posterior. Again the absurdity of the moment overtook him. That's all it took — over he went on his backside. Now the polyester pants and casual sports jacket were plastered with the magnetic mud.

* * * * * *

The pretty brunette sales girl indicated that Mr. Shelowder, the hardware store proprietor, had slipped out for a while. "Do you mind if I wait a bit?" asked the traveling salesman in the polyester casuals.

"Suit yourself," said the brunette, "but he may or may not be back."

"That's fine, I'll wait a few minutes anyway."

The traveling salesman liked hardware stores, especially October hardware stores. On display were shotguns and decoys, cases of shells and canvas hunting clothes. Carved pumpkins. He felt good in here looking out at a blustery October day. Other clients he'd called on in this small but healthy agricultural community on the prairies of central North Dakota had commented, "It sure is a duck day." He thought about the attorney he had visited with earlier. The man's gruff manner changed abruptly to a delightful attitude when a phone call interrupted their visit and it had become obvious to the salesman that the attorney was a duck hunter, getting the lowdown on feeding mallards from a farmer friend. He'd finally hung up.

"Hunt ducks, do you?" asked the salesman.

"Does federal make tax forms or shotgun shells best?" the lard-jowled attorney shot back. "Damn right I hunt ducks!"

And with that he had jumped from his desk chair, grabbed his coat on the run and told his secretary he'd be out until noon the next day. Three young trick-or-treaters poised to knock on the outside of the office door when the attorney boiled through were scattered aside along with their candy bags.

Meanwhile, the traveling salesman with the fine leather western dress boots stopped at the Phillips 66 station. "Lawrence around this afternoon?"

"What's that?" a voice yelled from beneath a car hoisted on a grease rack.

"I said is Lawrence around here someplace?" the air compressor was running and it was hard to hear.

"He ain't been around here for a week."

"On vacation, huh?"

"Naw, he goes to Disneyland on vacation. He's huntin' ducks . . . that's just routine around here this time of year. Don't know how you'd find him . . . damn it!" The mechanic cussed as he slipped with a wrench and cut a knuckle. "Geez . . . I could use a little vacation, too."

"You must not be a duck hunter," the salesman sympathized, "or you'd be laying in a burnt barley field instead of under that greasy car." The salesman departed quickly.

The salesman at the hardware store had been a dozen times up and down the sporting goods isle until he knew he'd stayed too long. He needed a bathroom — fast!

"Say miss," the salesman urgently queried the brunette, "could I please use your bathroom?"

"Oh my, are you still waiting for Mr. Shelowder? Bathroom? Oh, of course. Go down the stairs, but mind the steep steps now, then go straight back by the hanging light bulb."

The salesman broke for the staircase and carefully descended the ill-lit stairs. Successful, he left the toilet and started back to the stairs when he heard whistling. In the direction of the sound, in back of a wall of boxes, he noticed light. The happy whistling continued and now he could hear voices. Curious, he made his way closer and around the boxes. There two men sat at a long workbench. They both looked up simultaneously.

"What can I do for you?" calmly asked the man in a gray duster jacket with the name "Axel" stitched on the breast pocket.

"Sorry," said the salesman, "I just used your bathroom and then heard sounds over here . . . I didn't mean to interrupt you."

"Well, don't worry about it. We're just down here picking ducks and loading shells, This is our secret place . . . kind of." He hunched his shoulders and giggled.

The other guy wore a bus driver hat and green overalls. He was breast picking a beautiful drake mallard. Feathers fell into a 50 gallon drum. Several birds already picked, laid in a neat row.

"Axel Shelowder here," the guy in the gray duster held out his hand. "This here's Lawrence Phillips."

Phillips held out a bloodied and feathered hand, shook the salesman's hand and returned picking. "Sure is a duck day, eh?" Phillips pined.

"Feels and looks like it outside," the salesman said. "Darn sure is down here!"

The salesman reached for a hefty mallard carcass and admired its prime condition. "Where'd you get these birds, anyway?"

There was a long pause. The salesman wondered if he had posed a smart question. He may have better asked—and gotten a quicker answer—why nobody, including them, worked in this town.

Finally Shelowder spoke. "We shot'em over on the refuge road first thing this morning."

"Yah," Phillips teased, "just drove through with the pickup like nobody's business and potshot the best lookin' ones." Both men cackled loudly holding their sides while slapping each other on the back. The salesman knew he need ask no more about the source of those birds.

"By the way . . . do you duck hunt?" asked Shelowder.

"Nope," answered the salesman, "I don't have rights to a refuge."

Just as the salesman was about to leave, heavy footfalls came from up by the staircase. Someone else was in a rush to get to that little room by the single hanging lightbulb. Understanding the priority, the salesman moved aside from the narrow isle. Instead of heading to the lightbulb, however, the visitor, a large nervous, lard-jowled man decked out in camo and a Jones hat, jogged around the corner and ran directly into the salesman nearly sending him off his feet onto his polyester behind.

"Axel . . . Larry! I just heard from old man Rogstadder. Ducks are pouring into those flooded swaths south of his buildings. It's the mother lode! I'm telling you we got'em dead to rights this time. Rogstadder said they must be coming out of Weedbottom Slough . . . and into that wind . . . geez, they're just hangin' up there. That's what Rogstadder said. Let's go . . . let's get this show on the road!"

"Easy, easy Mr. Bradstreet. Just cool down. We can be expedicious without shooting ourselves in the foot," admonished Shelowder. "Let's plan this thing a little. Anyway, as you can see, we do have company here and we don't want to spill all the beans in front of a stranger, do we?"

Shelowder begged the salesman's pardon. The attorney shot a suspicious look at the salesman, as if he recognized him. Phillips kept picking ducks. The salesman thought it time to leave.

At 3:00 p.m. the salesmen, as was their custom when working the same territory, met for coffee. The October day had indeed turned into a duck day. Low cloud scud rolled from the north brushing the tops of the town's grain elevators. A brisk wind herded drying leaves along the gutters to stack up behind the wheels of parked cars. The two sat next to the window and shared the day's experiences.

Both had worked tirelessly all day, but few clients were seen. Few people were about, others could not be pinned down. Some sort of restlessness had settled on this town. It seemed tied to tempting waterfowl flights and closing weather. Was waterfowling this town's Octoberfest? If so, it was a concealed celebration. An infection few wanted transmitted. Yet by now, the two salesmen had lingered too long — they were smitten by some similar bug. Hunters by breeding and experience themselves, they felt the feverpitch of waterfowling carried in everyone's words. They sensed it in the fabric of the community. They heard it on the Halloween wind.

The salesman discussed their plight. They did have shotguns along, although mainly in case a gawdy ringneck presented itself along the road. Neither had prepared for a waterfowl hunt.

Two young men in canvas came in and sat in the booth behind the salesmen. They spoke in low, but excited tones. The salesmen looked at each other and shook their heads. They were talking ducks! Did it ever quit? They listened to the two talk about fat ducks feeding in large flights just north of the airport, only four or five miles north of town. Instinctively, the salesmen craned their necks against the window glass and looked to the north. Maybe they could see them from here . . . maybe.

Finally the salesmen relented. The infection demanded treatment. At the motel they quickly changed into the worst of their good clothes. One had only a fine pair of leather dress western boots. The worst the other salesman had was a pair of polyester casual slacks and a light sports jacket. It was 4:00 p.m. Any encounter with ducks would be brief. But it could be successful, even though neither salesman expected much from this ragged effort. At this late hour there was no reason to think the day could improve. Could Lady-Luck handle the goblin spirits of Halloween?

* * * * * *

The mud-covered salesmen looked like adobe bricks. Straw and heads of unharvested wheat stuck out from their mud-plastered clothing. Again they squatted close to the ground. Ahead of them, some forty yards, was the low unharvested patch of grain into which they had watched several small bunches of ducks alight. Just a few more yards and they could stand up to surprise the green-headed prizes.

Then an emerald, iridescent head stretched up through the standing grain and looked directly at them. Both salesmen froze.

162

They were close enough. With hand signals they coordinated their final plan. The Remington 870s were stuffed with No. 4s. Index fingers massaged the safety buttons. It was time to stand.

In perfect unison they unscrewed themselves from bent-over positions fighting for balance in the slippery mud. They could see the low spot better now. It wasn't an acre in size. Another green head peered over the grain. Then another. Nothing happened, nothing flushed. The salesmen signaled each other to move a step or two closer. Heavy mud-balled feet struggled for solid footing. Any time the flush would happen.

Then a new green head appeared on the edge of the standing wheat. He was nervous. His head twitched from side to side. Suddenly, he leaped straight up, rocketing away from the grain stalks, 25 yards from the salesmen. An 870 roared and down he came. At the same instant a dozen other birds rose from the grain patch. Green heads and brown in mixed confusion. Then another dozen lifted . . . and then more. And then . . . and then . . . the mother lode! Could there be two? Old man Rogstadder had told Bradstreet the mother lode was on his place, in the flooded swaths.

Birds were everywhere. It seemed as if the tiny low spot was carried aloft by a million fanning wings. Sheets of water fell from chestnut breasts and yellow feet. The last of the Halloween sun found a window in the clouds and cast its long light to create an avian kaleidoscope which, momentarily, lit the scene in shimmering colors of the spectrum.

And then it was strangely quiet. A few feathers slipped and slid earthward. The aroma of spent gunpowder hung over the grain patch. A dying north wind moved the haze southward. Seven prime mallards — somehow all greenheads — laid in the stubble mulch outside the tiny low spot. The salesmen — the hunters — stood silent. Mud dried to the fine leather western dress boots and locked onto the polyester casuals.

Three miles to the west on old man Rogstadder's place, not far from Weedbottom Slough, Shelowder, Bradstreet and Phillips shared a fenceline cover, waiting and waiting for the curly-tailed mallards sure to visit the flooded swaths. But the mother lode had vanished. Just as the horizon yielded stubbornly to the day's final sunlight, shotgun reports carried to the men from the east. Then the thickening overcast draped the prairie and the Halloween sun was gone.

North Dakota OUTDOORS, September/October, 1986

THINGS, TIMES AND PLACES

NEITHER RAIN, NOR HEAT, NOR GLOOM OF NIGHT...

A final careful check of the harness rigging showed everything in order as Ed Riedesel swung the bulky mail pouch in on the cabin floor of his homemade, horse-drawn sleigh, climbed in, and pulled away from the Cathay, North Dakota post office. It was Christmas Eve day, 1932. Other than having a bit more mail because of the holidays, it was no different than any other winter day in the life of a North Dakota rural letter carrier. A 27-mile route lay ahead of him and eager patrons awaited the last of the Christmas mail.

Route 1 was the full-time responsibility of Ed Siguaw, but Ed Riedesel had been his substitute since 1918, and because of some conflict he found himself handling this Christmas Eve day delivery. Four hours into the eight hour route Ed noticed ominous, darkening skies to the west. Soon a breeze carried an occasional large snowflake. Within minutes the wind increased and subconsciously Ed threw a few more pieces of coal into his small cabin heater. Before he arrived at the next stop, visibility was poor. Then suddenly, a white curtain dropped in front of him, and Ed lost all bearings, all sense of direction. He was helpless. He dropped the reins and prayed the horses would continue on, hopefully to instinctively seek shelter in a friendly farm yard. Luck was his escort. Within the hour the team stopped in front of the Tony Lill farm. Here Ed spent Christmas Eve and part of Christmas Day, arriving back home late and only after the remaining mail had been delivered.

This kind of dependability has been the hallmark of rural letter service. Perhaps the tradition began with the fleet-footed Persian messengers of 500 B.C. Herodotus, the Greek historian said of them, "There is not a mortal thing faster than these messengers . . . neither snow nor rain nor heat nor gloom or night stays these couriers from the swift completion of their appointed rounds."

Centuries later rudiments of the early postal system appeared in America and progressed through a colorful development. In 1692 a colonial postal system was established in America, and in 1789 Samuel Osgood was appointed the first postmaster general under the United States Constitution. In 1847 postage stamps were introduced followed by street letter boxes in 1858. In 1860 the famed Pony Express reduced time of the overland mail from 25 days, from St. Joseph to Sacramento, way down to only eight days.

The Pony Express romanticized the postal service, and won enduring respect for the inviolability of the U.S. Mail. The Pony Express lasted only 18 months, however, as the transcontinental telegraph linked East with West and reduced communication time down to seconds. In 1863 free city delivery began in eastern and some mid-western towns, and a uniform letter rate was also established that year. In 1864 the Iron Horse began its role of transportation of the mail.

By this time the country had experienced the rush of western expansion and with settlement of rural areas there arose a need for communication lines to these people. In 1896 the Rural Free Delivery (RFD) service was authorized to serve rural America and bridge a major communications gap between the rural and urban populus. From almost unnoted beginnings, and as a postal experiment, RFD service began out of Charles Town, West Virginia, and successfully advanced over the years to serve millions of people across the country. During the first week of service RFD patrons received 214 letters, 290 papers, 33 cards and two packages. They sent 18 letters and two packages. On October 1, 1971, the Rural Free Delivery service celebrated its 75th anniversary. Rural Free Delivery service began here in North Dakota in 1901.

Today Ed Riedesel is 85 years old. Retiring in 1972, he was a full-time and substitute letter carrier for 55 years, since October, 1917. Ed was four years old before there even was a Rural Free Delivery. He worked when the full-time rural letter carrier got $600 per year and supplied his own transportation, and when a 30-mile route was traveled by horse-drawn rig and took an entire day to negotiate. He was around when the Post Office Department issued a policy prohibiting rural postmen from using automobiles of any nature without special permission. Ed said, "The Department figur'd they were unreliable and didn't serve a route with regularity." Ed was a rural carrier when you could buy an open model buggy for $19, one with a top for $24 and a fancy surrey (with fringe) for $42.50. He has used most every type of transportation one can think of, including his faithful horses, which he remembers with fondness, were "the most reliable of all." Ed remembers being trailed by menacing wolf packs around 1915, but guesses that the prairie chicken was already disappearing from the Cathay area around 1920, because "much grassland was lost to the plow. Think it was 'bout 1920," Ed reflects, "when I shot a large prairie wolf . . . had to go to the next farm and borrow a shotgun. He weighed 90 pounds and I got a $5 bounty for him."

Another veteran North Dakota rural letter carrier is Edward Haykel of Orrin, North Dakota. This Ed does not have the 55 years service, but he does have 33 years in, along with a great investment of personal time in the business of running North Dakota Rural Letter Carrier's Association. He began carrying mail out of Orrin in 1942 when routes were still known as "horse drawn" routes and varied from 26-30 miles in length. "This was a conservative estimate of what a team could do in a day," says Ed. Horses had to be used until relatively recently because of the bad roads and poor maintenance. Ed says school reorganization helped to improve roads and, in turn, more modern transportation could be used. Early road maintenance was worse than nothing. A piece of county equipment would make a single swipe down the center of the road, creating an open lane for only a few days. Wind and drifting snow would then resculpture the lane into horrendous drifts. "We had to ride the ditches from then on."

A typical winter day in the early 1940s usually began around 5:00 a.m. when Ed got up to feed, curry and harness his team and start the cranky, hard coal stove in his rig. He then went to the post office to sort mail, leaving on his route about 9:00 a.m. and returning around five in the afternoon.

Many interesting things have happened to these men who braved the unpredictability of North Dakota conditions. Like Ed Riedesel's Christmas Eve day experience, Ed Haykel also recalls some experiences that made lasting impressions on him. For instance, the time his team left him standing by a partron's mailbox. Apparently the team had become accustomed to stopping at boxes, and after hearing the door of the rig slam shut, they would continue briskly down the road. On this occasion Ed had unintentionally allowed the door to slam shut while he was still outside the rig. It wasn't as serious as it first looked, however, because the next mailbox was less than a mile down the road. There he found his team patiently waiting at the mailbox for another door slam signal to move on.

Another recollection combined a bit of comedy with near-tragedy. Somehow a hot coal fell in Ed's boot, and in the excitement of trying to locate and discard the hot item he fell out the door and became hooked to the rig. The team spooked and took off running down the road, Ed still hooked on. Luckily the team was stopped by a heroine farm girl, and the only thing really badly bruised was Ed's ego.

After horses came the "high wheelers," automobiles specially-equipped with large tractor tires, tracks, or airplane tires to give added clearance. Model A's with truck transmissions were often used, and Model T's were similarly rigged. Usually the remade outfit would afford about two feet of clearance. Snowplanes also became a popular form of winter travel for many rural letter carriers. Ed Haykel said he had one but found it "troublesome." On one trip he accidentally cut the head off a neighbor's dog — along with 12 inches of propeller. "Before I could go on," said Ed, "I had to chop a foot off the other end of the prop to get her to go. Maybe I should've bought him a new dog, too."

The highlights in the RFD careers of both Ed Riedesel and Ed Haykel have been the various forms of service they have been able to provide patrons, not only with the mail, but with small favors they found opportune to offer. Much of their service fortunately covered the years when neighborliness was vogue. Often they provided the only visits and communications a rural family would have for weeks at a time. As such, they were extremely popular visitors, for they all carried a surprise piece of candy for the kids or a "chaw" or a smoke for dad. They provided an integral link between farm and city and kept the catalog orders coming. They were relied upon, for their own punctuality promoted somewhat of a dependence of the rural household on the rural letter carrier.

More than two men have done their jobs well for the North Dakota Rural Free Delivery to earn a reputation that is well understood far beyond the limits of Cathay and Orrin, North Dakota. Throughout the state, today, even when services are mostly official, the North Dakota rural letter carrier remains an important and popular person on the rural scene, and a credit to the history of Rural Free Delivery.

North Dakota OUTDOORS, Fall, 1976

Postscript

Ed Riedesel died June 19, 1982 at the Golden Acres Nursing Home, Carrington. He was 91 years old. Born in Cherokee, Iowa in 1891, Ed moved with his family to rural Cathay in 1898 where they began farming. He resided on the homestead from then until 1981 when he moved into Cathay with his wife, Bessie. Over the years Ed was active in community affairs, school work, community bands, sports and county farm programs. Of course, he carried the mail, too. For over 50 years Ed Riedesel helped carry the mail to rural homes around Cathay.

Ed Haykel started his 65-mile mail carrier route in February, 1944 when horses were still in use and it took most of the day to deliver the mail. He retired in September of 1983 running a 140-mile route in a fancy horseless carriage, handily getting the job done in a morning. To be exact, Ed says he worked as a mail carrier 39 years, 8 months and 18 days. He was state secretary of the Rural Letter Carrier's Association for 21 years and president one year. In 1965 he was president of the Midwest States Rural Letter Carrier's and served on the National Rural Letter Carrier's By-laws and Resolutions Committee. Ed also published the N.D. Rural Letter Carrier's Newsletter from 1964 to 1971. Orrin, N.D. is still Ed's summer home, but the sunshine of Apache Junction beckons irresistably come winter.

Spring, 1988 H.T.U.

THE MURRAY PLACE

I did a double-take, stopped the car and backed up to assure myself that I hadn't really seen what I thought I'd seen.

It was no illusion, though. There it stood, an honest-to-goodness sod shanty. Tumble-down and obviously in its final years, the tiny earthen structure was surely an artifact of North Dakota's settlement days. In my mind's eye flashed a potpourri of historical notions of pioneer life.

I got out of the car, crossed the fence that enclosed the one-acre site, took a dozen photographs, all the time wondering what story surrounded the place. I was fascinated. But I was also late, late for my antelope field checking assignment for the 1971 season in the Bowman-Rhame area.

Back in the car, I reluctantly drove on. I looked back, very conscious of a nagging compulsion to stay and discover the history of the site. Like an alluring book title, the face of the sod shack suggested that the authentic account of this piece of prairie could be found on the inner pages, in the life's text of someone nearby.

Two months later I had occasion to use the sod house photos to help illustrate an article for **North Dakota OUTDOORS**. Shortly thereafter, I received a letter, postmarked Rhame, North Dakota, from Mr. and Mrs. Allen Murray. Mrs. Murray (Martha) had seen the photo in the magazine and immediately recognized it as Mother Murray's (Allen's mother) homestead place. I read the two-page letter, in which was included a brief history of the soddy, and was very satisfied with Mr. Murray's account.

In the spring of 1972 while in southwestern North Dakota for the annual sage grouse inventory of strutting grounds, I stopped in Rhame and visited with the Murrays. We talked about the sod place and of their recollections of the life and times surrounding it. It was exciting, and a bit heart-stirring too, for it had been Allen's pioneer home—the place he and his mother, sister, and two brothers had come to settle. I pledged I would prepare an article so that other interested North Dakotans might know the story of one of North Dakota's remaining sod homes and a little about the people who built and used it.

Four years passed. In late September, 1976, I again visited the Murrays and sat with them in their white, wood-framed home in Rhame sipping a cup of the stiff, black coffee that has been Allen's kitchen-side trademark for years. Later, we all paid a visit to the homestead site.

I asked them for more information, more particulars about life at the homestead. Mrs. Murray left the room and returned with a 35-page longhand manuscript of the Murray family tree and other family facts. Included in it were the answers to almost all of my questions. Mrs. Murray had prepared the recollections to be published in a Slope County history, but she extended me permission to use excerpts for this article.

I am aware of this fine couple's sense of history and their scholarship in recording the details of their past. I have also enjoyed a rare form of hospitality, likely the same brand administered by Mother Murray to passersby of the Murray farmstead in settlement days.

******

John Allen Murray, born in 1899 of Irish stock at Minden, Minnesota, was five years old and living near Foley, Minnesota, when his father, John William, died in 1905. Shortly thereafter Allen's mother, Mary Ann (Mother Murray) became interested in homesteading in North Dakota.

Early in 1907 her eldest son, Paul, journeyed to western North Dakota near Petrel (presently Rhame) and took employ with the Chicago, Milwaukee and St. Paul railroad laying rail. At that time, he also filed a homestead claim. In the summer of 1907, he returned to Minnesota and successfully encouraged Mother Murray to claim a quarter section on the vast plains of western North Dakota.

In the summer of 1907 the two of them took the train to Dickinson and from there a horse and buggy on the 90-mile, two-day trip across country to Rhame. They stayed at a place called Midway (a large sod house, since disappeared, just northeast of Amidon, about one mile east of Junction 85 and 22) the first night, then continued to Rhame down the "cheese and cracker trail," so nicknamed because of the litter of cracker boxes, wrappings, bacon rinds, and other evidence of travelers taking their lunch.

Martha Murray filed on the quarter section immediately northwest of son Paul's. Legal matters completed, she left Paul to his railroading and returned home to Minnesota to prepare her family for the move.

In March, 1908, arrangements were finally firmed up and an immigrant railroad car was leased to haul the family's belongings to western North Dakota. Allen was only eight, sister Florence 11, 23-year-old Mary Olive was attending Normal College at St. Cloud, Paul was already in North Dakota, so that left 15-year-old Frank to ride alone in the immigrant car from Foley to Rhame, a 7-day trip stretched to ten by a reroute and inspection in Minneapolis.

Young Frank had quite a charge. The responsibility weighed heavily on his shoulders. The railroad car was loaded with all the worldly possessions of the Murray's and Frank had to see its safe passage to Rhame — all alone.

The car was crowded and stuffy. It contained a wagon, a walking plow, a team of horses, "Doll and Barney," two cats (that turned out to be the original ancestors of the present-day Rhame cat population — other settlers moved in catless), a batch of ducks, seven cows, roughly 25 chickens, china dishes, tools, and lumber and nails for starting a tar paper shack on Paul's quarter. Besides the live ducks, Mother Murray had prepared two roast ducks for Frank's between-meal snacks.

On March 17, 1908, the Murray family stood on the loading dock at the Foley railroad station and waved goodby to Frank as the immigrant car rolled away on its trip west. Anxiety welled up in Mother Murray. Perhaps a tear trickled down young Frank's cheek as the authenticity of the moment struck home. Flarety, the depot agent said, "best move you'll ever make." With that Mother Murray and kids brushed away the sadness of the moment and began final arrangements for the entire family's departure in May.

Young Frank arrived at Rhame on March 27, overjoyed with his safe arrival, and brother Paul's warm welcome. While railroading was the modern "in-way" to travel, Frank's association with the immigrant car left him a new definition about that kind of railroading.

The backbreaking job of unloading was completed the next day and temporary storage was found at the Frank Bacon ranch north of Rhame. As the buildings on Paul's claim were erected, belongings were shuttled by wagon the few miles east. Preparations reasonably complete, Mother Murray was notified to bring the family on when ready.

On a dark but fresh May evening Mother Murray, daughter Florence and Allen climbed down from the train at the west Rhame switch. Paul and Frank were there to greet them. The reunion was tearful but happy. Over the native sod, the highwheeled wagon carried the Murray pioneers eight miles north to their new home. A new way of life had begun for the Murrays. A courageous mother, $40 in a tattered handbag and a determination to carve a living from this new land was all that separated her family from success or failure.

In late summer of 1908, it was time to symbolically lay claim to Mother Murray's quarter section of land by erecting a dwelling, thereby satisfying a major part of the agreement she made with the federal government under the Homestead Act. Because of the unavailability of lumber, but an extensive supply of prairie sod, there was no decision to make. The claim shack would be made from sod.

Sod was stripped from the prairie with the walking plow, cut into pieces 4"x12"x24" and then stacked like bricks to enclose the 12'x14' house. A wood roof and floor were installed and wood-framed interior walls carried wallpaper and an essential shelf or two.

The sod house was cool in summer and warm in winter. Lignite coal, the soft ash-making grade, was plentiful and constituted the major fuel supply. Occasionally when Paul, Frank, and the neighbors made the 16-mile trip west to Pretty Butte to cut cedar fence posts, firewood was freighted back on a space available basis.

Paul's home, kitty-corner from the soddy, became family head-quarters where most homemaking occurred. The sod house served mainly as a guest house with its extra sleeping space and was frequently occupied. Neighborhood dances often ended late and those with some distance to travel often stayed on at the Murrays. If there were more girls than boys, the girls claimed the soddy, and vice versa.

Other settlers going to and from home often stopped at the Murrays. Mother Murray made sure they had full stomachs and always extended her warm hand of hospitality. The Murray place became known as the "half-way-place" because of its location midpoint between Bowman and settlers north towards the Little Missouri River. "How many times Mother got someone thawed out," says Allen, "our place was always busy and the sod house never seemed idle."

One man, locally known as "Milwaukee Anderson" because of his job with the railroad, frequently walked the 11-odd miles from his place north of Rhame to the little village of Griffin where he worked. He often availed himself of Mother Murray's charity and on several occasions happened to be one of those requiring defrosting. The sod shanty sheltered him more than once.

Another local character, "Pat the Wolfer," stopped at the Murray's in the early 1920s. As his name implies, he was a wolfer — that is, a wolf and coyote trapper (mostly coyote because wolf populations were likely very low). A grisly sort, the story goes that during one of his campaigns to evict some reluctant coyotes from their den (apparently along a clay cutbank) the cliff and den collapsed and buried Pat. His dog somehow aroused the curiosity of hands at the HT ranch nearby and they finally found Pat two days later barely alive beneath a pile of dirt.

But, Mother Murray must have drawn no distinction — everyone was welcome at her home. The Murray light shown brightly and was a welcome beacon to all.

After our visit the Murrays and I drove the short distance north to the farmstead. Inside the fence I stood quietly. On splendid September air a few leaves drifted earthward. Martha and Allen strolled around the soddy, stopping here and there to do some remembering. They touched the 20-foot tall cedar transported as a seedling from the breaks by Mother Murray. And on Paul's place, they pointed out a long row of white lilac introduced by Allen's mother from a sprout carried from Maple Lake.

Today, 1976, Mother Murray's sod house and Paul's farmstead across the road to the southeast are still, as they have been for several years. Wiry roots of prairie sedge grass bristle from the sod walls, like tufts of well-worn steel wool, unable to hold onto the earth they were wed to eons ago. Time and elements are harsh. The roof has sagged and the interior walls have buckled. The whole structure appears to be settling back into the earth from whence it came, its purpose fulfilled.

Paul's homestead place, too, has outlived its usefulness. Until 1975 it stood, (recently moved to Martha's brother's ranch), in fact, looking pretty good. A little shaggy though, 12 layers of tar paper still not enough to cover the walls and keep the persistent wind from exposing those stubborn Minnesota elm boards.

I tried to appreciate the pioneer's life—the Murray's life. No well water at first. The stoneboat or "go devil," conveyed water from a creek a mile away. Ice chopping in winter to reach water; frost-nipped chins and cheeks from riding horse-drawn vehicles; getting stuck in gumbo, creeks and snowbanks, first with wagons and horses then with horseless carriages; mosquitoes; flies; prairie fires; no rain; too much rain; flash floods, slave drivers and mule skinn'in on the Marmarth grade; wind; drought; blizzards; and primitive plumbing. Then in 1913—typhoid fever. It nearly killed Allen and Mother Murray. Perhaps these weren't the good old days after all.

Then again they might have been. It's all relative, like inflation. Fun times happened too. Buffaloberry jelly; Saturday night band concerts; wintering 500 sharp-tailed grouse; the town pump; gumbo lily; homemade ice cream on New Year's eve; and the hilarious scene of fiddler Billy Perry dressed in sheepskin and fur cap, lantern 'twixt his legs trying to keep warm, while fine dust rose from the wooden granary floor from the foot-stomping dances of his followers.

And to Martha, Allen's relatively new bride, a maiden Fischer, it was a good time. She met and was courted by Allen. Sometimes her parents would stop at the Murray place. Most times, she recalls "our parents were in too much of a hurry . . . the little place seemed to radiate warmth and fellowship . . . how I wished a wheel would fall off or something else would happen so we could stay at that cheerful farmstead." Finally married in 1959, it took Martha almost half a century to corral Allen.

I crossed back over the fence, returned to the car and waited for the Murrays. The sod house *did* have a history and here were two people that had made it and lived it.

Back at Rhame, Allen poured me a final cup of his heavy, black brew. Martha loaded me down with fresh garden favors and several jars of homemade jelly, and, would you believe, a quart of buffaloberry juice—for jelly.

Finally I hit the road—elementary, this newfangled locomotion. But why, at 55 mph, did my snythetic tires creak and groan and sound like iron rims against oak wheels? A gorgeous fall day too, but why cold hands and a nose as wet and fresh as a healthy coon hound's? But why not? I kinda felt like I'd laid up at the "half-way-place," the original froze-up neighbor and benefactor of Martha Murray's homespun care.

North Dakota OUTDOORS, November 1976

POSTSCRIPT

Allen and Martha Murray spend their time between a Bowman nursing home and their beloved garden at Rhame. Martha says, "the poor little sod house - the front still stands bravely - most of the other has fallen." Nephew Lawrence Fischer started a farmstead nearby some years ago, but the idle ground and the soddy remained fenced, preserved, at least for a time, as an artifact of the homesteading days in western North Dakota.

Spring, 1988 H.T.U.

KEEPSAKES BY COLT

"I couldn't even guess the number of times Hugh Swifthawk came in and pawned that forty-four for groceries. And he'd always come back to pay his bill, retrieve the revolver and collect his sinte (gratuity for bill payment), usually a black twist of strawberry brand tobacco . . . it went on for years."

Forest Otis, 72-year-old, retired Cannonball store owner and postmaster was sharing his recollections with me in his retirement home in Bismarck. And the farther back he reached for memories the more his eyes watered, disclosing the deep personal feelings he has for his past relationships with the Standing Rock Sioux.

"Finally - it must have been sometime around 1940 - I asked Swifthawk if he would sell me the revolver, inasmuch as I had possessed it as frequently as he had. Surprisingly, he sold it to me—I think I paid less than $10 for it."

Over the years, Forest Otis has purchased, traded or received as gifts, a variety of period artifacts from his life-long association with the Standing Rock people. This revolver, and another he was to acquire several years later, have become two of his most treasured possessions, and appropriate trophies of early Dakota.

As a boy he'd dreamed of living in the west-river country. Now, 60 years later, he looks back on his life and realizes that he lived that dream, almost to the letter. "I'd do it over again too, wouldn't change a thing!"

His consuming fascination with the West, that is, the West between Aberdeen and Thunderhawk, was the motivating force most responsible for making him a 30-year store operator on substations of the Standing Rock Sioux Reservation. In 1926, after some study at the University of Minnesota and a short stint as a rural book salesman, Forest, 21 at the time, wandered west and took a job, a temporary one just so he could stay in the country, assisting the licensed Indian trader at the Bullhead, South Dakota, substation of the Standing Rock. Later, in the same year, when the work fizzled, he left for McIntosh, South Dakota, where he enrolled in a six-week teacher's course, passed the exam, was awarded a teaching certificate and reluctantly returned to his native Aberdeen area and taught school from 1927-29.

But the lure of the west country was resistless. Finally, in 1929 Forest left his teaching job and again headed into the Standing Rock country where he landed an $80 per month job (that included room and board) at the head agency store at Fort Yates. During this time he met and courted his future wife, Mina, who was employed as a "little boys' matron" at the Fort Yates Indian School. In 1931 they were married. Shortly thereafter Forest seized an opportunity to purchase his own business and permanently settle in this land he had grown to love. In November, 1934, he bought a Cannonball merchantile business and for 29 years, until 1963, he and Mrs. Otis operated the Otis Store and post office. They retired to Bismarck in 1965.

With retirement and the move to megalopolis, they left behind a demanding but rewarding lifestyle that was typified by 10 and 12 hour days and often 7-day work weeks. Reservation trading posts or stores historically served, in addition to the Indians' merchantile needs, many personal and social needs as well. The Otis Store was no exception. Callers came anytime—morning, evening, afternoon, suppertime, Sundays, holidays, and before breakfast. They came to buy food, settle arguments, for explanations of confusing white mans' ways, and even for banking. Some Indians spurned real banks, but trusted the Otis', leaving in their care sometimes thousands of dollars. Just about anybody was extended credit. They accepted pawn and offered sinte when bills were paid. After 30 years of business the Otis' net loss was under $10,000.

In their earliest days in the store they handled the community's birth certificates and burial permits. They acted as cab drivers, nurses, and counselors. These civic services were sandwiched between their business duties. They were clerk and treasurer for the school district for over 30 years.

At first communication was a problem. Forest estimated, "probably only 15-20 percent of the people spoke any English." And so early resident whites, like the depot agent, section foreman, elevator man, school principal, and the Otis', had as much to learn about the Indian families they were serving as the Indians had to learn of them.

So, it was in this setting that the Swifthawk revolver surfaced — a Colt cal. 44 Frontier Six-Shooter, serial no. 201-165. And it was highly unlikely that Forest would ever again have a chance to buy another such shooting piece, especially for so little money.

Yet some ten or eleven years later — somewhere around 1950 — Forest's good friend Mrs. Annie Two Bears, North Dakota's First Gold Star Mother, came to the Otis Store with just such a proposition. The forty-four she carried had at one time belonged to a relative by the name of Shavehead, and it was for sale. Unbelievably, Forest had a chance to buy a match to his other revolver — they appeared very similar. The price? Mrs. Two Bears' firm figure was $10. Forest didn't argue.

It was later though, when Forest was closely scrutinizing the new purchase and comparing it to the other revolver, when he finally detected the peculiarity. He hesitated, then stared in disbelief. Incredibly, the serial no. on the forty-four purchased from Mrs. Two Bears was 201-162 — only three digits removed from the serial no. on the Swifthawk piece.

Both revolvers were patented in the 1870s. Thinking that they might possibly have been put into service in the 1880s with the reservation's first Indian Police, Forest wrote to Colt and requested manufacture dates. Colt said they were built in 1903, so they weren't around during Sitting Bull's last days. But they could have been around the reservation in late 1903, and certainly any other place between Colt's factory and this west-river country.

The hard rubber grips are well worn, and should the pieces be able to talk, the story of their travels undoubtedly would make exciting listening. How many owners did they have? Who were they — cowboys, sodbusters, a patent medicine man? What use did they make of these six-shooter, forty-fours? Did these big-bores settle any arguments? Did they take a life, or two or more? Perhaps none. Maybe they laid quietly for many years beneath a blanket in someone's chest-of-drawers. Surely they had traveled separate paths since 1903 when they rolled from Colt's production line. They were probably only a few feet apart though, so maybe they were shipped to a single destination in the same packing case. But after that they must have been separated — for 47 years! Then, against improbable odds, they retired, and at different times, to the same owner.

It is fitting they survived the trip through time and who knows what circumstances. They witnessed some of the final frontier times and passed relatively unscathed through a colorful era of North Dakota's past. Thankfully, they're not buried in the sod, bound to blue grama. It is fitting they are here, a mystic about them that solicits consideration and taxes one's historical imagination.

For Forest Otis these keepsakes remind him of his life with the Sioux on the Standing Rock, his west-river prairie, and that childhood dreams do sometimes come true. These things he wants never to forget.

North Dakota OUTDOORS, July, 1977

Postscript

Forest, now 82, and his wife of 56 years, Mina 81, get back to Cannon Ball and Fort Yates two or three times a year. "There is a great deal of pleasure in meeting so many friends of the past . . one of the biggest thrills is when someone says why don't you come back and open a store again . . . would not trade those years for any other time in our life." Forest and Mina now spend winters in Harlingen, Texas. "I still have the guns, and think a lot of them."

Spring, 1988 H.T.U.

EARLY NORTH DAKOTA CHRISTMASES

Christmas is surely a most important day in the life of American families. Yet for all its presumed fundamentality throughout the world — as American as apple pie and Chevrolet — we may be surprised to learn that the celebration of Christmas as we practice it today is a comparatively modern custom.

Who would have ever guessed that at the time of this nation's Declaration of Independence 200 years ago, December 25 was hardly recognized any differently than any of the other 364.

Religious leaders of our Pilgrim and Puritan ancestors, ironically, opposed recognizing Christmas as a religious or secular holiday. Massachusetts Puritans passed a law in 1659 making it illegal for anyone to stop their normal work and participate in church services.

They may have been prompted to this by a move several years

earlier by their European counterpart that outlawed religious services on Christmas and Easter. Church opposition to the celebration of Christmas lasted many years, in some parts of the country as late as 1855. If there was a celebration, Santa Claus, Christmas trees and gift giving were not too much a part of it.

Gradually religious opposition to the secular celebration of Christmas died out, and soon after the Civil War (1860s and 1870s) Americans began the celebration of Christmas with a set of customs borrowed from other countries and cultures, mixed them together and came up with a refreshing observance of Christmas that introduced Santa Claus and Christmas trees to young, spirited eyes and, the Messiah, Promise of the World, to young and old alike.

In the following paragraphs we're going to take a look at some of North Dakota's earlier Christmases, and at some of the people that found themselves living on our wintry prairie on this universal holiday. Some celebrations perhaps were limited by the original Puritan ethic. Others were limited by hardship, but a few adopted Christmas merriment much like North Dakotans would decades later.

The first white man to visit what was to become North Dakota and leave some record of his being here during the Christmas season was Pierre Verendrye. On December 13, 1738 this man and his party began their homeward march to Portage LaPrairie from a Mandan Indian village on the Missouri River. On December 24 they arrived at an Assiniboin Indian village somewhere near the southern part of the Mouse (Souris) River valley. Sometime before departure and/or enroute Verendrye became ill and perhaps for this reason no mention is made of Christmas. It is surmised that the hardships of this journey precluded all thought of celebrating the day in any way.

About 60 years later a geographer and explorer by the name of David Thompson, enroute to the Indian villages on the Knife River, made the area around Dogden Butte (near Butte, ND) his Christmas camp. The year was 1797. Apparently, a telescopic view of the route ahead revealed a party of Sioux Indians waiting in ambush for travelers. Thompson's party concealed themselves in a sheltered area near the butte where they probably spent a very nervous Christmas Day. At 7 p.m. on that day Thompson recorded the temperature of 15 degrees below zero, certainly another factor that took the warmth out of this normally cheery day.

On Thursday, December 25th in the year 1800, Alexander Henry, a partner in the Northwest Company, an outfit that operated fur trading posts in North Dakota and other points in the Northwest, spent what appeared to be a relatively pleasant Christmas Day at one of his posts either near the mouth of the Park River in Walsh County or at the mouth of the Pembina River. An entry in Henry's journal reads, "Treated my people with high wine, flour and sugar."

Probably the most significant exploratory expedition ever to cross North Dakota occurred in 1804 and 1805 when Lewis and Clark spent the winter at Fort Mandan about 14 miles west of Washburn. They arrived at the Mandan village a bit in advance of the severe winter weather and therefore were able to prepare adequate winter shelters before the long winter set in. For this reason and because they had successfully completed the first leg of a dangerous journey, they had ample reason to celebrate Christmas Day of 1804. An account from the Biddle text of the Lewis and Clark Journal reads:

> "Tuesday, 25th, we were awakened before day by a discharge of three platoons from the party. We had told the Indians not to visit us as it was one of our great medicine days; so that the men remained at home and amused themselves in various ways, particularly with dancing in which they take great pleasure. The American flag was hoisted for the first time in the fort; the best provisions we had were brought out, and this, with a little brandy, enabled them to pass the day in great festivity."[1]

Maximilian, Prince of Wied, who became a well known naturalist and scientist, left good records of his travels on the Upper Missouri. On Christmas Day in 1833 at Fort Clark also in the Washburn area he described festivities as follows:

> "At midnight the engages of the fort fired a volley to welcome Christmas Day, which was repeated in the morning; the 25th of December was a day of bustle in the fort. Mr. Kipp had given the engages an allowance of better provisions, and they were extremely noisy in their Canadian jargon. The poor fellows had no meat for some time, and had lived on maize, boiled in water, without any fat."[1]

On December 25, 1834, Francois A. Chardon, an American Fur Company clerk stationed at Fort Clark, related in his journal the celebration of that Christmas Day:

> "Thursday 25 Christmas comes but once a year, and when it comes it brings good cheer. But not here! As everything seems the same, No New Faces, No News, and

worse of all No Cattle [buffalo], last Night at one half past ten O'clock we partook of a fine supper prepared by Old Charboneau, consisting of Meat Pies, bread, fricassied pheasants [probably sharp-tailed grouse], Boiled tongues, roast beef — and coffee — the brilliant assembly consisted of Indian Half Breeds, Canadians, Squaws and children, to have taken a Birds eyes view, of the whole group, seated at the festive board, would of astonished any, but those who are accustomed to such sights, to of seen in what little time, the Contents, of the table was dispatched, some as much as seven to nine cups of coffee, and the rest in like proportion, good luck for the Cooks that they were of the Number seated at the table, or their share would of been scant as everyone has done Honour to his plate. . ."[1]

An unusual frontier character, Henry A. Boller, a member of the fur trading company at Fort Atkinson on the Missouri River which operated in opposition to the Fort Berthold trading post, apparently enjoyed frontier life and developed a sympathetic attitude towards the Plains Indians. His contentment on the prairie must have also permitted him to keep detailed journals. He makes the following comments about Christmas Day, 1858:

"A splendid day. Old Jeff says it is the pleasantest and finest weather he has ever experienced on the 25th . . . Everybody dressed themselves in their best; I put on a new pair of pants, a red plaid flannel shirt, black silk cravat, and coat. It seemed odd to be dressed up so much after being so long accustomed to a free and easy style. St. Nicholas did not desert us, up in these frozen N-Western regions. I gave Mr. McBride a bottle of old Brandy, (would that it had been a dozen); and he gave me a most magnificantly garnished bullet pouch and shoulder strap for a powder horn; the work of his squaw, Susanne; the finest thing of the kind I ever saw . . . Jeff Smith came over about noon, and his eyes fairly twinkled when the Bourgeois gave him a horn. After talking awhile, we went over to Fort Berthold to dine and did ample justice to the delicious prairie chicken and rabbit potpie, raisin puddings and pie; After a smoke, we returned, Jeff with us to Ft. Atkinson, where our Christmas Dinner was speedily set before us. It consisted of Mackerel, stewed oysters, sardines, bangs, molasses, coffee, and dried peach pie; the whole making a pretty fair spread . . . After eating to repletion, we returned to our house . . . the men from the Opposition had a regular frolic and stage-dance to the music of an accordian: they put on some squaws' leather dresses which I loaned them . . . They kept going for several hours . . . all deeply regretted the absence of any drinkables . . . We read nearly all the evening, but before I went to sleep, I thought of all the Christmases I had spent, and relived in my mind's eye the varied scenes in which I had been an actor, up to the present time and this, the first Christmas ever passed by me, away from the paternal roof."

"Cold — oh no -31 this morning and -30 tonight and not above -15 all day . . ."[1]

This statement taken from Ferdinand A. Van Ostrand's diary indicates the frigid weather experienced on Christmas Day, 1871. A young man, Van Ostrand represented the last of the fur traders in North Dakota and helped pull the curtain on the end of the era. By the mid-1870s the large fur trading companies passed from the Dakota scene; the frontier had been conquered and settlement had begun. Some additional notes from Van Ostrand's diary from Christmas Day read:

"Christmas has been lively enough in some respects. Too much of the ardent circulating to allow things to pass off happily — we had a very good dinner — all things considered. Tappan and Mr. and Mrs. Bradford dined with us. The Major gave the Indians something to make their hearts good. Marsh and I gave the folks in the fort a little stuff."[1]

The age of the explorer and trapper fur trader had passed. Fargo was no longer the gateway to the frontier as Northern Pacific rails were laid west 200 miles to Bismarck. With the railroads came the infantry and cavalry to protect the builders of the iron horse road. Then, transported by this rapid conveyance, came the settlers. It began in the late 1860s and by 1900 over 30,000 family homesteads had been claimed across much of North Dakota. Of course, Christmases continued, despite hard times and this generally unprosperous settlement period.

Mrs. Kate Roberts Pelissier was a small girl and member of one such family whose head was a restless type that took homesteads near Mandan and Medora, the latter being close to Theodore Roosevelt's Maltese Cross ranch (south of Medora). In *Reminiscenes of a Prairie Mother* Mrs. Pelissier, living at the Custer Trail ranch in the early 1880s and later on her father's own place just south of the Maltese Cross, recalls that times were bad, but not so bad they went hungry; however, "there had to be 'cash money' too." In her publication she states:

"Uncle Howard Eaton sent Anne and me each a lovely doll with hair [for her birthday earlier her two sisters
made her a rag doll stuffed with river sand and from a
buffalo forelock gave it long black hair]. He also sent
a little doll for Nell, and books for the older girls. How
happy we all were."[2]

On another Christmas a hired man provided the Pelissier girls
with the perfect present:

"He let us choose from among three things that he
would send away for. We picked out what we called a
'grind organ.' With it came about twenty 'rollers' for the
pieces it would play. For holding these he fashioned a
small cabinet, a pigeon-hole for each roller. To us children
this hand organ was very wonderful and we spent many,
many happy hours playing the records over and over."[2]

In the fall of 1884, the John J. Robinson family arrived from
St. Louis at the Bismarck railroad depot and made the 60-mile
and three-day trip to their new log cabin near Coal Harbor (near
what is now Riverdale). With the Christmas season advancing
quickly it appeared there was little to offer for a merry Christmas.
Young John Wade, currently a 98-year-old retired veterinarian
and pharmacist living in Garrison, recalls in his publication,
Recollections:

". . . There were no evergreen trees native to this area
. . . however . . . in exploring the area near the village
we discovered that there was an abundance of evergreen
'creeping juniper' growing profusely along the high bluffs
overlooking the Missouri River. This gave my oldest sister
Mollie the incentive to improvise a Christmas tree . . .
she gathered a quantity of juniper and selecting a suitable
small tree in the timber near the steamboat landing, she
set up the tree in the front room and covered the branches
of the tree by attaching the small strips of evergreen
juniper to each twig . . . With wild rose buds and thorn
applies threaded in strings the tree was decorated and with
a few wax candles it made a real addition to Christmas.
We had no oranges or apples that Christmas . . . but
Christmas morning we found our stockings well supplied
with nuts, stick candy and the old-fashioned gum drops
. . . My greatest thrill was to wake up Christmas morning to find a bright shining saddle with real stirrups . .
. So this was my very first cow-boy outfit and it appeared
with me in more than one early Fourth of July horse

race."[3]

The preceding accounts of early Christmases in Dakota remind us of the astonishing changes our Great Plains community has made in a relatively short time. The people who lived during these past periods were, by necessity, very close to the Dakota outdoors. Many were completely at the mercy of the four strong winds and depended on the bounteous but oftentimes obstinate prairie for all their needs. And in their holiday celebrations where merriment and joviality were earnestly embraced, like these Christmases, the outdoors, its prairie, its river bottomlands from which came their requirements controlled their festive moods.

Most late 20th century Christmases have been without privation. We are warm. Our fireplaces, cheerily aglow, are mostly for decoration. We are full, our stomachs packed to uncomfortable levels with gastronomic delights unheard of a century ago. We are clothed in synthetic get-ups designed mostly for looks and seemingly less for practicality. We are soft because of automobiles, motorboats, elevators and snowblowers.

More than ever we have reason to be thankful. More than ever we have reason to be generous and loving to others. And more than ever we should remember the good news and the real meaning of Christmas.

REC Magazine, December, 1977

REFERENCES

[2]Pelissier, Kate Roberts. 1957. Reminiscences of a Pioneer Mother, **North Dakota History**, Vol. 24, No. 3, July, 1957, 12pp.

[1]Reid, Russell. 1946. Early Christmas Day in North Dakota. **The Museum Review**. Publ. by the N.D. State Historical Society, Vol. 1, No. 12, December, 1946, 7pp.

[3]Robinson, John W. 1975. **Recollections**. Publ. by Tumbleweed Press, P.O. Box 1857, Bismarck, N.D., 299pp.

PEOPLE ON THE RIVER ARE HAPPY TO BE...

What do you want out of a few days of summer outdoor recreation?

Would a little peace and quiet be important ingredients? Do you want to leave crowds and associated frustrations behind? A carefree schedule, is that worthwhile? You probably want to relax, unwind. You may want to experience some sort of close relationship with your outdoor heritage. Or you may want to pursue summer outdoor recreation because it's simply the in thing to do. For these and reasons ten-fold, you will be among thousands of North Dakotans making a summer pilgrimage to find your place in the sun.

Many will embark to capture the spirit of the great outdoors with a full complement of modern recreational devices. And it would seem that they will have added to, not subtracted from, their workaday frustrations. To each his own.

Others will seek fulfillment by backpacking, still using the latest lightweight technology to aid them, but refusing luxuries that cannot be transported on their backs.

Somewhere between fits the river people — the floaters — those who let river currents decide their course and move their shallow-draft, motorless crafts on voyages that are strikingly reminiscent of those embraced by the likes of Huck Finn and Tom Sawyer. To the river they have commended their precious vacation time and cast their fate.

Few are disappointed. Many return. As the stories of satisfying river experiences are retold, more join the ranks of floaters to become equally fascinated by the simple but impressive communion they have shared with a river.

Floaters might be called water gypsies when set adrift on a waterway. Almost instantly a sense of liberation and wanderlust is felt. Hustle and bustle fades in your rippling wake. Drifting peacefully, quietly, already your civilized mainspring begins to unwind. Your world has suddenly shrunk to what is at hand. For several days, for 50, 60, 80, or 120 river miles you and your companions will be paddling your own canoe.

Slowly you will begin to understand the river — see that it has moods. You will note soon that you are not only *on* the river, you are *with* the river. You will go where it goes. The river does not retrace its steps, nor can you in your motorless craft.

The river may be slow, fast, deliberately straight, or cautiously crooked. It has its quiet moments on broad and shallow protected reaches (which you will never "hear" motoring by). It has its temper tantrums in the narrows where lodged debris causes the surface to boil and churn. You will be relaxed or attentive accordingly.

The shoreline tells of the river's past moods. A giant cottonwood tree, likely over 200 years old, leans precariously riverward on a water-cut bank, most of its root system exposed. Another spring flood will surely topple the old-timer, unless the aspiring beaver who has recently begun a job, completes it.

Once cut loose and committed to the course of the river you have no use for money. For days no one needs or can spend a penny. A fifty-dollar bill is useless. You might as well use it to light your pipe at day's end. You've got what you need and for the rest there is no charge. On second thought, light your pipe with a twig retrieved from the fire and keep the fifty-dollar bill. It'll buy you two more float trips on two other rivers. No, you say, that can't be? How for $25 can you buy a $1,000 experience?

The river trip is totally an uncomplicated venture. This brand of river travel begins with a light load of essentials and few luxuries. A seaworthy craft (canoe, johnboat, pram, etc.), a map to trace your progress, life jackets, paddles or oars, a sleeping bag and ground cloth, pup tent, a change of clothes including something for all kinds of weather. The rivers are on the northern plains, a region of extremes in weather. In a week expect, rain, sunshine, heat, cold, wind, hail, and perhaps even snow. You should have a first aid kit. Matches, limited cook gear, and good food. A camera. Perhaps a fish pole for amusement. In all no more than two waterproof duffle bags per individual is necessary.

You can do it all with minimum paraphernalia and rediscover a resourcefulness you may have thought you'd forgotten. For instance, your pocket knife will be summoned constantly for dozens of critical camp chores, not merely for such homely tasks as fingernail cleaning.

A small gas stove for emergency use may seldom be used as you discover how well the woodfire treats your food. And campfires — campfires on riverbanks are best for water gypsies — like a cookfire in a railroad right-of-way is for a hobo.

Boiled coffee will rival the mellow brew, trademark of Norwegian ladies at church socials. The pot, blackened by a week's worth of campfires, testifies to the sweet reasonableness of such uncomplicated dining.

You'll recall how silty river sand efficiently cleans knives, forks, and camp kettles.

You'll be reminded that rain ponchos really do work to keep you and your clothing reasonably dry in the absence of artificial shelter. Bodies and gear so covered, rain is no reason to abort the day's run.

You'll know the pleasant satisfaction in kindling a roaring blaze on a rain-drenched shoreline, erecting a canvas shelter and huddling together, smugly content, victorious over the elements. Then you'll especially appreciate a huge cottonwood, felled years before by some ambitious beaver, as you hunker beneath it to escape a pummeling of marshmallow-size hail.

You'll appreciate your bed at home when you discover that only a ground cloth and some foam padding do not always the best pallet make. But on the third or fourth day out, body well-soiled, hands cut and scratched from constant exposure to the raw earth, arms and back aching from unfamiliar strains, your primitive rack is perfectly acceptable.

River people know the wind as more than a breeze in the face.

It means deeper, longer paddle strokes to move your craft downstream, but with difficulty upwind. Then a sharp river bend makes for an opposite course. Spirits rally. A canvas is rigged for a sail and the tiny craft verily leaps through the water to the next bend—but, only to require more paddle work.

Mechanical contrivances of river travel are minimal. A motorless craft means no gas to carry, shear pins to break, exhaust to smell, and noise to tolerate. It means, however, that all chores are hand-executed. The degree of blistered palms and stiff arms and backs mathematically equate to river miles traveled and winds encountered. Besides time, you get the "feeling" for what else is invested in a river mile--lest you take for granted the gargantuan efforts of the Lewis' and Clarks, and native redmen who coursed these waterways—upstream.

To go with the river is to go on a carefree vacation. A vacation that will let you relax, unwind, and be happy. Maybe on a river, and with a river, you can find your summer place in the sun.

North Dakota OUTDOORS, July 1978

GREENER PASTURES — WE'VE GOT SOME TOO

*Iigh in the Colorado Rockies a man surrounded by friends lounged close to the evening fire. What a beautiful experience, he thought. He had come from North Dakota and had been a guest in Colorado's high country for several days of elk hunting. Thanks to Colorado people and successful game management he had been afforded this rewarding opportunity. Nowhere in North Dakota could he find the natural resources for a similar experience.

*The greatest trees on earth crowned out at dizzying heights hundreds of feet in the air and dwarfed the North Dakota family. The family stood awestruck before the rangy giants, as if they were observing a moment of silence in thankfulness for their preservation. The 60,000-acre Redwood National Park in California is a natural wonder of our country. Nowhere else in this country is that majestic environment duplicated. The family had to leave North Dakota to see the great sequoias.

*They had made the trip many times. One of a number of groups of North Dakotans who eagerly awaited spring's arrival, once again planned for another trip to the wilderness of northern Canada. There they would taste not only firm walleye flesh, but also savor the fundamental aesthetics of a relatively untamed land where northern lights dance sprightly across the heavens in step with wolf concerts. They had made the trip many times, but each new time they relished more. Such things are not found in North Dakota. But in Canada they are.

*Slipping silently across quiet, glassy waters at dawn the first canoe, carrying two North Dakota Boy Scouts, nosed around the weedy point. The giant moose stood in water up to its knees, head down, immersed in an aquatic breakfast. At 25 yards a tin cup fell from the duffle to the canoe floor in a metallic introduction of the scouts' presence. The bull plowed quickly to shore and disappeared before the other canoes in the party rounded the point. But the scene had been captured on film and the likeness would be forever cherished and would remind the boys of that exciting trip in a land noted for its natural beauty — Minnesota's Boundary Waters Canoe Area. A magnificent piece of Minnesota real estate, the BWCA hosts visitors from across the country, including North Dakotans.

And so it goes. Annually, thousands of North Dakotans, like those mentioned above, leave the state for summer vacation, spring fishing trips and fall hunting forrays. We go to other states and provinces to sample scenic vistas and subdue wild trout streams and elusive game animals that do not exist in North Dakota. We expect to find the sights we seek and we expect them to remain unspoiled for us to enjoy another time. To degrade them would constitute a national sin. These are the "greener pastures" of our minds. These hinterlands we want protected in ironclad contracts from those who would see them traded to visionary development.

For all of us North Dakotans who furlough beyond our borders there is perhaps an equal number of nonresidents who view our living natural resources with the same degree of reverence as we view theirs.

*A Minneapolis hunter and his teenage son finished placing their decoys just as the sun peaked over the eastern horizon. A strong wind and low, incoming clouds would keep waterfowl in motion and make for an unforgettable duck hunt. The Minnesotan couldn't believe he was finally back in North Dakota within the great prairie pothole region of the U.S. He had planned his vacation so his boy would miss as little school as possible even though, he reasoned, the kid's education really would not go lacking. On this mid-week day the hunters were alone on the marsh, in fact, alone on the entire section. They had no numbers on their backs, had not been assigned a particular blind or area, had paid no fancy access fee, and were not restricted to a handful of shells. They were in waterfowl's last frontier — North Dakota. Hope for the future of this country's waterfowl resource is found in few other places.

*It had been a banner season. Spring rains supplemented winter runoff and the rich North Dakota farmland soaked up additional summer rains to let this breadbasket of the world produce a bumper crop. Equally prolific had been the production of waterfowl. An Indiana photographer came to film the feathered crop now on the wing. A wildlife biology class from an Iowa university came to witness the last of the prairie pothole region and the teeming waterfowl that comprises much of the total Central Flyway population. Visitors from forested states of the nation stood on short-grass knolls to look for miles across the undulating plain, amazed at the seemingly uncountable wetland basins and the breadth and beauty of the prairie. In his book *Our Wildlife Legacy*, Durward Allen said, "Duck hunting hath charms to soothe the civilized beast." And those who pursue hunting for such sensations number into the millions. Millions also describe those who acknowledge and appreciate the non-consumptive values of watching, observing, and simply registering the presence of this resource.

And so if we subscribe to the idea that Colorado save for us her mountain vistas, California her towering redwoods, Canada her enchanting wilderness, and Minnesota the Boundary Waters Canoe Area, then we have an obligation to protect for them our prairie wetlands with all the associated benefits.

Perhaps we need reminding that North Dakota, too, has a unique resource in her wetlands. First, simply because they are here in North Dakota like nowhere else in this country; secondly because they are so vulnerable to drainage; and finally because they represent the last hope for maintaining much of North America's waterfowl resource. To this resource we have no fewer responsibilities than do states mentioned above for theirs. We owe it to ourselves and to the nation. Greener pastures? Look again, we've got our share, too.

North Dakota OUTDOORS, February, 1979

LITTLE GEMS OF COMMUNICATION

—Thank goodness for them, for in today's suffocating blanket of bureaucratic correspondence there is nothing so refreshing . . .

. . . as a good dose of original comedy to help make your day. A potion, an unsolicited prescription for improved mental health, humor springs from anything that tickles your funny bone and lightens your load. It is everywhere and this business of game and fish management is no exception. We get serious letters, obnoxious ones, common and routine ones and ones that tactfully point out grievances in a delightful way — like telling you to "go to sin" in such a way that you figure the trip can't be half bad. Printed materials cross our desks that make us pause and smile, chuckle and laugh. They refresh us before unreviewed stacks of reports, statements, regulations and memoranda.

I giggled for several minutes the other day when I read where the Illinois Department of Conservation received a letter requesting information on the Illinois elephant season. The writer wanted to know if elephant hunting was legal, the cost of a nonresident permit, the bag limit and if Illinois offered a cow or bull season. Anticipating success, he also wanted to know if he must retain the head for identification.

Of course, the Illinois Conservation Department could do only one thing. They replied to the letter saying indeed Illinois did have an elephant season. The bag limit is set at "all you can carry" (including decoys that you are required by law to use). Retaining the head for identification is unnecessary, they said, but it is a must that the permit be affixed to a fleshy aperature beneath the victims tail . . . Further, since elephant hair bracelets are growing so popular, it has been made legal in Illinois in October and November to run alongside a mature bull and shave its hairer spots. Some additional nonsense was included before the Department letter-writer thanked the inquirer for his goofy correspondence which wacky content had immeasurably brightened his day.

Anyway, the above reminded me of other correspondence that has come to rest on the desks of our Department personnel. In hopes that these might brighten your day we include a few choice samples for your review.

Lately a man wrote to the Department expressing dissatisfaction with the deer season:

"Just a note to let you know how things went. It took me 5 days to get a deer. When I shoot it it was all green inside . . . I hunt for the meat not the sport. The meat was all rotten so I came out in the hole."

Another man attached a note to a fishing questionnaire he returned to the Department:

"Last summer my 6-year-old knotted up every reel I own, my 2-year-old made camping unbearable, my business loused up every weekend that might have been available. The other weekends I mowed the lawn. I may run away from home if things don't improve this summer."

Such are the frustrations of *grown* outdoorsmen!

This one is an especially precious piece of communication that leaves no question about one man's concern for rabbits:

"To the Game Warden of North Dakota:

"I think you better make a law of how many rabbits can be shot per person or close the shooting of rabbits because − − of − − North Dakota is caning them making sausage out of them + hambergers and gos hunting every day for fox pluss rabbit but he gets 20 rabbits a day and he shoots them every day he can drive his pickup to shoot them. If you think this is a bunch of bull well go to his place to buy eggs or pretend to go there for derections and or look in there deep frezz or down the basement on the shelf you will see to many dead rabbits (even spi on them you will see its true) and if you dont do anything fast to save rabbits people around here wont even know how a rabbit looks like. And I hope you care for these rabbits cus there's a lot of persons who does like me. this is all true."

Here's a day-brightener apparently written by a grade-schooler as an essay assignment for a British Columbia teacher:

"Geese is a low, heavy-set bird which is mostly meat and feathers. His head sits on one end and he sits on the other. Geese can't sing much on account of the dampness of the moisture. He ain't got no between the toes and he's got a little ballon in his stomach to keep him from sinking. Some geese when they get big has curles on their tails and is called ganders. Ganders don't haff to sit and hatch but just sit and loaf and go swimming. If I was a goose, I'd rather be a gander."

The ingenuity of North Dakota outdoorsmen knows no bounds as indicated by this humorous account of how one trapper tried to cope with 1978 regulations.

"When I saw how trapping regulations were set up this year I realized I would have to try something brilliant to keep fox and badger out of my sets until October 21. I assumed fox and badger could read, since this is the only way I could think of to warn fox and badger away from my sets. I set a small poster at each of my sets to keep fox and badger out. However, I found fox and badger were illiterate as shown here, or maybe they are just to hasty, as he did take a long and wishful look at the sign after he already blundered into the trap. I suggest if you keep the present regulations regarding trapping, you should educate the animals involved while still young. Such an educational program shouldn't be too expensive and would save some animals a sore foot.

"P.S. Maybe they have trouble reading the sign in the dark. If this is the case, let me know, and I will attach a small light to each sign. However, this starts to get expensive. Maybe it would be easier to open all trapping seasons for fox, badger, coon and coyote on Oct. 21."

Which do wives hate more, footballholics or weekend and

holiday hunters? This note hastily scribbled on the back of a 1978 deer hunting questionnaire leaves little doubt. I've never heard of a wife threaten stoic Bud Grant or Vin Scully. But an unsuccessful, frustrated North Dakota deer hunter said:

"Would have liked to have hunted on the 23rd (Thanksgiving Day) buy my wife said she would kill me, A. Link, Jim McKenzie and probably Chris Grondahl in that order if I did."

(She didn't — I saw Governor Link just the other day.)

And this late news bulletin just in from South Dakota suggests that the deaths of scores of rabbits, canned, stuffed to sausage and ground into hareburgers have been avenged by the ghosts of two western South Dakota jackrabbits. Seems an unidentified motorist was returning home somewhat lightheaded from a holiday party. When the guy's headlights illuminated the white forms of two jackrabbits sprinting down the road the man decided to run them over. The bulletin says, "That was a mistake. The powerful Chevy quickly closed on the twin rabbits and went crashing into them. Really crashing. The driver was surprised, to say the least, to discover that the 'jackrabbits' were the white stocking feet of an otherwise all black horse. The car was totaled, the horse was dead, the man was upset, and all the jackrabbits in the vicinity were probably snikering smuggly."

Well, there they are. Just a few little gems of communication that have put fun in a few of our minutes. Those stacks of unreviewed paperwork seem less intimidating now.

North Dakota OUTDOORS, February, 1979

RED LIGHT FOR RETROSPECTION

Our battered little red Volkswagen careened through Bismarck's quiet holiday streets transporting my three-year-old son, Michael, his dog, Tigger—a year-old, not quite Lahsa Apso—and myself home after picking up the Sunday paper prior to mid-morning church services.

At the intersection of 6th and Boulevard, gateway to North Dakota's beautiful capitol grounds, we forced our screaming little "krautwagon" to a halt in respect of the red traffic light.

The intersection was unusually quiet. No other cars were coming or going from this normally bustling crossroads where on any weekday hundreds of cars per hour rush in all directions, many north to the imposing skyscraper capitol building where their occupants retire to execute the state's business.

The red light persisted, belaboring its shiny brightness. In the comparative tranquility of the moment, with the surroundings stripped of work-a-day pandemonium, I was struck with a desire to reflect — to ponder a landscape that I hadn't really considered for years.

Aside from business visits, I'd essentially been away from Bismarck for over 16 years. Since then I'd only used its streets and avenues to speed me in and out of town noting little else than vehicles and pedestrians. But now I was back at my birthplace. Here in Bismarck my children would grow, learn and experience all the childhood fascinations that this new environment could offer.

I looked north across the roadway to the beautifully landscaped real estate that aproned the 220-foot capitol building on the knoll a quarter of a mile away. My mind lingered on the vista. I wondered if my kids, if little Mike standing next to me, would develop some association with these grounds like I had in my school days. Could these grounds be just as invitingly explorable to my kids as they once were to me? I had special feelings for this place, but the spinning world had blurred old horizons. To the man on the street they weren't of earthshaking consequence, but to a sprouting child they became the mortar and block in the fabrication of a healthy development.

Now, at this peaceful corner melancholia welled within me. Really, what I looked at across the road was the playground of my youth. Within a stone's throw of these executive buildings I wore my sneakers and galoshes treadless. I ice skated and sledded, played ball and snared gophers. I built forts and flew monstrous kites six feet tall held earthbound by heavy chalkline. Yes, I'd been by here many times since those unforgettable days 20 years ago. But the pace had become more hectic with each passing year and time needed to reminisce was stolen while adult pursuits became more complicated — where new challenges and experiences held priority over remembering old ones. But now, right here, the perspective, at first cloudy, cleared and I saw a medley of adolescent adventures dance across that sovereign property.

Finally, the light turned green, but instead of heading home the Volks chugged north across the intersection and hesitated. "Come on Mike," I bid to my little fellow and his foxy-looking dog, "let's take a long, overdue look at my old playground."

In front of us the massive bronze statue, memorializing our Dakota pioneer families, sat perfectly centered on the south end of an immaculately manicured 10-acre lawn. Many times I had crawled to the faces, 15 feet above the turf, to touch a nose or cheek and feel the sense of mission portrayed in the metal eyes of those sculped symbols. I played there in 1953.

Around the curve the slow grade of the pavement, flanked by wide grassy boulevards, made its dignified way to the hilltop. There, on our right, stood those stately cottonwoods guarding the wide sidewalk I used on countless trips to school two decades ago.

The splendid Indian summer day, perhaps the last one before fall's final exit, sweetened my recollections. The Volks slowed, then jerked to a stop in front of the Liberty Memorial Building. Twenty years hadn't changed that giant monolith at all, even though legions of other kids had since scampered about its jutting sandstone construction and marble stairways and pillars. And the lawn, sloping at a fast angle down and away from the building still looked thick and durable and able to cushion the falls of beginning somersaulters and half-pint warriors and cavalrymen who fought the Little Bighorn beneath the shadow of the building that once housed its tragic history. And inside, where our heritage was displayed, flowing marble stairways rose three floors, each level with its own story and own impressions to leave on young awe-struck minds. Today the new North Dakota Heritage Center, constructed just east of the Liberty Memorial Building, contains our history.

Michael was too young to understand. But he stood beside me as if he did, and seemed to tolerate my cogitation. And Lil' Tig, wet nose pressed to the glass, appeared impressed too, though I suppose mostly with what virgin scents might be found in the ground's greenery and be sampled by a canine newcomer.

We proceeded north and saw the new highway building. It had claimed a large piece of ground on which once stood a small parking lot and more trees and romping room. An old wood-framed workshop was there then too, that headquartered penitentiary trustees who helped maintain the extensive lawns and gardens. Behind the shop over a garage door — the inside of which had been festooned with girly pictures — a ragged basketball hoop hung. I remembered myself and a friend spent the afternoons of a teachers' convention one year, playing basketball with those con men. The best player of the lot was a little guy who played with a cigarette in his mouth, greasy ducktail combed to a wavy valley, and a pack of Lucky Strikes rolled in his T-shirt sleeve. I played with them in the late 50s.

Another 100 yards and we bent forward towards the windshield looking for the top of the prairie skyscraper. When this capitol building was proposed to take the place of the burned, territorial house, many people said that prairie winds and skyscrapers would never mix. But it was built and it has stood in spite of our Great Plain's gales. Seventeen floors. We ran up them for best time, and down too. From the observation room we spied our homes, watched snow fall in Morton county and shuddered watching a window washer suspended two levels below us. The revolving doors, massive brass cylinders with three compartments, spun us in dizzying circles, until Ferd, the janitor, would scold and shag us on our way.

"Michael! Listen! I'll blow the horn in the tunnel."

But the broken horn wouldn't work and Michael waited for a sound that only I heard — the echo from the horn of my dad's '46 Buick.

Through the tunnel the west lane sloped back down toward the intersection. This side of the grounds held memories too. President Eisenhower's motorcade rolled slowly down this lane on a warm June day in 1953. "There Mike, over there, I'm sure I stood and waved at the President from that very spot."

The long, gently sloping straight lane also made it a natural for Bismarck's soap box derby. What beautiful cars! How I envied those big kids as they rolled off the wooden ramps, crouched low in the cockpit, only the tops of white helmets protruding as each raced for victory. Then Minot claimed the derby before I reached the age to compete.

To the west of the pavement across the lawn and through the hedges and bushy lilac, a man-made forest once offered the perfect setting for our games of cowboys and Indians and military campaigns. In winter huge drifts accumulated high into the tree tops where tunnels and snow caves became our winter hideouts. The governor's mansion sits on most of the ground now, but there's some room left and surely today's kids do the same.

Another hundred yards down the hill I looked back, slowed down and tried to assimilate the whole landscape. Had I missed anything? There must be more to remember.

"Hey, there's the clearing . . . sure that's it . . . we played football there one year every day after school." I was a sixth grader then. The clearing had grown smaller because the surrounding spruce and pines had aged and grown bigger. Maybe kids use the big lawn now, I thought, they throw longer passes these days.

I slowed some more, hugging the curb to let an impatient motorist pass. I wanted to postpone arriving at the end of the lane. The car rolled at a snail's pace as if allowing me every chance to shake hands with each memory that a turn of the head produced.

No use. The intersection was just ahead and a green light beckoned us onward, back onto life's thoroughfare. Again I hesitated. I looked at Michael and wondered on which playgrounds in Bismarck he would spend his youth. Just a little guy, he had a lot of childhood left. A lot of doing to do and memories to make. I hoped he would have at least the opportunities I had. I hoped his playground would be as rich in equipment as mine. I hoped his young experiences would turn to warm and pleasant memories in adulthood. Maybe this place would be his playground, too.

Finally, Michael spoke. "Let's go home, Dad." So we passed through the intersection westbound for home just as the traffic light turned red.

Only minutes before, we had stopped for a red light that must have twinkled in some special way. For it not only stopped the car, it also stopped that relentless conscience of presence. It released the power of retrospect which took me on a journey through my childhood that I may have never taken otherwise. On to church now, with a thankfulness for memory and a prayer for time to tarry with it.

Written, November, 1976
Prairie Peoples Magazine, Winter, 1983

MOUNTAIN TALK

These mountain men who surfaced from every background, lettered, illiterate, of French, French-Canadian, English and Spanish descent, characteristically were of similar bent. They all carried a "hair of the black b'ar."

They were a breed compelled to wander and live with hardship and hazard. They were "contemptuous of luxury, generous without limit, bravest of the brave, capable in emergency with quick determination and fixedness of purpose, and loyal to death." They possessed a passion for absolute freedom. They starved one day and banqueted in abundance the next. They wrote a brief, albeit romantic chapter in American history.

These fierce and uncouth figures exploited the beaver business, and unwittingly pathfound for further westward expansion. They developed at least one other distinction—and that was their language. Mountain man vernacular was coarse and to the point, colorful in expression and communicative punch, and fraternally enriched until it belonged to no one else. Mountain talk used imagery and a gross sampling of metaphors to create picture communications. One mountain man describing another's penchant for stretching the truth said "lies tumbled out of his mouth like boudins out of a bufler's stomach."

Mountain life was always superior to that of a "Saint Loui'y Dandy." One trapper couldn't return to civilization because he got "half froze for bufler meat and mountain doins." He wanted to catch up with a "pretty smart lot of boys . . . on . . . a might handsome location away up on old Missoura."

When a rendezvous was held "to," mountain men got together to barter and trade goods. And when they drank, so did they brag about their guns, horses, women and lastly themselves, ". . . and when it came to that 'ware steel!' "

Later talk might come up, "you seed sights that spree, eh, boy? The way the whisky flowed that time was some now, I can tell you."

And remember Jake, "clever man as I'd ever know'ed trade a robe or throw a bufler in his tracks." He was a good old hoss, "as sure as my rifles got hindsight and she shoots plum center."

And that Englishman, the one with "the two-shoot gun rifled, them English are darned fools; they can't fix a rifle any ways, but that one did shoot some, leastwise he made it throw plum center." I gotta admit, "he had the best powder as ever I flashed through life."

The golden age of mountain trappers and plentiful beaver at $5-6 a plew (pelt) prompted a wise old trapper to remark, "such heaps of fat meat was not goin' to shine much longer."

When too many Indians were about one nervous trapper might decide to break from his companions to look after his own topknot. "Do 'ee hyar now boys, thars sign about? This hoss feels like caching." Another might say, "break or you'll go under. This childs goin' to cache" (hiding).

Regarding another kind of "caching" a trapper moaned, " . . . this old hoss is gettin' old . . . but when it comes to caching of the old traps, I've the smallest kind of heart, I have."

A mountain man planning to cache because of Indians about, talked urgently to his skittish horse: "Do 'ee hyar now, your darned critter. Can't 'ee keep quiet your old fleece now? Isn't this old coon putt' in out to save 'ee . . . now, do 'ee hyar? This hoss sees sign, he does, he'll be afoot afore long if he don't keep his eye skinned, he will. Injuns is all about. Can't come around

206

this child - they can't, wagh!"

One old hunter upset with a greenhorn's ineptness at cutting buffalo meat scolded him: "Ti-ya - do 'ee hyar now you darned greenhorn, do 'ee spile fat cow like that whar you was raised? Them doins won't shine in this crowd, boy, do 'ee hyar now, darn you? What! Butcher meat across the grain! Why, whar'll the blood be goin' to, you precious spaniard? down the grain, I say, and let your flaps be long, as out the juice will run - do 'ee hyar now?"

The girl left behind was always "some punkins," or the ultra of female perfection. One Mary Brand was that and when asked what she was like a trapper said, "She's some now, that *is* a fact, and the biggest kind of punkins at that."

Another defended his life of simplicity and freedom when he explained, "its against natur' to leave bufler meat and feed on hog, and them white gals are too much like pictures and a deal too foofaraw."

These then were some of the words of mountain men, put together over the short space of only a few decades. Their language was as peculiar as they were and just as short-lived.

Quotations from:
Ruxton, George Frederick. 1915. In The Old West, Nelson Double-day, New York. 345 pp.

AMERICAN HUNTERS
HAVE IT MADE
– AT LEAST BY CZECHOSLOVAKIAN STANDARDS

Still crying in your beer about not getting a deer permit last year or having to wait another year to apply for wild turkey? Do you think license fees are going out of sight? Mad because you can't shoot a dozen ringnecks per day or hunt anywhere for Canada geese? Ticked off 'cause someone got up earlier and beat you to a favorite duck blind? Yup, somedays it just doesn't pay for the average American hunter to clear the sack. Indeed, life in the great American outdoors is confounding.

Hey! Listen up! You think you've got it tough in the good old U.S. of A. – just thank your lucky stars you're not a would-be hunter in Czechoslavakia.

Want to go hunting? Sorry. You can't buy a hunting license down at the hardware store. In fact, you can't buy a license anywhere. You have to study your way into a hunting club through an academic and practical course of a year's duration that ultimately qualifies you for admittance to a club—providing there is an opening.

Jaroslav Figala, a biologist from Agricultural University in Prague, Czechoslavakia, hosted by the University of Minnesota, recently spoke to a group of North Dakota wildlife research and management people on the general theme of wildlife management and hunting in Czechoslovakia. The distinguished biologist's descriptions of the hunting scene there were in utter contrast to what we hold dear, or should, in this country.

Though socialism was not discussed, it is apparent that this political system has affected Czech hunting traditions. Game, like in America, belongs to the State. But the land, unlike America, is in collective farms under government supervision. Hunting clubs, of limited membership, are managed by a national committee associated with the collective farms. Wildlife on the average 1,600 acre farm is handled by a club manager and member volunteers. Club size and membership is usually based on one hunter per 16 to 28 acres. Aspiring student members earn "points" for management work, especially in predator control in the areas of crow and fox trapping.

Figala said anyone has the right to try and pass the exam to become qualified for membership in a hunting club. However, one must have time to study and prepare for the difficult test. He said women are not omitted, and although more women are gaining access, the majority of clubs are comprised of men only.

Passing the exam after the one-year course still carries no guarantees of admittance to a club. Generally, apprentice hunters continue to work an additional one to two years on club projects like maintaining winter feeders, trapping and transplanting game, or serving as a driver or beater for other club gunners. Eventually the well-trained hunter takes his place in the club, usually when a death occurs or when a member leaves for other reasons.

Limited hunting may be allowed by invitation as a guest of a certified member. High ranking government officials, diplomats, and certain dignitaries are provided special hunting areas.

There are approximately 18 million people in Czechoslovakia, but only 150,000, or 0.8 percent, are hunters. (In North Dakota approximately 14 percent of the populace hunts). Perhaps more Czechs would hunt if they were less limited by time, money and class.

Figala said that to belong to a hunting club in Czechoslovakia is to find oneself well-stationed in life. Clubs eschew hunter mediocrity, are highly social and stiff with tradition and ceremony. Ritual is practiced afield and in the club house. For instance, horns sound when guns can be loaded and a hunt can begin. At the end of the day game is separated by species and lined up carefully for display while the hunters, all in a line themselves, fire the "last shoot" in honor of the game harvested.

Violation of national game regulations may cost a hunter suspension or loss of his hunting club membership. Infringement of individual hunting club rules may bring about appropriate peer disrespect. Minor oversights may be pooh-poohed, but one may face the cost of several rounds of rum to buy back dignity.

Club-harvested game can be purchased by members with the balance marketed to the public at large. Those who can afford game eat it. Perhaps many can't because Figala reports that 90 percent of the Czechs serve carp for holiday meals and coot simmered in milk is considered a delicacy.

Not all game is harvested by shooting. Clubs also live-trap and sell game to other clubs and nations. In 1973, for example, 33,000 Hungarian partridge were sold for breeding stock. (From 1923 to 1936 North Dakota consigned for over 8,000 Hungarian partridge, many from Czechoslovakia. In 1923 we paid $9.00 per pair for 25 pair of Czech Huns.)

The European hare is the most popular game animal in Czechoslovakia, followed by the pheasant and Hungarian partridge; Czech figures for 1973 shows harvest of these three species as 1.4 million, 1.3 million, and 48,000 respectively.

Biologist Figala did point out some similarities in management problems between Czechs and Americans. Czechoslovakia, too, has found indiscriminate use of chemicals and pesticides limiting factors to wildlife populations. Bigger agricultural equipment has also meant larger and larger field sizes, less edge and a tendency to monoculture. Human populations with more recreational time also puts additional pressures on Czech wild lands. These changes the hunting clubs are helpless to fight, for they have no control over land use on the collective farms.

Another similarity is that of the hunter himself. It seems that regardless of geography, hunters are hunters. Figala said hunters everywhere like to verbalize the hunt and chase, philosophize concepts and ideologies. Wherever he's been, Figala asserted, he has seen a lot of beer and rum consumed getting the job done.

This latter affinity we can all live with; however, that's where I'm happy our similarities end.

Yes, I'll have to wait another year to apply for a wild turkey license and maybe shooting one or two ringnecks per day will have to suffice. I guess I'll take America first—and then North Dakota—where our tradition guarantees me the right to buy a license and participate democratically in sports afield.

North Dakota OUTDOORS, February, 1985

10/10